LOSS IS MORE

Phil Morgans

Published by

Llyfrau Cambria Books, Wales, United Kingdom.

Cambria Books is a division of

Cambria Publishing.

Discover our other books at: www.cambriabooks.co.uk

To Lucy, Rhys, Huw and Katy.

I didn't give you the gift of life, but life gave me the gift of you.

CONTENTS

HOME	1
THE FRONT	71
HOME	141
CAMP	189
HOME	293

HOME

1

George fanned out his cards on the top of the beer-stained table-top. He paused for effect and then dragged the small pile of cigarettes towards himself. He smiled at the others around the table and asked, "another hand?"

Two of the other four players stood up and announced, almost simultaneously, "no, I'm off home."

One of them adding, "otherwise I'll be getting a locked door."

George added, "and cold tongue for supper."

William Marsden, an Englishman recently moved into Treafon, and one of the two men who had stood up said, "a bit late for supper, I think," in a West country accent.

George, who had lost his watch and chain in a card game a few months before, had no idea of the time and shouted out to the man leaning behind the bar with a cigarette dangling from his bottom lip "what's the time Maldwyn?"

Before Maldwyn could answer, a voice from further across the bar shouted, "it's 11.30 and time you was home with your wife and little ones George Williams."

George smirked and shouted back, "I think she'd give me more beer money to stay out. She says I'm more hindrance than help when I'm home."

The voice shouted back, "if I was married to you, I'd give you money to stay out too."

This brought a few laughs from those still in the pub.

George replied with a broad grin, "is that a proposal, John Walters?"

The whole bar laughed at his response.

George put the cigarettes, his winnings, into his pocket and stood up. The two players who had left the game shouted their goodbyes and left the bar.

George went to the bar and said, "one for the road Maldwyn. Can I pay with ciggy's?"

Maldwyn, a barman with a face that looked as if it carried all the troubles of the world, walked behind the pump and said, "you certainly cannot."

George shrugged and pulled some change out of his pocket and spread the coins on the bar. He looked around the room as he waited for Maldwyn to pull the pint of ale. What he spied was not a very inspiring sight. The walls of the room had a dirty creamy layer of peeling paint at the top of a small rail which ran halfway up the wall, and a dark brown colour below it. Both above and below the rail there were streaks of grime which had seemed to slip down the walls in runnels and collect at the bottom.

Suddenly, the door of the Castle Vaults burst open, and two men rushed in. Everyone turned to look at the men.

One of them, who George knew vaguely, shouted out "there's going to be trouble, Charlie Price has wound them up in the Punch House and with a few men from the Globe, Cambrian and the Red Lion they are going to make the Jews pay." With that, they rushed back out.

The mutterings of the men in the bar suddenly increased, and there was louder shouted conversation and after many boring days spent in the local pubs and bars, they became excited by the prospect of activity. The men sat at the tables looked around, and their excitement seemed to transmit an energy to each other. About a dozen men stood up and made their way out of the door, followed by George Williams, unusually leaving an unfinished pint of ale on the tabletop.

Outside, despite the late hour, it was a moonlit night and as it was the middle of August; it had only darkened in the last two hours. Once out in the street, George could see men arriving from the adjoining streets and the whole scene began to fill.

George turned to his left and noticed Brinley Evans, a fellow worker in Lower Treafon colliery. A foot taller than George and a few pounds heavier, Brinley had known George since their school days. George claimed Brinley was the scruffiest man he knew.

Continuing to watch the activity around him George said, "What's this all about Brinley?"

Brinley, his big red nose twitching, looked back at George and said, "well, I was in the Punch House when Charlie Price and a few of his mates came in about quarter past eleven. He got up on one of the tables and shouted out that they were going to make the Jews pay. He said that one of them, Joseph Cohen, had charged his tenants double the normal rent for the houses he owned up in Five Lanes. He said that rich Jews were taking advantage of poor local people. Then he stopped, and suddenly he started pointing fingers at the men sat at the tables, looking them in the eye and asking 'have you ever seen a poor Jew?' The men shouted back 'no'. Price shouted out his question again and the men shouted 'no' back, and then they all followed Charlie Price outside."

George looked at Brinley and said, "this has been coming a long time and to choose this time on a Saturday night with the men having bellyfuls of beer, well...."

Brinley continued, "the men outside the pub went mad, clapping and cheering and Charlie said he was going to do something about it."

The huge gathering of men started to move away, and Brinley and George Williams moved with them. They proceeded down Salisbury Street, a street with a mixture of a few small shops and terraced houses and gathered outside Joseph Cohen's Draper's shop. A large man, Charlie Price, got up on top of the back of a cart, which George thought it had looked as if it had conveniently just been taken there. Charlie Price could always be guaranteed to be in the thick of any trouble. He had his cronies, who were always with him, and he would always claim the rights of the downtrodden worker. He was a big man and would seek to intimidate those who thought and spoke anything that seemed to contradict him.

Price shouted above the noise of the men and moved his hands up and down in a gesture to quiet the crowd, whose conversations fuelled by beer seemed louder than usual.

Once the crowd had quietened, Price started in a booming voice, "we can all complain about people taking advantage of us. We sweat blood in the work we do with no thanks for it and others get rich on the back of our labour. Earlier today two workers in Llanelli were shot dead while they protested about their working and living conditions." This news produced a mixture of surprise and exasperation amongst the men and the level of noise rose again. Price held his hands out for quiet and continued, "let us here say, we have all had enough!"

He waited for effect and some of the men cheered and shouted back, "Yes!" in response.

The men then went silent and were now all listening to him. As their conversations died down, he continued, "let's act for what we believe is right."

With that, someone handed Price a half brick, which without hesitation he immediately hurled through the plate-glass window of the shop, breaking it into shards of glass and showering the men closest to the shop. A huge cheer went up and several men could be seen to be moving or bending down to look for anything they could hurl. Joseph Cohen didn't live at the shop, so no one came out to remonstrate with the crowd, but several oil lamps were lit in the houses alongside the shop as people came out to see what was happening. In fear, many went straight back into their houses and bolts could be heard being replaced to secure their safety.

The mob had increased in number and as Charlie Price got down from the cart, other men could be heard shouting for them to move

5

to the main street.

George moved along with the mob as they progressed towards the top of town, more in curiosity at this exciting event which had not been seen in the town for many years, and many thinking that if they didn't follow the action, they would be devoid of conversation or an opinion on Monday morning during their shift as they had not witnessed the spectacle first-hand.

The mob stopped outside Bernstein's Outfitters. Several men picked up stones and some could be seen prising up edging stones alongside the roadway. These were immediately thrown through the shop windows, which shattered. As the mob moved on, George noticed several of the men climbing into the windows and grabbing at the shirts and trousers on the tailor's dummies in the window. Others pushed down the thin wooden back to the displays and could be seen going into the shop itself to see what they could find.

The mob started to disperse, with groups going in different directions. George headed off with the main group, who ended up at the end of the high street outside a jewellery shop. The window here had been smashed and three or four men alighted from the shop as George arrived. Though he had been drinking for some time during the evening, George was sober enough to realise he did not want to be caught outside a jewellery shop that had been ransacked. He turned, and with several others, made their way back across town. As he came to Elstayn's Tailor's shop, he could hear a refrain of hymn singing. Standing with his hands in his pockets, he shook his head in disbelief that the mob bent on pillage and destruction could be singing hymns at the same time. He smiled as he thought that it could only happen in Wales. The whole scene was one of unusual wildness that to any bystander could be misconstrued as pantomime, with a humorous undertone if it had not been so serious.

As the mob turned, he found himself at the front, alongside Charlie Price. Price raised his hands for quiet and shouted, "we are all in this together. We will have justice," and with that, he thrust half a brick into George's hand. George mesmerised, looked down at the half brick as if he had never seen such a thing before. Price nudged him and nodded towards the window. George came to his senses and quickly realised what he was being asked to do.

The mob began to chant "Jews out, Jews Out," and Charlie Price started to become agitated at George's slowness in reacting and gave him a second nudge and nodded towards the window, making it clear he expected George to throw the half brick. Before George could assess his own actions and because he felt he could not back down in front of the mob, he turned and hurled the weapon through the window. It gave him a strange sense of power as the glass showered him with small shards sticking to his clothes and in his hair; one of them cutting his cheek. He quickly wiped away a smear of blood as the man behind him patted him on the back. Feeling elated, George thought that the last time he had felt the same way, was when he had thrown the winning dart to beat the Railway Inn some three years before.

When he later thought of this, he could remember saying "yes!" and clenching his fist, but he could not remember a compelling reason for doing it.

George suddenly realised that nearly two hours had passed since he had left the bar and he thought he had better start making his way back home. He wandered across to the top of town and then stopped and looked back at a scene of destruction. It looked as if Attila the Hun had led his marauding hordes across the town, pillaging and ravaging as they went. The edges of the road were strewn with bricks and broken glass, as well as chunks of paving slabs that had been dug up to use as weapons. In amongst this rubble were discarded items taken from shop windows, including boxes, clothing and pieces of carpet that men had tried to take but had found them too heavy or too cumbersome with their arms already full of other items. He noticed that one or two of the other shops, not owned by Jews, had also had their windows broken and men seemed to be wandering in various directions, some of them carrying a variety of items, which appeared to be mainly clothes, both women's and men's.

A large group of men had gathered outside the Synagogue in Morgan Street. George halted and stood back, wondering what would happen next. The men began to pick up stones and bricks as weapons as they had outside the shops, but a slightly built man George knew as Richard Elias shouted, "no, not here, this is a place of worship and if you damage or destroy this place, it will be eternal damnation you will bring upon your heads." This caused a muttering amongst the men, none of whom seemed to want to be the one to cast the first stone. George could hear stones being dropped to the ground and the mob began to drift away, as someone shouted, "come on boys, no one's been to Samuel's yet." This was a pawnshop on one of the streets running off the main street. George didn't feel like walking all the way back up to the top of town and realised that after a week's work and the effect of the beer, he was beginning to feel very tired. As he wandered down the adjoining street, he noticed two men coming towards him with large wide-brimmed women's hats on, making the scene even more bizarre. One of them was Brinley, whom he had spoken to earlier.

Brinley shouted out as he passed, "a present for the missus."

George nodded and as he went by, he noticed three policemen walking towards him about fifty yards away. He quickly turned and shouted after the two men they had just passed, "Oy, Brinley, men in blue, starboard bow."

Brinley and his companions quickly whipped the hats from their heads without looking around and threw them into the bushes alongside the road. Brinley shouted back without turning, "cheers George, I owe you one."

Twenty minutes later, on arriving at his house, George pushed open the gate slowly so that the squeak of the hinges did not wake the three-year-old and the one-year-old inside. The thought flashed through his mind that the gate was going to give him away one day. He tried to register that he must try to get hold of something to oil it.

8

Thankfully, Maud, his wife of five years, had left the front door unbolted and he crept in. The room felt cold, as the ashes in the fire grate had burned out some time before. He undressed at the bottom of the stairs and dropped his clothes in a heap. He slowly made his way up the stairs in his underclothes, remembering to avoid the fifth stair from the top, which he remembered creaked.

He quietly crept into bed as Maud turned and in touching his leg, momentarily woke. She said, in a sleepy, slurred voice, "you are freezing," and then she turned back and seemed to go back to sleep.

George said nothing and eventually slipped off into a deep sleep, knowing he did not have to get up for work on the following morning, a Sunday.

2

George woke to the cry of a young child the following morning. He shouted down the stairs, "can't a working man have a bit of peace on a Sunday morning, without being woken with that racket?"

Maud came to the bottom of the stairs and shouted up, "it's Will that's crying. He just fell over your clothes at the bottom of the stairs, so I'd keep quiet if I were you."

George thought better of a reply.

Maud shouted up, "we're off to chapel. No good asking if you are coming, I suppose?"

George shouted down, "not today."

He could hear Maud say, "not any day, in your case."

The house suddenly went quiet as Maud and the children left and George got back under the bedclothes.

The next thing he was aware of was the banging and crashing of pots and pans as Maud had returned from chapel and had started to prepare a meal. She had brought George's clothes to the bedroom while he slept. He got up and dressed, pulling his trousers up and placing braces over his shoulders.

It was August and a warm day and so there was no need of a shirt while he was indoors. He went downstairs and was grabbed around the legs by a three-year-old Willie. Joan, only just one, was fast asleep in her small cot in the next room. George pulled Willie onto his lap and his son cuddled into the chest of the person he idolised.

The kitchen was typical of a small, terraced house of the time, and due to Maud's efforts was spotlessly clean, though smoky, dark and dismal. The one wall was taken up by a large grate, where pans and kettles could be boiled on metal grills or hung from a metal rod above the fire. One wooden armchair was placed next to the fire grate and a wooden table with three chairs was placed against the adjoining wall. The chairs and table had all been passed down from earlier generations or given by friends. The chairs were all different and all showed signs of having been repaired. At the other end of the kitchen was a small scullery, which was reached by going down two steps. George had fallen several times after coming home worse for wear, missing his footing and tumbling into the scullery. The only ornamentation was two small china ornaments on a shelf under the front window and two pictures, one on each of the walls opposite and adjoining the fireplace. Maud had rescued these two pictures from a box she had found on the banking above the river at the back of the house. She thought someone had been ready to throw the box of items into the river and had become distracted or had changed their mind. The room, like almost all the houses in the street, had paint peeling off but the occupants had neither the time nor the money to spend on such luxuries.

Maud had been a very attractive twenty year old when George had first met her as she did the family shopping one Saturday afternoon. She had bright eyes and a small dimple in the cleft of her chin which held his gaze. Probably for the only time in his life George spent all his money and attention on Maud, even foregoing his nights in the local pubs just to spend time with her. George was well known as a charmer and she enjoyed his wicked humour and eventually succumbed and agreed to marry him; despite her family's protestations and detailed detective work on his activities in and around the town.

Maud came out from the scullery and said, "what time did you get in last night?"

George looked vacant and said, "no idea. I don't have the time on me, remember."

Maud said, "well, you would if you hadn't gambled it away. That was a wedding present from your mother and father. I would have thought you would have treated it with a little more respect but that's you, isn't it?"

George, who was sat with his head in his hands, said, "don't have a go at me today, love. I'm not well."

Maud laughed and said under her breath, "you'll be well enough come next Saturday night."

There was silence for a moment and Willie climbed down to run off and play in the back garden. Maud went to open the door for him, shouting, "no out of the back gate, mind you."

Willie replied, "no mam."

Maud came back in and stood in front of George, asking, "were you involved in any of that trouble last night? It was the talk of the chapel. Apparently, the town is in ruins."

George tried to look innocent replying, "it was a bit rowdy, but I came home. Didn't want to get involved."

Maud said, "yes, I bet. What did you do to your cheek?"

George suddenly remembered the cut on his cheek, and he touched his face, wincing at the sharp pain. He remembered that he had received the cut the previous night from a shard of glass as he threw the half brick through Elstayn's window. "Don't know how I got that."

Maud said, "so drunk you don't even know when you injure yourself?"

George said, "I wasn't drunk."

Maud continued, "no, I suppose you just sat sipping tea for the seven hours you were out," and then returning to the subject, "the talk is that more police have been drafted in from surrounding towns and twenty men have already been arrested. I don't know what they did to some of those men, but people seem to think that they were pressured into giving the names of other men involved, and more were then arrested at home."

For the first time, George began to take a little more interest as he remembered standing with a brick in his hand. "Did you hear any names of those arrested?"

Maud said, "the only name I heard mentioned was Charlie Price, and the rumour is that he was actually throwing bricks through a window when he was arrested."

She asked, "do you know what it was all about?"

George said, "well, all I heard was that a Jewish shop owner had charged very high rents for families living in some of his properties."

"Who was that?"

George replied, "Joseph Cohen."

Maud frowned, "I don't like that man, very arrogant, always showing off his smart clothes, never speaks to any of the local people - not a nice man." She stopped, and then added, "but, no one should take the law into their own hands and do damage to him or his shop."

George said, quite sheepishly, "quite right." He continued, "I think the men were up in arms because two men were shot dead in Llanelli yesterday during the railway worker's strike and the men are still angry about the way the workers were treated in the Cambrian Combine strike last year when the troops were sent in. South Wales is not a happy place for a worker at this time. The government and the rich businessmen think they can treat people any way they like."

George waited to see if Maud was going to offer an opinion. She didn't, so George continued, "and it's not just Welsh workers, some said Chinese workers in Cardiff had been attacked. I don't know what the world's coming to with people beating up others and even killing their own people."

Maud stopped preparing the dinner and wiped her hands on her pinafore. She turned to George "All very well, workers are treated badly and have always been treated badly. The Chartists themselves went from this very town to march on Newport over seventy years

13

ago and little good it did them, but this is 1911." She stopped for effect then added, "and actions must be within the law of the land and within God's law."

George looked fed up and replied, "fat lot of good that's done in the past. The Chartist leaders were transported off to hard labour halfway around the world and the government's answer to any grievance is to send the troops in, while they get rich off the backs of the workers."

Maud simply replied, "act within the law and you'll come to no harm."

George added, "and stay poor."

The discussion came to an abrupt end as Joan could be heard crying from her cradle and Willie came in to draw their attention to the fact that his sister was crying.

Maud turned to George and said, "nurse Joan while I get the dinner on."

George went to pick Joan up and went out to the back garden with Willie. The back garden was a patch of grass with a vegetable plot below a wall at the bottom with a chicken run alongside the wall between George's house and next door. He sat with Joan on his lap on the opposite low wall. After working underground for long periods, it was lovely to sit and feel the warmth of the sun on your body and he sat for some time with his eyes closed. Joan had just slept and so was cheerful and happy. He could see Willie playing with small bits of wood that George had carved into makeshift soldiers having a battle on the grass. He thought all was well with the world, unless you were a Jew living in South Wales.

After dinner, Maud, taking off her pinafore, said that she was going to visit her sister Annie with the children. George, who rarely visited any family, said he would be going out for a walk to make the most of the sunshine.

George left the house thirty minutes later, after washing and shaving. He was a vain man despite being poor and always tried to make an effort with his appearance whenever he left the house.

Looking in the mirror, he would say to himself, "you never know who you are going to meet; if it's a lady, she will at least give you a smile."

He put a stud in the collar of his clean shirt and brushed his trousers down. After leaving the house, he turned left at the end of the street and crossed over the large metal railway bridge, which became enveloped in smoke as a goods train, loaded with coal on its journey down to Newport docks, passed beneath. He thought cynically, these trains went out but only to make the mine owners rich. They quibble about giving small rises of a few pence a week to their workers while they ride around in fancy carriages wearing posh clothes.

He crossed over the road to enter the park that had been bequeathed to the local community by an 'ironmaster'. The huge park had been the ironmaster's garden which he had left to the people of Treafon. George thought that this was probably the only decent thing ever given by one of these rich men to the town.

As he made his way through the park, he took in its beauty, on this lovely, calm summer evening, flowers blooming and the trees giving a degree of shade; making the walk a pleasant one. A slight breeze gently moved the leaves, and George found the whole scene relaxing. He stopped to smoke a cigarette as he leaned on a railings surrounding the duck ponds and then he proceeded towards the bandstand. There seemed to be very few people around for such a pleasant evening. He left the park at the top set of gates and wandered across to the top of the town where he was immediately shocked by what he saw.

The contrast between the park that he had just walked through and the scene of devastation in front of him was as if he had entered another world. He noticed that almost all the shops had been boarded up, whether they were Jewish owned or not. He couldn't work out if

15

this was because of damage done or as a precaution against further attacks. The road was almost impassable because of rubble strewn across it and the town was full of people who had come to look at the scene. Children were enjoying themselves playing with the stones and rocks which covered the edge of the road. These were the discarded weapons from the previous evening. Every so often a stiff breeze would lift the dust from the roadside and adults and children alike would try to shield their eyes from the wind-blown particles.

There were policemen everywhere, some George had seen before who were based in Treafon, while there were others who had clearly been drafted in. He wandered across to one of the policemen who had obviously been posted at a crossroads and stood alongside him. George was a short, stocky man and the policeman towered over him. He stood in silence for a few seconds and then said, "this is a hell of a mess. Who'd have believed it?"

The policeman, who had very impressive side whiskers, turned to George to check him out and to assess whether he was respectable enough to engage in conversation answered, "yes I think we've got the main culprits, but investigations are still going on."

George ventured, "I've not seen you here before. You are not from Treafon, are you?"

The policeman drew himself up and replied, "no, brought over from Abertillery, though I live in Blaenavon. Police here from all over. Rumour is, if there's more trouble tonight, troops will be brought in."

George thought about what the constable would like to hear, and said, "quite right too, it's a quiet town normally. We don't want damn fool people running around smashing up the place."

The policeman said, "if I had my way I'd close the pubs down for a few weeks, that would make the troublemakers think."

George replied, "completely agree officer, temperance me, shouldn't be open at all to my way of thinking. Well, I'd better be off, ready for chapel soon."

"Afternoon then, sir," said the policeman, touching the brim of his helmet.

George grinned to himself and continued his walk across the town where some shop owners were still sweeping up the glass and masonry. He started to head home, going past Joseph Cohen's shop where the riot had started, where he noticed Brinley standing in front of the damaged shop front.

"Shwmae," said George, in a half whisper, not knowing who might be listening as he sidled up to Brinley.

"Shwmae," replied Brinley, "thanks for the warning last night."

"No problem, any time," said George, "what's today's news?"

Brinley said, "sixty arrests so far, apparently. Detectives have come up from Cardiff, Newport and Pontypool and are putting the thumb screws on some that they think will give more names. They arrested Robert Ryan, the Irishman, works over in the metalworks in Ebbw Vale but his missus told me he was tucked up in bed last night. I think someone's got it in for him. He's Irish and some of the men are anti-Irish. Smashed the town up pretty good though."

George said, "I think a lot of it was the blokes letting off steam. They are fed up with the way they are being treated and the Jews copped it. Poor buggers! But mind you, I have no sympathy with the likes of Cohen who are intent on making money out of the fact that there are simply not enough houses for everybody in the town. Have you been up to Five Lanes lately?"

Brinley shook his head.

George said, "they've got two and three families to a house. You get a strong smell of shit from about half a mile away. It's like something from the dark ages. Word is Cohen owns half a dozen houses there."

Brinley said, "you on your way home now? If you are, you need to

17

go past Kern's Shop. People reckon he's standing outside with a shotgun, to protect his property."

George waved goodbye and set off home. On his way, he went past Kern's Shop and sure enough, outside the shop was Gerald Kern, standing in the doorway of the shop cradling a shotgun. George was going to cross the road for a chat but thought the better of it; in case Kern was a bit trigger-happy.

3

Suddenly, there was a huge metallic crash as the gates of the cage were thrown back, and the miners stepped out. George chatted with a few of the other miners as they walked towards the lamp room to return their lamps and check discs; an essential act in the running of the mine. All the discs were numbered and a tally listed alongside the name of a miner. If there had been a problem underground, the miners returning to the surface would immediately return their lamps and discs and the foremen and managers of the mine would know exactly who were still underground.

After handing in his lamp and signing out, George carried his tommy box, in which he had carried his lunch, out towards the gate of the colliery. He was exhausted after a nine hour shift and the dried coal dust which had slipped down the back of his collar had begun to itch. Never mind, he thought. A bath in front of a warm fire will soon put that right. He lived only half a mile from the colliery, which he could easily see from his back door. As he went through the colliery gate, two uniformed policemen, one a constable and one a sergeant stepped forward to block his way.

He stopped, and cast his eyes up to the sky, finding enough breath to ask, "what is it you gentlemen want with the likes of me?"

The burly sergeant stepped in front of the even larger constable, and momentarily stood there in silence. George was thick set and heavily muscled, but he was only five foot eight inches tall. The two policemen were as broad as George, but both were well over six feet tall. The constable was perhaps six feet four.

The sergeant had taken a good look at the coal black face in front of him and said, "can't say I recognise you at the moment, but perhaps with a clean face I might. It is George Williams, isn't it?"

George wondered how the policemen could identify one man from another as the sea of black faces passed them but then realised that he must have been pointed out by a fellow worker innocently responding to the inquiries of the two policemen.

George had been in trouble for minor offences in his youth, but he was now thirty years old with a family and less inclined to be involved in any local trouble. The sergeant had only been in Treafon for about two years and so would not be aware of any of George's earlier transgressions.

George offered, in a very tired voice, "you wouldn't recognise me sergeant because I have never been in your presence," and after a few seconds and with a cheeky grin, "unless you are in the same chapel choir as me and I haven't noticed you."

The sergeant smirked and replied, "well if you've done what's been suggested by some, I think you could be asked to surrender your presence in the chapel choir," and after a moment's hesitation, "not that I would ever think you were in it in the first place."

George looked quizzically at the sergeant. "If you've done what's been suggested by some. What does that mean?"

The sergeant said, "well, I don't think this is really the place to discuss it. Perhaps we could move to the station."

George rolled his eyes and momentarily refused to move with the two policemen. He asked, "could I not go home for a bath and some food and come a little later?"

The sergeant didn't bother to reply to the request and turned to the constable, saying, "do you know this man?"

The constable shook his head.

The sergeant turned back to George, "do we need to put cuffs on you or are you going to come quietly?"

George laughed and said, "after a nine hour shift down there, I defy anyone to come with you in any other way than quietly."

The three men moved off towards the police station, which fortunately for George was only about a half mile from the colliery

20

but unfortunately in the opposite direction from his house.

On arrival at the station, George was asked to sit on a bench opposite the main counter of the station. George looked around at the bleak, white-washed walls, only broken by a large notice board which was plastered with all sorts of pieces of paper overlapping each other, all faded and some with blurred pictures of men and even one or two of women you would not want to meet even in broad daylight.

The sergeant went behind the counter and asked the constable to escort George to the washroom along the corridor where he would find a basin, some water and a towel. George, in his exhausted state, dragged himself off to the washroom, where he found a small basin with cold water. He tried to wash off the worst of the coal dust but ended up trying to wipe most of it off in the towel. He walked back to the counter and placed the filthy towel on it. The sergeant picked up the towel between one finger and a thumb and dropped it on the floor behind the counter. He then indicated for George to sit back on the bench. George waited for what seemed like two hours or more, asking several times if he could go home or if he could have something to eat. Faced with refusal, he eventually allowed his eyes to close and slipped sideways across the bench in the subdued light cast by a gas lamp.

He was shaken awake sometime later by a man possibly in his fifties, in a suit, with a gold watch chain hanging from his waistcoat. George woke in an aggressive mood after falling into a deep sleep, but after a few seconds remembered where he was. The man in the suit turned to the constable and said, "take him into the interview room and stay with him. I'll be along shortly."

The constable half saluted and replied, "certainly Inspector."

George was shown into a small room and the constable ushered him to an upright chair on the one side of a desk. Almost immediately, the door opened, and the Inspector came in and sat on the other side of the desk. He opened a file and looking down, he read silently for a few minutes. Then he picked up a pen and without looking at George said, "name and address?"

George wearily offered his name and address.

The serious individual on the other side of the desk put his pen down and studied George for a second. He then said, "I am Inspector of Police, Collins. I'm usually based in Pontypool, but I am here in Treafon to investigate the incidents of last Saturday night in the town. We have interviewed over fifty people since then. Some have offered information; some have been released without charge and others have been charged with a range of offences. At one of those interviews, your name was mentioned as being involved in the troubles during that evening. What do you have to say to that?"

George became more animated with his rising temper. "You think because some shit has decided to drop me in it because of an argument in the past I'm guilty of something?" George realised that an agitated response would do him no good at all, so he calmed down and shrank back into his seat.

Inspector Collins waited for a few seconds, and said quietly, "now sir, I know you are tired, and we have both had a long day, but we need to move on. Where were you on Saturday night at around midnight?"

George realised the seriousness of his reply and thought calmly before he spoke, then answered in a more measured tone than before, "up until midnight I was in the Castle Vaults having a quiet beer and playing cards, there are about twenty people that can tell you that. Someone came in, don't know who it was, and said that there was a disturbance in town. Most of us went out to see what was going on. I was in a crowd of people who stood watching for a short while, others that I didn't know were smashing the windows of shops. After a while, I got fed up and to be honest, I was disgusted at the damage that was being done and I decided to go home. That's it."

The inspector asked, "did you try to stop any of the people throwing bricks and stones?" Before George could answer, the Inspector followed up with, "and what time did you get home?"

George quickly answered, "I didn't attempt to stop anyone, there were just too many of them, and I have to say since Saturday I have regretted that every minute. I should have been braver, and I was a coward. Those poor people! Oh, and I got home about 12.30." George was now becoming nervous and wondering if the inspector had any further evidence to implicate him.

The Inspector was not impressed by George's false remorse and followed up with, "12.30, are you sure? We can always pull your wife in to verify the time, though she might be put out by having to drag two small children, is it? Just to give us the truth."

George said, "well, it might have been a bit later. I'm not really sure as I've lost my watch and the missus was fast asleep when I got in."

The Inspector thought in silence for a minute and then rose and left the room.

George sat in weary silence for what seemed like ages but was probably no more than fifteen minutes.

The door opened and the Inspector returned and sat down. He said, "after the problems on Saturday, the riots, because that's what they were, spread to Bargoed, Pontypridd and Merthyr. As a result of the numbers involved, the police have asked for assistance in controlling the riots and I can tell you that troops will be arriving in Treafon later today or tomorrow. We don't seem to have enough evidence at the moment to charge you. We have one witness who said he saw you throw a brick through a window, which I don't need to tell you is wilful damage and carries a prison sentence. If we get more witnesses who corroborate that, we will be calling you back in.

For the moment, you are free to go, but before you do let me give you a bit of advice. You are not a youngster. You probably have a loving family, and for a while, the control of this town will be in the hands of the army. They do not take kindly to lawbreakers and deal with them differently from us and under these circumstances; they are within their rights to do so. You don't appear to be a stupid man, so go home, go to work and above all, keep the peace. Goodbye Mr Williams. I hope I don't see you again."

George nodded, stood up and left the room and the police station.

He pushed open the front door to his house. It was late evening, and the children were already in bed.

Maud was sat in front of the fire but stood as he entered.

She said, "where in heaven's name have you been? I've been worried sick. I was just about to call in a neighbour while I went to the pit. I thought there had been an accident."

George very wearily replied, "I've been to the police station. They thought I was involved in the problems Saturday night, but it was all a mistake."

Maud shook her head and said, "I don't know what your food is going to be like. It's probably ruined."

George trudged past her and said, "no problem - I'm too tired to eat anyway. I've got to be up in a few hours, so I'm off to bed." He dropped his boots at the foot of the stairs and dropped the rest of his clothes at the foot of the bed and crawled under the blankets.

Maud was about to ask him whether he had bathed but thought the better of it. She sat back down in front of the fire thinking about the following day's chores and that if George hadn't had a bath she would have to wash the sheets again. She sighed, "Oh god, more work."

4

The following morning, George walked over the railway bridge to get to the colliery. This was a large metal bridge that overlooked the station. He looked over the bridge, and from his vantage point, he could see a lot of activity on the station platform.

A long train with carriages and goods wagons had stopped alongside the platform. Groups of soldiers were carrying bags and boxes off the goods trucks, and other soldiers led horses out of wagons designed to hold cattle.

It caught his attention and he stopped to watch them for a few minutes, fascinated by the uniforms of the soldiers. Many of them had braid tucked through their shoulder epaulettes. A very large man stood to one side, with a clipboard and pencil. He had a sergeant's stripes and rows of medal ribbons on his chest. He guessed the sergeant had probably seen action; perhaps in the Boer War, which was some ten or eleven years before.

George let his mind wander to that time when, as a young man, he had been impressed watching lines of soldiers and then gun carriages and wagons following them as they marched through the town on their way to the railway station and off to that war. George had always had a fascination for soldiers and battle stories from the time he was a boy and was often found playing soldiers on the grass at the back of his parent's house, with small pieces of wood which he had whittled into the shape of soldiers. He had painted up the small pieces of wood in different colours to represent the different regiments.

Suddenly, George was aware of others passing him on the bridge over the railway line, rushing to begin their shift at the colliery. George shook himself out of his reverie and began to speed up his pace to ensure he arrived at the gates on time.

At the end of his shift, he made his weary way to the colliery gate and noticed the two uniformed policemen that had stopped him on the previous day. He blew through his teeth and was about to say something to the sergeant when he brushed past him, touching the brim of his helmet to George as he went by and quietly saying, "Mr Williams, good day to you," very politely.

The two policemen apprehended a fellow worker, as they had done with George. He murmured, "thank God for that," as he made his way home, though, he thought, obviously enquiries are still going on. When George passed the railway station for the second time that day, all traces of the soldiers had disappeared.

George went through the front door and shouted, "shwmae," to Maud. She came through to the kitchen from the small scullery and George noticed how ill she looked. "You ok, cariad?" he asked.

She replied, "tired is all I am." She sat opposite George and said, "the little ones are hard work and Willie is not well. He went to bed early with a rasping noise in his throat and a cough, and Joan has been restless all day. I had to try and prepare food and clean and wash and run back and fore seeing to them." She stood and went back into the scullery to serve up George's dinner.

George said nothing regarding Maud's comment on her day. It was generally accepted in the community that the men worked long and hard shifts underground and that the woman of the house dealt with everything else. That meant the preparing of food, the shopping, the cleaning and the washing and caring for children if they had any.

Maud felt that she was in no position to complain, and she rarely did, as some women had seven or eight children or even more. She knew Mrs Evans, 'down the tip', had thirteen children and ran a shop from her front room. The only advantage was that as children grew up, they could help with the running of the house. There was little or no time for rest and relaxation, even if the family could afford it.

Maud and George had been married for five years and apart from two charabanc trips to a nearby beauty spot and a local lake a few years before, they had not left the area. Maud's relaxation was a visit to members of her family and sometimes to George's family.

26

George's forms of relaxation were his visits to one of the pubs in town on a Saturday night, when he would often come home blind drunk and stay in bed through Sunday morning. Maud didn't complain, though she disapproved. She left that to the members of the Thomas family next door. Mr Thomas was a deacon in the local chapel and he, his wife and his mother who lived there, strongly disapproved of George and could barely bring themselves to speak to him.

George finished his dinner and as it was August and the evening still light, he picked up his jacket and shouted to Maud that he was going out for a walk.

Maud shouted back, "don't be late, you've got work in the morning."

George said, under his breath, "timekeeper in work and now a timekeeper at home." He shouted a weary, "yes love," back into the house.

He wandered up the street, past the railway station and into the park. It was a beautiful evening, though cloud was starting to gather, and George momentarily thought it would have been nice for Maud to come out with the children. He quickly put that thought to one side. Maud still had work to do and anyway, Willie was ill. George would never have considered that perhaps if he had stayed home to help Maud, they would have had time to go out together. It was not how things were done, and he didn't want to start that, otherwise he didn't know where it would end. He was a bit concerned about Willie. He thought that Willie was ill far too often, but perhaps he just needed toughening up.

He paid three pence in every pound he earned to the Medical Aid Society, and when Willie needed medical help, he could visit the nurse or the doctor, but finding time to go and wait in the surgery was difficult for him and Maud. Doctor Bowen had asked George if Willie's room was damp, and George had said that it was and that he had tried to patch up the damp walls, but it had made little difference.

27

The doctor had replied that Willie's perpetual cough was probably caused by the damp. George thought, well, there's nothing I can do as all the family sleep in damp rooms. He had told the doctor that he had mentioned the damp to the man who came to collect the rent, and he had assured George that something would be done; but that was twelve months ago, and nothing had happened.

He came out of the top park gates and wandered across the main street. He noticed the shops were still boarded up, though one or two had people outside trying to clear up the small shards of broken glass. Alongside the shops were large panes of glass ready to go back in. He stopped outside Cotton's Grocers, one of the non-Jewish shops that had been attacked. Mr Cotton and his son were bagging up all the old glass and bits of wood. George wondered whether someone had broken Cotton's window as an act of revenge as he knew that William Cotton was very strict on not allowing any credit.

George stood next to Mr Cotton. "Shwmae, William."

William Cotton stopped what he was doing and wiped the old putty off his hands on his apron. "Shwmae George," and then, "what a mess, eh?"

George shook his head "idiots," feeling just a little guilty as he thought of himself on the previous Saturday, throwing a brick through a similar shop window, and trying to justify it to himself. "I know you can't defend it, but perhaps you can understand those who damage the property of Jews." He stopped to look at William Cotton to see if there was any agreement.

Cotton said, "they work hard same as us, there's no justification for damaging any person's property like this."

George didn't want to get into an argument with William Cotton and so decided to turn away. "You're right William, no justification. Ah well, best of luck with the new window," and he moved off.

George was just about to cross the road and make his way back home when he could see that he had been spotted by an elderly couple

28

walking along the road towards him. He could not now avoid them. The smartly dressed elderly man moved towards him. "Hello George, how are you?"

George looked around. "Hello sir, very well thank you," nodding to the elderly man, George's father, Owen, who looked like an older version of George, about the same height and facially very similar, but with a goatee beard and moustache. He then turned to the elderly but equally smart woman, Ann Williams, saying, "mother," and then, "how are you both?"

George's father, an upright and very stern looking gentleman, looked up, "very well George. How are Maud and the children?"

"Very well, sir," George replied.

George's father, looking across at the row of shops, said, "a bad business this - all this meaningless destruction. I can't say that I particularly favour the Jewish community. I don't like their attitude and I don't agree with their religious thinking but how anyone could do this is beyond belief?"

Before George had a chance to respond, George's father looked at him with piercing eyes, "were you out on Saturday night George? Nowhere near this battlefield of sinful destruction, I hope?"

George suddenly felt very guilty, as he had many times in front of his father, who was a lay Methodist preacher in Salem, a chapel at the top end of town. Owen was a well respected figure in the town and people often went to O.H. for his level-headed advice. George continued to look at the floor, which had become a habit while being addressed by his father from about the age of four. "No sir. I did come out for a beer but was long gone before the trouble started," he lied.

"Still drinking the devil's brew, then?" O.H. asked.

George replied, "thirsty work underground," suddenly remembering that his father had worked underground all his life up until the last five years when he had given up work and at no time had

29

he drunk any alcohol.

His father shook his head, "no excuse, no excuse. Well, we had better get going." Suddenly George realised that his mother had not spoken, when she looked across at him and said, "tell Maud to come up and see us, and be sure to bring the children."

George was about to tell her that Willie was ill again and then thought that any comment would only prolong a difficult conversation and that would entail his father telling him he should be spending his money on medicine for Willie rather than beer. He could guess where the conversation would lead, and he was suddenly glad to be on his way.

He waved goodbye to his parents and crossed the road and began to head home. As he came to the bottom end of the town centre, he spied two soldiers standing, as if guarding the outside of the post office. He crossed the road and called, "shwmae," to them.

The taller soldier of the two nodded to George and replied, "howdo," in a Birmingham accent.

George said, "think there'll be any more trouble?"

The soldier said, "hope not, I've got a leave coming up and my missus will not be pleased if I don't make it home for her birthday."

The other soldier nodded in agreement.

George asked, "what regiment?"

The more talkative soldier of the two said, "Worcestershires. Pulled us out of barracks in the middle of the night they did, to come down here to keep the peace with you Taffys," and then, "no offence like."

George said, "none taken. Some say there's trouble in other towns?"

The soldier replied, "yes, we're nicely bedded down 'ere but there's trouble in Merthyr and somewhere called Ponty something and is it

Bargoed?"

George replied, "Pontypridd."

The soldier said, "yea, you started something 'ere and now it's spread. Not you personally like but perhaps your mates. Don't like Jews myself. Finds they keeps themselves to themselves, don't bother much with other people. We got 'em in Birmingham, but they don't cause no bother to no-one." The second soldier, with what was more like a cockney accent, said, "what's the word on what happened here to spark it off?"

George said, "high rents on some of the properties they own, and like you said, they don't bother much with the locals, so they become a bit of a target, and that's about it really."

The conversation dried up a bit then George said, "so how old was you when you joined up? Always fancied the army myself."

The first soldier said, "got into a bit of trouble when I was eighteen. My old man kicked me out, so the army was the only choice really. Been in now for six years. John here is older than me. He's done ten years and a stint in India."

George turned to the second soldier who suddenly piped up, "don't want to be going there mate, too fucking 'ot. Loads of mates died of disease, though the women are cheap."

George laughed along with them and said his goodbyes as he thought he had better make his way home. As he walked alongside the railway sidings where the ground was covered in a layer of coal dust, he thought about the troubles in the town. He wondered whether the riot would be an end to it. The men would have blown off steam and now perhaps everything would settle back into the tiresome routine that existed before. In his thoughts George had little sympathy for the Jewish community and considered selfishly only how his own life had been disrupted.

31

5

A few days later, George had just finished his dinner and Maud had gone out to answer a knock at the door. She could be heard speaking to someone, but George couldn't think who it was. After a few seconds, she came back in to reach down a small jar from a shelf in the scullery. George knew this was where she kept a few coins to help her with the housekeeping. He became curious and took advantage of her return to go out to see who it was. Bending down in the back yard was a small figure with corkscrew dark curls that framed his face. He was olive skinned and he had bright, shining eyes. He had almost a child-like appearance and he looked up when George appeared with a welcoming smile.

George leaned back to see the person's face. "Isaac, how are you? Haven't seen you for a long time."

The man stood up, stretching, and in a strange accent said, "George, this is where you live. You are a lucky man. Maud is a very nice person."

George chuckled, "you going to put in an offer, Isaac?"

Isaac, with a stern look replied, shaking his head in mock shame, "please George, don't joke, she is a lovely lady."

George said, "how's business?"

Isaac replied, "not good. After the problems last week, people don't want to have anything to do with me. I'm not sure whether they are afraid of us Jews or afraid of what other Welsh people will say if they are caught buying from us. I don't understand, they smash up the shops and then they won't buy from me. It's like a double punishment for us Jewish people."

With that, Maud came out of the house and passed over a few coins to Isaac Gaba to pay for the cotton reels and needles she had just bought.

Isaac Gaba was a Jewish packman. He was born in Germany and

had lived in London, but he had moved to Treafon about four years before. He sold a range of small items that he carried in two boxes that he strapped around himself, one on his back and one on his front. George had helped Isaac a few months before when he was carrying out running repairs on the straps he used to hold the boxes. George had given Isaac some tape he had found in his pocket and held the box while Isaac had repaired the strap. Since then, George had stopped to chat with Isaac several times. He walked everywhere and he had told George before that he visited surrounding towns up to a distance of eight miles away, often leaving home at two o'clock in the morning and sometimes returning home after midnight. He worked every day except a Saturday, the Jewish Sabbath, when he attended the synagogue with his family. George respected his work ethic and liked Isaac's cheerful manner, and it mattered little to him that he was Jewish, though he knew that others in the town would have a different view.

George said, "did you have any trouble, Isaac?"

Isaac replied, "my wife, Rachel, has been jostled while in town with the two children, and nasty things said to her, but nothing we have not experienced before. I made a mistake of passing through town last week at about eleven o'clock at night as the men were coming out of the pubs and one man pushed me while another threw my goods into the road. I spent nearly an hour picking everything up from the road in the dark and some things had to be thrown away as they were damaged, but two men on their way home stopped to help me."

He continued, "mind you, as we were picking up the goods that were strewn all over the floor, some men went past and one of them said loud enough for me to hear, serves 'em right for being Jewish." He stopped for a second and then looked at George and said, "you don't know what it means when people are unexpectedly kind. It allows you to forget some of the nasty things people say and do."

George immediately felt guilty again, thinking how he had contributed to the pain inflicted on the Jewish community. He moved to go back inside, then stopped and threw two pennies to Isaac.

Isaac thanked him and began the process of putting the straps holding the boxes over his head. "Goodbye George, see you again."

George raised his hand as he went back indoors.

All thoughts of remorse for the damage done on a previous Saturday night had left George as he turned from the bar with the three pints of ale for himself and his friends Rhys Jones and Gareth Sullivan. Both these men worked underground with George. Rhys was a Treafon man through and through. His pathway through life, as with George, seemed almost pre-ordained; school, where neither excelled though neither was without ability, down the mine at fourteen, married, though Rhys was married three years before George and then out on Saturday nights to try to relieve the depression of a working week made palatable only by the camaraderie and the humour of fellow workers.

Gareth was different. He was a wilder entity altogether, deeply religious, or so he said, a son of Irish Catholics, he would drink to the point of not being able to stand, sometimes he would go home that evening and take his drunkenness out on his wife but would think that all would be well if he then went to church to confess his sins. He believed that church almost gave him carte blanche to do whatever he wanted as he could then confess, and everything would be alright. Gareth worked in the same gang as George and he considered him a friend but his wildness frightened George and Rhys, as when drinking he was capable of anything.

George would relate one story where two men were arguing outside Gareth's bedroom window one night. Gareth looked down from the window and asked them to keep the noise down and one of the two told Gareth to "fuck off back to bed." Gareth immediately leapt from the bedroom window onto the man below, knocking him unconscious. Gareth got up off the man and turned to knock on his front door, asking his wife to let him back in. The other man was left speechless, staring at the house and the prone body of his friend lying in the road.

George placed the beer on the table, realising that this was the end of the first round of three beers. If any of them suggested any more after this, it would be six beers, or more, and dangerous territory. They chatted about the events of the riots, the role of the Independent Labour party and its links with the trade unions, the poor season the local soccer team were having and a deep discussion on the physical qualities of any local women they had noticed during the week.

Eleven o'clock came and George rose his hand to the other two as he was now incapable of speech. He stood up, probably too quickly and immediately his head began to spin. He rushed to the door of the Treafon Arms and fell over the doorstep. Sprawling across the pavement, he vomited into the gutter. He lay there for a minute while working out how he could get to his feet. Eventually, he pushed up with his forearms, shook his head and swung around, as he noticed someone asking if he needed a hand to get up.

Richard Elias stood looking over at him as he peered up, looking with one eye to help him focus. George got to his feet and after swaying a little, slurred, "how are you, Richard?"

Richard said, "are you going to be ok going home, or do you want a hand?"

George thought for a few seconds and replied, "I'll be fine," and then after a few seconds of silence, "but thank you for asking."

Their conversation was curtailed by the door of the pub being swung open and two men bodily throwing Gareth Sullivan out onto the pavement. Sullivan fell headfirst and groaned but did not move. George was about to ignore this and carry on his conversation with Richard Elias when he noticed two policemen rushing up the street, responding to the commotion.

George turned to Richard and quickly said, "bye, bye," before rushing off in the opposite direction to the oncoming policemen, and in his haste being spun sideways into a wall by a horse and cart which caught his arm as it passed up the street.

George's recollection of the evening ended at that point and the next he felt was an almighty headache as he woke in the wooden armchair alongside the fire grate in his kitchen the following morning. He spent the rest of the day avoiding Maud or the children and eventually escaped to a small bench overlooking the river at the back of the house to sleep off the horrendous hangover.

For many days after, any attempts at conversation with Maud were met with stony silence. After over a week of this and after many sincere apologies to her and promises not to get drunk again, and a following Saturday night spent at home, Maud asked him if he was going to go to his mother's birthday tea on the following Saturday. At first, he tried to offer all manner of excuses as to why he could not go, but it became clear that the barrier put up between Maud and himself would only be removed by his agreeing to go. He reluctantly gave in.

George walked alongside Maud, holding Willie's hand as Maud pushed the battered pram with Joan in it. George had shaved and dressed in his best suit, shirt and tie and Maud had told him that he looked very smart and that he looked as he had on their wedding day. George liked to look smart, and he smiled as Maud's comment made him feel good.

George glanced up at the others around the kitchen table. Maud sat quietly next to him. His younger brother, Ben, sat to his left. Ben was more like George. He was an exuberant character, with an infectious sense of humour, and was popular with a wide circle of friends. George's parents sat at the end of the table to his left and George's elder brother by three years, Thomas, sat opposite, next to his wife, Elizabeth. George also had a younger sister, Esther, but she was away attending a friend's wedding in Cardiff.

George kept unnaturally quiet in this company. He found his parent's company overbearing and while his mother could be good company on her own, she became silent in his father's pious presence. Thomas was, if anything, more overbearing than his father. He was bright and if the family could have afforded it, he would probably have gone to university. He had studied while in school, and after, and had become a solicitor's clerk in Caerphilly. He had met his wife, Elizabeth while working in Caerphilly and they had got married shortly after. They had been married for eight years but had no children.

In George's opinion, Thomas had become 'old before his time'. He was taller than George, but he had put on weight and George believed this was due to his sedentary occupation. His demeanour lacked humour and he was difficult to engage in conversation about any topic other than religion and the law. George's father enjoyed his eldest son's company as their views on the world corresponded so closely. O.H. was minister in his local Methodist chapel, Salem and Thomas was a deacon in his local Methodist chapel in Caerphilly. He had already announced that he and Elizabeth would have to catch the early evening train to Caerphilly in order to be home for the following day's Sunday service and George had noticed his father nodding in understanding and approval. The conversation revolved around the damage done in the riots of previous weeks and the need for people to control themselves after drinking heavily, which Thomas and his father felt was the cause of the riot.

O.H. looked up at George and said, "I spoke to Richard Elias earlier this week. He said he had bumped into you on his way back from a prayer meeting in Siloh."

George was momentarily taken aback as he had only a vague recollection of the drunken conversation with Elias and had forgotten that Elias attended Salem Chapel regularly. George quietly said, "oh yes," wondering what his father would say next.

George's father continued, "Elias seemed to have quite strong views on the dangers of drink, and how it contributed to the damage done by the rioters. He has told me how he intervened as the mob attempted to destroy a house of worship. Shameful, shameful."

George noticed Thomas nodding in agreement.

George remained quiet, hoping the conversation would move onto a different topic. He was relieved when Thomas started to outline one of the cases he had been working on in the solicitor's office. He took the opportunity to glance up at Elizabeth, Thomas' wife. George was always struck by her very obvious demure beauty, fair-haired, slim and very pretty. She had blonde hair which she usually wore piled up on her head and she had amazingly blue eyes. She seemed to become lovelier every time he saw her. She said very little, and George wondered if Thomas' overbearing attitude ensured she remain quiet, and that she should know her place. Maud was quiet but that had nothing to do with any influence George had over her; as in reality he had no influence over her at all.

Willie got up onto his grandmother's lap and she continued to have a quiet conversation with him. George took the opportunity to take a few more cheese sandwiches, which his mother had prepared, until he had a stern look from Maud, which suggested he had had enough, and not to take any more.

As Thomas was getting ready to go, he mentioned the soldiers that they had seen as they came up towards the house. He said, "I see there are troops still in the town. Dreadful that they are needed to keep the local population quiet."

Thomas turned to those in the parlour with a parting comment, "if all followed the Lord's word there would be no need for armies to keep the peace."

O.H. responded, "amen to that."

A little later they said their goodbyes and George felt a little relieved that Thomas was leaving but a little disappointed that he was taking Elizabeth with him, as during what otherwise was for him a boring Saturday afternoon, she had been something pleasant to look at.

An hour later, as George, Maud and the children were about to leave, O.H. shouted back to his wife, "I'll see them out."

Ann came to the parlour door wiping her hands on a cloth after doing the washing up and said, "it's been lovely to see you all, don't wait too long before you come again." She quickly kissed the two children and hurried back into the kitchen.

O.H. held open the front door and Maud shepherded the children out.

As George went to leave, his father grabbed his shoulder and pulled him back. He said quietly, "don't forget I've spoken to Elias. He described to me the state you were in." He gritted his teeth and squeezed his words between them, barely in control, "you are becoming a disgrace to this family, and it is the demon drink that is leading you there. You were in the middle of the riot, you were seen." He attempted to turn George around to face him. "After drinking, yes after drinking, you were seen inebriated last week, lying in the gutter." George managed to shake himself free, but O.H. continued, "learn to control yourself. You are not a child, and you have a family to look after."

George said nothing as he walked away, keeping his lips pursed in controlled temper.

6

George had quickly shovelled down his food and had just rushed up to the bedroom to collect his banjo and case. As he came back downstairs, he bumped into Maud who had just come in from the back garden carrying a large basket piled up with washing, "and where are you off to in such a hurry?"

George said, 'minstrel practise today in the Temperance Hall. I told you yesterday. We've got a concert in two weeks."

Maud scowled, "George Williams, you never mentioned anything of the sort."

George replied, "I'm sure I did, but if it slipped my mind, I'm sorry. I have to go. I'll be late."

Maud put down the basket and blocked his pathway and with her hands on her hips, said, "I've promised Annie I would go up and help her hang a new pair of curtains. How am I going to do that now? I can't take the children up with me. We'd never get anything done if I did. I was hoping you would look after them this afternoon and now you are going out and goodness knows what time you'll be back and in what state."

George said, "did you not hear me say the practise is in the Temperance Hall, that means there'll be no drink there. The practise will be about two hours and I'll be back by four o'clock at the latest. Can you not go up then?"

Maud pursed her lips and said, "not got much choice, have I? Make sure you are here by four, or so help me…

George didn't wait for Maud to complete the sentence but pushed past her and rushed out of the door with his banjo and case.

George was a member of the Kentucky Minstrel Band who regularly held concerts in various venues in Treafon, and the surrounding towns and villages, providing they had venues large enough. The Minstrel Band was a large one, with thirty banjo players and over twenty other singers and musicians. At their concerts, they filled the stage and George was always impressed with the sound of thirty banjos all paying in harmony and in tune. It required a certain skill to play at the required speed and to stay in tune.

The practise ended just after three o'clock and George made his way out of the hall with his banjo and case. He had gone perhaps two hundred yards when he noticed Sammy, the newspaper vendor. George would rarely go to the expense of buying a paper, but he would chat to Sammy, who had already read the papers and would relate to George what was in them. He looked down at the board where Sammy displayed the headlines and read out what the board said, "Phew! April 15th 1912, Titanic sunk with possibly fifteen hundred lives lost." He looked up and said, "makes you decide not to travel by ship."

Sammy smiled and said, "dreadful business. Happened two days ago, hit an iceberg so they say." He looked at George and said with heavy sarcasm, "it's not going to put you off going to New York though, is it George?"

George laughed and said, "when I do, I'll be drinking straight whisky, no ice for me."

Sammy shook his head, laughing. George started to make his way home. He could hear someone behind him calling his name, but he tried to ignore it as he knew Maud would be cross if he was late home. The person behind him was clearly getting nearer and more anxious and was running to catch up to the point that George could no longer ignore him. He stopped and turned to find his brother Ben, arriving breathless.

Putting his hands on his knees and leaning forwards, Ben gasped, "did you not hear me?"

George said, "I was trying to ignore you, could you not tell?"

Ben said, "I need you. It's an emergency."

George looked quizzically at his brother. "What sort of emergency? Is mam or dad ill?"

Ben said, "no, nothing like that."

"What then?"

Ben said, "the Harriers have got a side together to play Abertallin this afternoon. At the game there is to be a collection to help set up a children's ward at the Cottage Hospital, well, to help equip it by paying for bedding and things. Because of shifts, we could only get fifteen together anyway and this morning Gwilym Roberts has pulled out. He's ill. We can never play Abertallin with fourteen men. It will be hard enough with fifteen. So, basically, we need you to play on the wing."

George laughed, "oh, play on the wing is it? Not good enough to play anywhere else? A few years ago, I always played scrumhalf for the Harriers, now I'm on the wing. Keeping me out of the way?"

Ben looked a bit sheepish. "I suggested you could play scrum half but the blokes thought you were..., well.., a bit old now."

George said, "thank you for the vote of confidence," and turned to walk away.

Ben grabbed at his coat. "George, you have to. It's for the children in the town. Think if Willie or Joan were to get sick. We'll never be able to arrange this game again. We'll never have enough money to give to the hospital, and..."

George said, "yes?"

Ben looked down and said, "and it's down to you."

George looked up to the sky and gradually turned around. "Lord, why do I do this? Ben, why do I listen to you?"

Both brothers turned and rushed up to the top of the town and took a left turn to go across to the Recreation Ground. The ground was created from a flattened area of coal tip at the side of the valley, with changing huts and a small shed at the town end of the ground. The pitch was a patchwork of small clumps of grass and areas of small coal. A crowd was already beginning to build as they went into the small hut to change. A few of the players nodded to George and as he sat on one of the small benches the captain threw a shirt, shorts and socks across to him and shouted, "anyone got a spare pair of boots for George?" George carefully placed his banjo case under his seat.

Gareth Sullivan, a second row for the Harriers, shouted across, "he can have my old ones."

George picked up the boots that had been thrown across to him and immediately realised Gareth was considerably bigger than he was and consequently, his boots would be considerably bigger. He said, "these are no good, they are huge."

The captain looked across and with a wry smile said, "all we got, George, take it or leave it."

George could feel his frustration growing. He thought, I'm going to be in trouble with Maud as it is, and they can't even give me kit that fits.

George managed to find three pairs of socks and put those on, hoping to fill the large boots as much as possible.

As they were ready to run out after their pep talk from the captain, Gareth Sullivan looked down at George's feet and said, "shame Gwilym couldn't play today. Big boots to fill without him," and then fell about laughing at his own joke.

George glared at Gareth, "fuck off you Irish clown."

After an hour, with the game well into the second half, George had still not touched the ball. He was worn out running on the muddy surface and trying to lift these large heavy boots as he ran. The Harriers were winning by five points, and they had been told at half time that well over thirty pounds had been collected for the hospital ward from the large crowd that were watching.

George was still concentrating on the game when one of the Abertallin players took the ball and hoisted a huge kick into the Harriers half. George could see the ball coming towards him from a height and was determined not to mess up his only touch of the ball. He caught the ball cleanly and went to kick it into touch but when he tried to lift his kicking foot his boot caught in the muddy ground. He seemed to have plenty of time as none of the Abertallin players were anywhere near him and he attempted the kick again, but his feet still refused to budge. He made one last effort just as an Abertallin forward appeared in front of him, raising his arm and leading with this into George's chest and head, catching him and knocking him backwards. George's head took the main impact of the blow and as he hit the ground he momentarily blacked out. That was the last thing he could remember of the game.

He eventually stood up and wandered around, not having a clue where he was. In the meantime, the game continued. The Abertallin forward had picked the ball up and charged over the try line. The conversion was kicked, and George was helped off the field, shaking his head. Now, down to fourteen men, the Harriers were easily overpowered and lost the game by twenty-eight points to thirteen.

Ben could see the scowls on the Harriers player's faces. He could hear one say, "we would have won if we'd had a decent winger." Ben looked around but he couldn't see George at the end of the game. He had spent the last ten minutes a forlorn figure leaning against the railings, which surrounded the playing area but facing away from the game.

Ben then spotted someone in a Harriers shirt heading away from the changing hut wandering towards the mountainside. He raced after his brother and after catching up with him turned him around, "hey, where do you think you are going?"

George looked up at his brother and with a stupid grin giggled, "who are you? You look a bit like my brother, but you've got mud on your face and he's better looking than you," and he giggled again.

Ben could see that George was in a daze and shepherded him back towards the changing hut. As he got to the doorway into the hut, he noticed Doctor Stewart coming towards him. The doctor could often be seen at the Harriers games but most of the players would avoid being seen by him as he was not really deemed competent and was reckoned to be drunk most of the time when attending to people in his surgery.

The doctor shouted, "I saw what happened. He's had a bump on the head." He reached into his pocket and lifted out a small package out of which he took two large tablets. He looked at Ben and said, "give him these, he'll be as right as rain in no time."

Ben put the tablets into George's mouth one at a time and held his mouth closed until he had swallowed them. Some of the players had already left when the two got into the changing hut and Ben sat George down on the bench and said, "don't move." Ben then proceeded to get dressed after washing his face and arms in a bowl that someone had brought along, and which was now full of filthy water. Ben then moved to George, wiping his face and taking his shirt and shorts off, as well as his boots and the three pairs of socks.

Ben was just about to leave when Gareth Sullivan called out, "I'll swap, give me back my boots and you can have this banjo and case."

Ben passed Gareth's boots back to him and took George's banjo and case.

As he left the changing hut, the team captain, Dai Evans, a large man with a fashionable drooping moustache, shouted across to Ben, "see you down at the Globe. There's going to be a bit of singing and another collection for the hospital. Dai Globe, behind the bar, has promised a half-penny in the kitty for every pint bought, should make a tidy sum."

Ben said, "I think I'd better get George home. He's not himself."

Dai Evans laughed. "I don't think George has ever been himself.

45

I've seen him on a few Saturdays when he's definitely more like somebody else, and I bet his missus wishes there were times when he was somebody else. Don't worry, he looks fine to me. We'll look after him. Just the one pint in the Globe."

Ben thought, "can't do any more harm. George is going to be the same whether he goes home now or in half an hour's time."

7

The short journey to the Globe pub was eventful as George suddenly decided to run in front of a fast-moving horse and cart and had to be pushed out of its pathway by Ben's quick thinking. A little further along, Ben stopped briefly to speak to a friend and when he turned around, George was nowhere to be seen. When Ben sighted him and eventually caught up with him, he made a grab for his collar, but George managed to shake Ben's arm off saying he had to visit Mr Elstayn to apologise for breaking his window.

Ben had no idea what he was talking about but he realised that George could not be left alone, and with some difficulty he was able to steer him carefully to the pub's doorway. VNot an easy task as he had to hold George with one hand and carry his kit bag and George's banjo case in the other hand.

On entering, Ben sat him down in the corner away from the door, where he remained sitting upright with a stupid grin on his face. Ben placed George's banjo case under the seat. He then went to the bar and instructed Iestyn Thomas, a fellow Harriers player to keep an eye on his brother. The pub quickly filled up with many coming in to take part in the singing that would now take place, and most were happy to oblige by offering a few coins to the fund for the local hospital.

During the next hour, Ben continually kept telling George to keep his voice down as he insisted on singing the song that had been sung previously and sometimes drowned out the singer. This produced an unholy cacophony with many in the pub telling George to keep quiet. He would respond by scowling at those who shouted at him in a very exaggerated way. Ben became concerned about him as he was acting this way without having had much to drink.

George continued to sip his beer while pulling strange faces at those around him. A few of those singing were soloists who did not take kindly to George's rendition of other songs at the same time that they were singing. He then noticed his banjo case under the seat and pulled out the instrument to play with the strings, tightening some and loosening others.

At one point when Ben's back was turned, George got up onto the small stage and proceeded to sing 'Ten Green Bottles', all the way through, with a banjo accompaniment. When he finished, he proceeded to sing it all the way through again, reacting to the jeers by saying that he hadn't sung it before. All the positions of the strings on the banjo had been changed and so it was very out of tune. He tried to sing and play a few Music Hall numbers but he realised he couldn't remember the words and so hummed through most.

Gareth Sullivan bellowed out, "for fuck's sake George give it a rest."

George just pulled a face, and shouted back, "quiet, I'm singing."

Gareth replied loudly, "ok, I've had enough." He stormed onto the small stage, grabbed George's banjo and smashed him over the head with it. George sat for a while with the broken banjo around his head.

Sullivan looked at Ben and shouted, "take him home quick Ben, before I decide to put that banjo somewhere else."

Ben was enjoying the evening but felt that unless he took George out of the pub the two of them would be lynched. He found it confusing that George was acting so strangely after only perhaps two beers, but it was obvious that he was upsetting everyone in the pub.

Ben got George outside the pub and proceeded, with some difficulty to take him down through the town to the park gates. It was eight thirty in the evening, and the park-keeper was about to lock the gates. As Ben got nearer to the gates, the park-keeper told Ben he would have to hurry as his mate Rob was about to lock the bottom gates. Ben hurried George along as a trip through the park would save perhaps ten minutes. For a few minutes, George seemed to be more compliant and rushed along with him. Suddenly, Ben slipped and when he regained his balance, George had disappeared into the bushes.

Ben stood looking around him, not knowing which way George had gone. He stood and shouted, "George, stop playing silly buggers, come out. I have to get you home, and then go all the way home myself before I get a locked door."

Ben stood and listened to see if he could sense movement in the bushes. He stood for several minutes and could hear nothing. He decided to continue along the path. He realised that if he did not make an effort to get out of the park, he was in danger of being locked in, but he still felt a duty to get George home safely. Ben wandered the park for some considerable time with no sign of George. He eventually gave up and wandered up to the top gates of the park, knowing that if the gates were locked, as they were very likely to be, he could call at the park-keeper's house next to the gates and persuade him to open them up.

Meanwhile, George wandered the park and suddenly began to feel very tired. He mechanically followed the path to the bottom park gates but found a pad lock and chain drawing the two gates together. The park was surrounded by a stone wall with high wrought iron railings topped by iron spikes from the time that the park was an ironmaster's personal garden. Despite his strange stupor, George knew that he could not master the railings without serious injury, if not from the top of the railings, certainly from the drop on the outside. He began to walk back through the park and remembered the wooden building known locally as 'the Ladies Shelter'. He didn't know why it had been so named and he didn't much care. He was more concerned with his tiredness. The day had been long, and his body seemed battered and exhausted. He lay across the benches which surrounded the shelter and immediately fell asleep.

George was awoken by the unusual sounds of birds very close by. He opened his eyes and realised that he was out in the open. He was freezing cold, and he tried to ward off the effects of the cold morning by drawing his jacket around himself. He moved into a sitting position and immediately wished he hadn't as his head felt as if it was just about to fall off. He noticed some people moving in the distance and gradually came to his senses and remembered where he was. He very slowly walked down towards the park gates nearest to home. Every movement hurt in every part of his body. His muscles hurt from the exertions of the previous day's rugby and his head hurt. He felt a sigh of relief as, when he got to the gates, he found them open. He had no idea what the time was, but he noticed a boy wheeling a baker's cart along the road towards a row of houses. He asked the baker's boy the time and the boy replied that he wasn't certain, but it was about seven thirty.

George's thoughts were crowding into his head. He suddenly remembered that he had promised to be home the previous afternoon. Still in a confused state on arrival at his house, he decided to try to sneak into some part of the house and pretend that he had fallen asleep there the night before. He thought that this might at least in part assuage some of Maud's venom.

He decided to go around to the back door and try to gain entry there. As he got to the back of the house, he quickly drew himself back below the outer wall as he noticed Maud pegging clothes onto the line in the back garden with Willie passing them up from a small basket. He realised that for the moment, that avenue was closed. He suddenly felt very tired, and his body ached.

He noticed next door's gate was off the latch and he could see that their shed door had not been locked. He smiled as he thought he might hide in there until Maud finished hanging the clothes and then he could try to get into the house unseen. He crept through the shed door and cast his eyes around for the best place to hide. He was drawn to an old deckchair placed in the centre of the floor. He smiled as he thought of Mr. Thomas hiding in here from the two women of the house and then realised that was exactly what he was about to do. He sat on the deck chair and couldn't believe how comfortable it felt. Suddenly, his eyes felt heavy.

George was woken up by a commotion outside the shed. Before he had time to escape from the shed, the door opened, and the inside of the shed was cast into the light and then almost immediately into deep shadow. The shadow was created by the form of the very large constable who had escorted him to the police station some time before. Around the large body of the constable George could see the face of Mrs Thomas, the old lady from next door.

She said, "there, I told you there was an intruder on my property."

The constable said, in a deep booming voice, "thank you maam, I think I can deal with it now." He stepped back and George stepped out of the shed.

The constable turned to Mrs Thomas and said, "do you know this man, maam?"

Mrs Thomas screwed up her eyes and folded her arms. She hesitated in thought as to what to say. "Unfortunately, yes constable, he is the drunkard from next door."

The constable looked down at George from what seemed a great height. "Do you mind telling me what you are doing in there, sir?"

George wanted to remind the policeman that he had spoken to him before but then he realised he would have to admit having visited the police station to Mrs Thomas.

He concentrated on trying to think quickly of a plausible excuse for being in the shed, but his head hurt. He looked up with a disbelieving face, "borrowing a barrow constable."

Mrs Thomas in frustration and a little anger said, "hmm, I don't think so."

The constable turned to Mrs Thomas and said, "do you want to press charges maam?"

George looked at Mrs Thomas pleadingly. It seemed an interminable time before the old lady spoke, "for Maud's sake no, I suppose."

George moved beyond the shed to the wall to have something to lean on, "thank you ma, I'm very grateful and when I get chance I'll explain it to you," he stopped and closed his eyes, "but my head hurts something awful at the moment."

Mrs Thomas looked at him with a piercing gaze. "That'll be the beer I suppose. You'll be getting no sympathy here, George Williams." She moved alongside the policeman, "get him out of my sight constable before I do something I may regret."

George screwed up his eyes and said, "don't worry, Maud will do that when I get in."

The constable escorted George around to his front door and knocked quietly. Maud came to the front door with the classic pose of the angry woman, arms folded and a steely look. The constable asked, "excuse me maam, sorry to bother you, do you know this man?"

Maud unfolded her arms, "no constable, never seen him before."

George said in a pathetic attitude, "please Maud, I've had a hell of a night," and then as he couldn't think what else to say to fill the silence he continued, "and I've broken my banjo."

8

The sergeant major barked out his orders and the twenty-five men in front of him responded. They marched up to the one end of the Drill Hall and following a command, turned and marched the short distance to the other end. After repeating their drills for some forty-five minutes, the sergeant major commanded them to "fall out," and they moved to the back of the hall to allow a second contingent to drill. The hall was simply too small to accommodate all the volunteers. When the weather was fine, they could drill outside in one group, but as snow was continuing to fall outside, they had been forced to drill inside. It was December 1913.

George thoroughly enjoyed the time when he met up with others for practise drill. He had joined the 3rd Battalion Monmouthshire Regiment twelve months before and he was proud to be a 'Terrier'. The regiment was formed as a reserve force following the change from volunteer regiments to reserve regiments in 1908. He was one of the older members of the company and he was making the most of the remaining three years he would serve in the Territorials, as the men had to leave when they were thirty-five.

Several of his friends and work mates had also joined, Gareth Sullivan, the wild Irishman, Brinley Evans, Rhys Jones and Charlie Price, following a spell in Cardiff prison for his part in the Jewish riots. George often felt exhausted after drilling for ninety minutes following a day's shift underground, but it kept him fit and healthy, and he loved it. He had done two summer camps earlier in the year, one of them with a contingent of the Royal Artillery, and those were particularly enjoyable. He met men from other areas of the country and aside from the thrill of stealing eggs from the local farms for their breakfast while they were in a camp in the Breconshire countryside, and having the opportunity to carry out military manoeuvres, sometimes on horseback, they would also hide hip flasks of whisky and sometimes kegs of beer and party all night before their return.

They had to be careful though, as discipline was tightening up as the threat of war increased. Many talked about a possible war and consequently the drills and manoeuvres became more important and more serious.

George talked with his workmates and with his fellow soldiers about the possibility of war and all were supremely confident about their ability to defeat a foreign foe. Some would even define the potential enemy as likely to be Germany, who they would speak about in condescending terms. Germany had been 'sabre rattling' for the last few years and the British press had highlighted this, and it consequently became the main topic of conversation in many pubs and clubs.

Last night's conversation had focussed on the fact that at least two German families had left Treafon in recent weeks to return home. Rhys and Gareth had suggested that perhaps these families had received secret information about an impending war, causing them to book their tickets home.

George could only offer "I used to get my meat from Schubert's butcher, now I'll have to look somewhere else," and got a laugh in response.

At the end of the session, they walked to the end of the hall and handed in their wooden rifles. Gareth Sullivan piped up, "Sarge, is it right we'll be getting real rifles to drill with after Christmas?"

Before the Sergeant Major could answer, George shouted, "no, we're going to smash the Germans with these rifles and hope they get splinters."

The Sergeant Major said, "very funny, Williams, every regiment needs a comedian. I'm sure your jokes will be much appreciated by our enemy, who'll laugh themselves to death."

'Thank you, Sergeant Major," replied George with a smile.

"Now bugger off home and worry someone else," the Sergeant Major added.

The following Saturday, George sat with his pint of ale in front of him. He was making an effort and drinking slowly, but he was in a round with Rhys, William Marsden and Brinley who were berating him for slowing down the round of drinks. After three pints of ale, George decided to buy his own so that he might go home early and in a reasonable state.

Brinley asked, "do you think it'll be war?"

Rhys replied, "I don't know. You hear about the threat from Germany from time to time, but I can't afford to buy a newspaper and so I rely on other people's views. I doubt anyone will be asking the likes of us what we think."

George had been listening and eventually said, "we shouldn't be afraid of war. Our army is well equipped, and we have the best navy in the world. Do you want to know what I think will happen?"

Rhys and Brinley nodded waiting for George to impart his knowledge.

George said, "they'll send the navy to the German coast and tell them to just sit there. They'll starve the bastards out, like the siege of castles in the old days. If they do that it won't matter what the army do."

Rhys said, "I think it'll be more complicated than that. I was talking to Ifor in work, and he said he was frightened that German aeroplanes would come over here and bomb us." He waited a few seconds and added, "and what about the submarines? They could sink the navy without anyone even seeing them," placing his pint glass on the table with an air of finality.

George said, "if we are talking about all this, do you not think that the people in London have not already thought about it? No worries, I say, we'll fight the war and be home before you know it. My only concern is that the threat of war drags on without anything happening. I've only got three years until I'm thirty-five and then I'd have to leave the Territorials. That would really piss me off."

George left the pub early and walked the quiet streets back to the house. As he got to his gate, he noticed Mrs Thomas, the old lady from next door, arriving at her gate adjacent to his at the same time. She could not be avoided.

"Evening Ma," George gave his usual greeting.

"Hmm," said Mrs Thomas, "no need to ask where you've been."

"Prayer meeting, Mrs Thomas," replied George with a smirk.

"Praying for the price of beer to drop, while in the Castle Vaults, no doubt," said Mrs Thomas acidly.

"Now, now Mrs Thomas, let's not be unkind, another few hours and it'll be the Sabbath, not a time for unkindness," replied George, adding, "you're out late Ma, fancy man?"

Mrs Thomas, realising she couldn't verbally fence with George all night, finally said, "you should be home looking after your family, not gallivanting around the town. You're not a youngster anymore, George Williams," and with that, she shut the door.

George suddenly remembered he was intending to ask the Thomas' for a loan of their barrow to collect manure the following day, which wiped the smile off his face.

At lunchtime the following day he went around to the Thomas' house with Willie behind him. Mr Thomas, a severe looking man, answered the door and reluctantly agreed George could borrow the barrow, with a parting comment "not too happy in agreeing to support you working on the Lord's Day, but I suppose that's your choice, even if it is a bit of a heathen one. I'll leave the shed open for you." He closed the front door without a parting goodbye or any acknowledgement of Willie's presence. George shrugged and took Willie around to the back of the house to collect the barrow.

Willie carried the shovel and off the two went, down the street, stopping at each pile of manure left by the dray horses, to lift it into the barrow. Willie said, holding his nose. "Poo, that stinks."

George replied, "that's goodness, that's what that smell is. It'll be great for the garden."

Willie thought for a second and said, "I'll keep all my poo from now on then."

"No, no, don't do that Willie, it only works with animal poo," said George with a broad grin.

When they got to the bottom of the long street, Willie had to rest as he had started coughing. He sat on the edge of the pavement to get his breath back. George sat with his arm around him. When he had recovered, George took Willie home and went with the barrow and shovel to the back garden where he shovelled the manure onto the vegetable patch. He then took the barrow down to a small stream at the back of the house to clean it before returning it to the Thomas' shed. By the time he got back to the house, he could hear Maud upstairs speaking to Willie. She had taken him up to bed with a glass of water and a bed warmer, which she had warmed on the fire.

Maud eventually came down and said, "I won't go to chapel this evening. I'll stay and keep an eye on Willie. He seems to get ill more often, and he doesn't seem to put any weight on. He often says he doesn't want any food. I'm really worried about him. His room is damp, and I think we are going to have to get the doctor to him again."

George didn't say anything, as he knew that his views on calling the doctor would not agree with Maud's. It was the damp room that was causing Willie's poor health and there was little the doctor could do about that.

9

"Go on, take a swig. It won't bite," said George, passing the hip flask to his younger brother Ben.

Ben quickly took the flask, and after a look around to make sure no one was watching, he took a big gulp. He doubled up coughing and spluttering as the whisky hit the back of his throat.

Both of them were standing around the corner, hidden at the back of Salem Chapel, but both could still feel the warmth of the July sunshine. George thought it was a lovely summer scene. The grass was long and had not been cut for a while and the wildflowers that grew there attracted bees and butterflies.

George closed his eyes and said, "Duw, this is a little bit of the countryside in the middle of the town."

George took another quick swig and reluctantly said, "come on, we'd better get back inside, or someone is going to come out looking for us, and that would give the game away."

It was July 1914, the afternoon of George's younger sister, Esther's wedding. George was close to Esther, and he thought she looked gorgeous on her wedding day. The contrast of her dark curls and the lace collar of her white wedding dress was breath-taking. He had given her a big hug after the service and wished her the best of luck. He shook hands with Evan, her new husband and turning to Esther said, "I'm glad you married the second-best looking bloke here." Esther and Evan tutted at the comment and laughed. She had married Evan Best, from Rhymney, over the valley from Treafon, and Esther would be moving over to Rhymney after the wedding. George teased her at every opportunity, coming up behind her and repeating in her ear, "Esther Best, Esther Best," until Maud sternly told him to grow up.

Later, as George chatted to Evan, he noticed a short, stocky man with a broad chest standing behind his new brother-in-law. Evan became aware of someone behind him and turning immediately greeted the man with a huge smile, "Gwynfor, I didn't see you there." Evan turned back to George, and while holding his brother's handshake firmly he pulled the shorter man forward, "George, this is my older and as you can see, balder big brother, and he's shorter than me." He laughed and so did the brother, who George could see had a jovial nature, and was a little less serious than Evan.

Esther, who had been speaking to her mother, then joined the group. She said, "George, I see you've met Gwynfor." She smiled and turning to Evan said, "Gwynfor said I can go looking for him if I get fed up of you," and with a wicked look at Evan she continued, "so you'd better behave."

A little later, a cameraman that O.H. had hired called them all together for formal photographs. The family formed up around Esther and Evan with Thomas and Elizabeth on one side and George and Maud, with Joan and Willie in front, on the other. Ben stood next to George while O.H. and Ann sat either side of the bride and groom. The fussy cameraman moved Ben across to Thomas' side as he thought it gave the picture a better balance. The Williams family then moved aside for the Best family to have their photograph taken. O.H. generously promised that he would pay for a copy of the photograph to be sent out to each of the families present.

George and Ben went back into the chapel vestry and noticed most of their close family were sat around one of the trestle tables. George leaned over to Ben and said quietly, "looks like a war council, doesn't it? Have you ever seen such a collection of more miserable buggers?"

Ben laughed and went to sit down.

O.H., Evan, George and Ben were sat around the table. George's mother, Ann had taken the children for a walk as they had become bored. The ceremony had taken place five hours before. All the guests had eaten at the reception, and most had made their way home.

Thomas had gone into the chapel with Elizabeth to talk to the chapel pastor, who was now eighty-two, and who had preached in the chapel before O.H., and who now had difficulty hearing.

George could hear Thomas shouting to the pastor in order that he might be heard.

He then turned his attention to the conversation between O.H. and Esther's new husband, Evan.

Evan said, "I know the wedding was a bit short notice but with all that was happening in Europe we thought it was better to get married before war broke out, as we both think it will."

George, emboldened by the whisky, laughingly blurted out, "thought it was a quick wedding for another reason."

For that, he got dagger like looks from his father and he sheepishly slid back into his chair.

"Why should that matter to you, Evan?" O.H. asked.

He replied, "because it looks like war, and I want to do my bit for my country and go and fight."

George said, probably a bit too loudly, "here, here." O.H. responded with another piercing stare.

Evan was finding it a bit difficult to make his point without being rude to his new family, and so he decided to keep quiet.

O.H. dropped easily into preaching mode by grabbing the lapels of his suit jacket and then proceeded to look upwards as if for divine support. "Has the world not seen enough troubles? Was the killing of the heir to the Austro-Hungarian Empire not enough for everybody? Does he have to be avenged and in this drag other peoples into it? Why do we need to shed blood for people half a world away?"

He closed his eyes and shook his head and then continued, "I travelled to Merthyr last week to hear Keir Hardie and the Scotsman, Maxton, speak. The phrase that has rung in my ears ever since was when Hardie said 'they are no enemies of ours, but faithful friends'. I came away heartened by the numbers that were there and the huge support for peace." He paused for effect, leaned forward and then continued "not war."

George felt that only one side of the argument was being given and said, "the newspapers are saying that Austro-Hungary are going to send an ultimatum to Serbia and if Serbia don't agree the terms, there will be war between them, and that Russia will then support Serbia as fellow Slavs. Austro-Hungary will then expect Germany to support them, and the Kaiser has said he will. France will then be expected to support Russia," he waited "and so the two sides line up."

O.H. then interrupted, "all speculation and at no time have you mentioned Britain."

George responded, "we will have to make our minds up whether we support France as a result of treaties we have made in the past."

O.H. replied with heavy sarcasm, "a wonderful ally, France. We have gone to war against France more than any other country in the world, and now they expect us to support them in this ridiculous argument."

Ben said, "well, I can see sense on both sides of the argument."

O.H. stood up. "There is no sense on any side that supports killing another man. I will always speak out against those that take up arms against each other."

With that, Thomas came through the chapel door into the vestry, with Elizabeth following, who then squeezed in next to Ben. Thomas remained standing. O.H. was about to move away but stayed momentarily to see if Thomas offered an opinion.

Thomas, noticing that everyone had gone quiet said, "there's quiet you all are, talking about us, were you?" He laughed, but the seriousness of the discussion persuaded no one else to join in.

George said, "father was expressing his opinion on whether men

61

should go to fight another war."

Thomas was quiet for a minute and then said, "well, I'll not be going for one, you can be assured of that."

The statement struck George like a thunderbolt. He knew that Thomas was older and so might not be called to fight anyway. He had thought all along that O.H.'s position on the possible war was really irrelevant, as he would be too old to fight. Evan was clearly going to war while Ben was undecided, but George was sure he would go if called upon. But what would happen if there was a war and Thomas was asked to fight and then he refused to go. George was shocked at Thomas' stance. He wondered if he was just copying his father so as not to offend him, or whether he really would refuse to go.

Thomas ended the discussion by moving around to the head of the table and grabbing his lapels, as O.H. had done a few minutes before. George was struck by the physical similarity in the stance taken by both men, physically and ideologically. The only differences between them were the obvious age difference, which gave O.H. a few more wrinkles around the eyes, and he had a beard whereas Thomas, his eldest son was clean shaven, but otherwise they looked and to a point even sounded the same.

Thomas said, "we don't know if there will be a war, we don't know whether Britain would choose to stay out of a war between other countries and we don't know whether we'd be made to fight if there was a war." After a few seconds of silence he continued, "anyway, nobody's going to make me fight, it is an abomination of God's law, remember the Sixth Commandment, thou shalt not kill." Elizabeth cleared her throat as if about to speak and everyone turned to face her. Whether she was about to speak or not became irrelevant as Thomas interjected, "do not press my wife for her opinion. We have discussed it and she understands my commitment." Elizabeth remained silent.

Several of them looked up as Ann returned, nursing baby Joan and with Willie trying to get underneath the trestle table to sit on his father's lap. Ann took note of the last few comments made and just as O.H. opened his mouth to speak she firmly said, "no more talk of war in front of the children, it will frighten them, and I think on Esther's wedding day we should be speaking of happier things." Ann had spoken and no one was prepared to challenge it. O.H. quickly closed his mouth.

A few seconds later, Maud and Esther returned to the vestry after saying their goodbyes to family members, and Thomas and Elizabeth were preparing to leave to return to Caerphilly. George knew that the goodbyes would take some time and he took the opportunity of the confusion to sneak out to the back of the chapel and have another swig from his hip flask.

George did not return to the topic of war until he, Maud and the children were on their way home. Maud was pushing the pram and George was carrying Willie, who had fallen asleep. He said, "well, Thomas saying he wouldn't go to the army was a real shock. I wonder how people in the community will take that and what the government would do to people who refused to fight? O.H. can sound off as much as he likes and people can choose to listen to him or ignore him, but Thomas…" He shook his head in disbelief.

Maud said, "it's a pointless discussion. You're either a soldier or you're not. If you choose to fight you go and if you don't then you carry on with your job, and at the moment no one is being made to fight."

George said, "that's as maybe, but to say at this stage that you wouldn't fight under any circumstances, well…" He left the statement unfinished and kept his thoughts to himself.

As they came down through the town, they passed the front of the Punch House, a small public house. George could hear the hum of conversation through the half-opened door. They had only gone a few paces past when George said, "I can hear Brinley in there. I wanted to have a quick word with him about work. You carry on and I will catch you up." Willie had woken up and George had carefully placed him on the pavement, from where he had rushed to his mother's side.

Maud stopped in her tracks and turned to face George with an angry grimace. "Why can't you be honest, George Williams. You've been drinking all day. I could see the outline of the hip flask in your pocket and smell it on your breath."

George pulled a sulky face. "It's my sister's wedding."

Maud took a step nearer to him. "You are so selfish. You expect me to carry two children and push a pram while you go in there and have a skinful of beer, which means we won't see you for the rest of today and most of tomorrow, and you expect my permission?"

George took in what Maud had said, and his demeanour suddenly changed, boosted by his intake of whisky "permission, permission," he shouted, "after a week's worth of shifts underground you think I need your permission to relax with my friends."

Maud started to move away and then she stopped and went back, pushing her face right in front of George. "I hate myself when I use bad language, but as God is my witness, you are getting worse. You don't think of us for one minute, you, you …" She hesitated and then shouted out "you are a selfish bastard," and then she stormed off muttering under her breath.

George stood stunned for a second and then, noticing some men he knew who also worked underground who had stopped to watch the scene, he shouted after her, "I am the breadwinner in our house, and I will do what I like."

The two men who stood a few yards away started to clap and one shouted, "you tell her George."

George turned, tut-tutted and pushed open the door of the pub.

64

10

George sat on top of the farm gate smoking a cigarette and looking out across the gentle green landscape. There were several sheep grazing in the field just a few feet from him, penned in by a high stone wall. He watched them grazing and they seemed totally unaware of his presence. It was a calm, peaceful scene and was helped by the bright sunshine. He sighed with satisfaction. He had sat on the gate with little or no movement for the last twenty minutes. The rest of the party he was with couldn't see him as he had walked along to a position where he was out of sight, shielded by a small grove of trees.

Maud had worked hard to persuade him to come along to the chapel picnic. She had not spoken to him for a few days after the shouting match outside the Punch House, but George had to relent and apologise when he had to make his own meals for a few days. She had wanted to attend the event with her friends and had needed George to help with the two children.

She had managed to get Joan to sleep and had put her into the pram, and Willie had gone off with two other children to pick blackberries in the bushes alongside the field. George had sat with Maud for a while on a blanket that had been laid out and he helped himself to the sandwiches and cakes, which everyone had provided, but he had wearied of the conversation of the women around the blanket.

There were several older children who had gone off for a walk and there were three other men sat around the blanket, one was a retired miner who was now the chapel preacher, the second was the husband of one of Maud's most outspoken friends and consequently he sat and said nothing and the third was a teacher in the local school whose conversation was meandering, and exceedingly high-brow and George found that he could only understand half of what he said.

George had finally agreed very reluctantly to go. Just before they had set out, he had sneaked down to the chicken shed in the back garden, supposedly to check on the chickens before leaving, he had told Maud. In truth, it was to pull out a whisky bottle he had hidden the week before. The bottle was wedged behind a loose brick at the back of the chicken run and George was careful not to be seen and to replace it without any evidence of it having been there. He had filled two hip flasks and put one into each of the two side pockets of the jacket he would be wearing to the picnic.

The group met first at the chapel and then collected others along the way. There were over twenty women to the four men and George marvelled at the way in which the other husbands had managed to get out of attending the event. One woman said that her husband had badly sprained his ankle the night before, while another said that a garden wall had collapsed a few days before and this would be the only opportunity for her husband to rebuild it.

George flicked away the stub of his cigarette and brought out one of the hip flasks for a quick swig. He thought it peaceful and quiet on the gate and from there he couldn't hear the women's constant chattering, which had bored him into a stupor. He sat for a further five minutes with his eyes closed, listening to the birds in the hedgerow.

He reached into his pocket to take out the hip flask for one more swig when the three young children crept up behind him and shouted "boo!"

He almost fell off the gate and almost fell a second time when he tried to put the hip flask back into his pocket without the children seeing.

He climbed down from the gate and laughed as the children ran around him. The other two children ran off with the bag of blackberries, keen to show their mothers what they had collected. George went back more slowly, swaying a little, holding Willie's hand, as he listened to him explaining how he had to climb very high to reach the biggest blackberries.

George went back to sitting around the blanket. He listened to the drone of conversation without taking it in. He excused himself a few times, supposedly to go to the toilet in a nearby small wood, but really to continue to swig the whisky. He returned to the blanket and lay down on the edge of it with his eyes closed.

The women's conversation quietened a little and he was surprised when the man that he had never met before, but was apparently a teacher, burst into singing a hymn. He had a good tenor voice and after a while some of the women joined in. After five or six hymns, the singers started to opt out and eventually there were only two of the women singing. George thought the singing was a welcome change from the boring conversation and so he decided to sit upright and begin to sing himself. He was considered to have a reasonably good voice and he hit the right notes almost immediately. He began singing 'Boiled beef and carrots', a music hall favourite, and one or two of the women joined in. A group of children sat and listened and started to laugh out loud as George, now completely intoxicated, grabbed Maud. He pulled her up, put his arm around her waist and started to dance while pulling funny faces at the children at the same time.

As he swung Maud around, she leaned further into him closing her eyes against the strong smell of the whisky and with menace she put her lips close to his ear and said, between her teeth, "put me down immediately, you are embarrassing me."

George started to feel dizzy and suddenly, he lost his balance and collapsed onto the blanket, knocking over some of the plates and cups that remained. The children looked up at their mothers and seeing that the mothers were scowling, the children immediately stopped laughing and went quiet. George then sat up and began to sing again, progressing to 'Any Old Iron', and then to more bawdy songs, ending with 'Dinah, Dinah show us your leg', and finally 'the Good Ship Venus'. George looked around and realised he was all alone. Over the time of his rendition, more of the women, and then the men had collected their plates, cups and any food that had been left. They grabbed their children, and made off across the field, all headed in the same direction, towards the farm gate. He continued to sing, sometimes repeating songs he had already sung, and as he could no longer see Maud or the children, he staggered across to the farm gate at the far end of the field. As he looked back, he could see Maud and some of the other women had gone into the next field and were returning to the blanket by taking a huge detour, obviously to avoid him. He laughed to himself and shouted out loud, "stuck up sods," just before losing his balance and sliding into a hedge.

He couldn't be bothered to walk all the way back to the blanket as he knew Maud would be angry with him, so he decided to continue on his way home. He was cross with himself for agreeing to go on the picnic in the first place and justified his behaviour by saying to himself "stupid fuckers, shouldn't have invited me."

He staggered across the street when he got back to Treafon and found himself looking at the front door of the Castle Vaults. He could hear laughter and loud conversation from inside and he stumbled through the door, making such a spectacle that the whole pub stopped to see who it was. George threw his arms out and shouted, "I'm back." Nobody moved or spoke, so he shouted, "it's me, George Williams," in a very slurred speech.

He managed to get to the bar and order a beer and then he slumped in a chair alongside the bar, spilling half of his beer. The man across the table, Ieuan Davies said, "you look as if you've been having a good time George, where've you been?"

George said in a voice you could barely understand, "a fucking chapel picnic."

The men on the surrounding tables all laughed, disbelievingly, at what they thought was clearly George's way of making a joke. George became very indignant at the men laughing at him and he immediately stood up holding his fists in front of him, "I'll fight any fucker who says otherwise," and he began to roll his sleeves up.

John Walters came into the bar, looked at George and said, "I

68

thought I recognised the voice from outside, even when he's pissed."

George spotted him and lurched towards Walters, grabbing him and suddenly remembering that he had been singing earlier, he once more launched into a song, dancing around the spare bit of pub floor with John Walters, in a sort of bear hug.

The entertainment went on for some time, with George standing up to tell the men in the pub a series of stories, some of the time losing his way and failing to remember the end, but the men were entertained and didn't mind. At other times he sang, but once again he couldn't always remember the words. After spinning around several times to illustrate one of his stories, he lost his balance and fell into a chair. He slumped forwards onto the table and immediately passed out.

John Walters felt responsible for getting George home and tried to hold him up while he opened his front gate. George had sobered up a little and insisted that John leave him at the gate. John disappeared up the road and was soon lost in the darkness while George searched for his key.

At that moment he could hear next door's front door opening and he quickly hunkered down under the wall between the two houses, sitting on the floor and closing his eyes in an attempt to make himself invisible. He could hear someone going down to the small shed at the bottom of next door's front garden, opening it and then going back up the path. He waited for several minutes to ensure that the person had gone back indoors. When he stood up, quickly turning to look over the wall into next door, he cringed as there was Mrs Thomas, right in front of him, the old lady staring back at him. He shut his eyes and said, "hello, Ma."

Mrs Thomas pulled a face at the strong smell of drink and replied, "that's some sort of state to be coming home in," and before George could say anything she smiled with a look of satisfaction "Maud's not there. I spoke to her earlier. She seemed very upset. She had the two children with her, and a big bag and she said she was going up to her sisters to stay the night." She waited for that to sink in and then added, "you couldn't blame her if she never came back, living with a drunkard like you." She tossed her head and turned to go into the house. George was about to say something, anything, but then thought the better of it. He thought to himself, if I did, it would be one more person I would have to apologise to in the morning.

THE FRONT

11

George managed a side-long glance at Rhys, his mate from Treafon. The guns could now be heard in earnest, and he could feel the ground under his feet vibrating. The sergeant, just ahead of him, shouted back to the following company of men "fall out."

George allowed his body to slide onto the grass bank alongside the roadway, crossing his legs and moving his foot inside his boot to relieve the pressure. "This cobble stuff will be the death of me."

He was just about to take off his boot when the sergeant came across and sternly gave him the command, "leave them alone. If we have to move in a hurry, you'll be walking on bare feet. Let's be setting a sensible example to the men, corporal."

George said "yes sarge, of course sarge."

It was now February 1915. The battalion first mustered in Abergavenny after the outbreak of war, and then moved on to Oswestry. George had first been made a lance-corporal while the battalion trained in Oswestry and then a full corporal while in camp in Northampton. Rhys had remained a lance-corporal. George was very modest about his promotions and had written home to tell Maud he had only had promotions as men unfit for foreign service had been filtered out and returned to reserve battalions, and so they were left with few options. One of those who had clearly suffered medical problems was Charlie Price, who had been sent back after he had failed a medical because of a possible heart condition. He thought, as a corporal, at least Maud will have more money to support the kids.

George turned to Rhys. "Where do you think we are?"

Rhys replied, "Belgium."

George was tired and beginning to lose patience. "I know we are in fucking Belgium. We've been in fucking Belgium for two days."

Rhys replied, "why'd you ask then?"

George stood up to get some feeling back into his legs and shook his head at Rhys' response.

After what seemed a very short time, the sergeant called them back into line. "Come on, come on, get the lead out of your legs."

George and Rhys got back into position and the route march continued. Eventually, they came into a village, which had clearly suffered some bomb damage. George noticed a sign as they entered the village and said out loud, "Steenvorde."

Rhys turned to him and said sharply, "are you any the wiser?"

Rhys was about the same height as George and quite slight. George considered Rhys a bit daft but appreciated that he was fiercely loyal to his friends. Many was the time that Rhys had stood by him when others might have abandoned him.

Rhys, George and two other privates were billeted with a family of three on the edge of the village. They all sat down for a meagre meal at the kitchen table and efforts were made at conversation. However, the British troops could speak little or no French, or any other language that the Belgian family might speak, and the family could speak no English.

George took out his packet of cigarettes and was just about to offer the man of the house one when he noticed the man's wife scowling at him and shaking her head. George, Rhys and one of the privates went out through the front door to smoke outside.

As they looked towards the horizon, they could still hear the bangs and crashes of the guns in the distance, and they could see the flashes of the flares lighting up the night sky.

The young private, John Watkins, looked up nervously and stated, "someone's copping it."

Rhys replied, "that'll be us soon."

George glared at Rhys and tried to reassure the young boy. "The boches haven't faced the 3rd Mons yet boy, have they. We'll be fine."

George was struck by the strong smell of cordite in the air, which had got stronger as they had moved nearer to the front line.

Private Watkins turned once again to George. "What's that smell, Corp?"

George laughed. "That's the madam of the house cooking I would imagine."

George quickly moved the conversation on to something less emotive.

The three eventually lapsed into silence. So much had happened since war had been declared the previous August. Following muster at Abergavenny, they had been shunted around from camp to camp all over England and Wales. They had been paraded before the King and crossed the English Channel, Northern France and now Belgium.

He said out loud, "so much to tell 'em in the Castle Vaults when we get back, eh Rhys?"

Rhys looked up. "If we get back."

George threw away his half-smoked cigarette. "Duw Rhys, look on the bright side."

For the next ten days, the battalion completed courses in trench digging and the making and hurling of bombs and grenades. They formed up in the centre of the village in the early hours of the morning and were told they were to be moved out.

George said to Gareth Sullivan, the Irishman from Treafon who was standing next to him, "God, I'm glad to be leaving here. That billet was the most miserable experience of my life. Here we are fighting to help these Belgians, and do they appreciate it, do they hell? The missus in our house moaned all the time, rambling on in this foreign language, upset if we smoked, upset if we made too much noise. The little boy in the house was a nice kid. He wanted to come with us this morning, and who could blame him, getting away from that miserable cow."

As George finished the sentence, a loud rumble could be heard which appeared to be getting louder by the second. The men had got used to being told nothing. They usually looked to the sergeant for his reaction and as he seemed unconcerned, they visibly relaxed. The noise came from what was deemed to be a safe direction and so the men simply stood and waited. As the noise got louder, the men all looked apprehensively to the right and to everyone's surprise, what should appear from behind a row of houses but a London bus.

Gareth said, "well, bugger me."

George replied, "thanks, but no thanks."

Several of the men made jokey comments, and it required a command from the sergeant to quieten them.

With that, several more buses appeared and parked up next to each other.

Rhys laughed. "Well, that was the last thing I expected to see."

The men were ordered onto the buses and though this proved difficult for men equipped with full packs, they were glad of the ride rather than the route march they had made into Steenvorde.

George mounted the steps to sit on the top deck shouting "any more fares?"

The following day, George was sat on a grass banking poking a small stick into a hole in the ground. Rhys was lying beside him.

George said, "I've never been so bored in my life. We march from village to village all over this god-forsaken country. We have instructions on how to dig trenches and how to fire guns, throw grenades and mills bombs and we are kept back from the front line. How are we going to win this war if they don't give a man a chance?"

The battalion had just been told to fall out after a parade where

75

they had been informed that a new unit was being put together; a mining battalion. The men had been addressed by a Colonel and a number of 'brass hats'. They were told that some men had already been posted to this new unit and that they were looking for volunteers who had experience of working in the mines. Hands went up and Brinley, who was stood next to George, whispered, "go on, stick your hand up - you're an experienced miner."

George whispered back, "piss off, so are you and if you think I've come out here to go back underground, you've got another think coming. I'm a trained fighting man, highly skilled in shooting and bayonetting. They need me in the front line, not digging tunnels."

The men who had put their hands up were taken off to register with their new unit and the other men had 'fallen out' to await their next orders. George glanced across and noticed that Gareth Sullivan was one of those being marched off to join the mining contingent. As Gareth was passing, he raised his hand and winked at George and Rhys. George chanced his arm and shouted across "all the best, you stupid Irishman. See you after the war."

As they sat on the banking, George said, "I reckon they are holding us back to make the Germans think they can win this war easily and then crack soldiers like me and you will be brought into the front line as shock troops." He turned to wonder why Brinley had not answered, only to find him lightly snoring. George said, "well, one crack soldier, and you, Brinley Evans, wouldn't frighten my boy Willie at this moment."

As George lay back, Rhys Jones moved along the line of men on the banking and sat next to George. He offered, "that sergeant over there says they are taking that lot off to dig tunnels under the German lines. They put explosives in the tunnels and blow up the German trenches."

George looked sceptically at Rhys. "How do we know that the boches are not doing that to our trenches?"

Rhys thought for a second and replied, "we don't," and then after

76

a few seconds more, "perhaps they'll ask us to be quiet in the trenches so that they can listen to see if we can hear the Germans digging."

George was rapidly losing interest in the conversation and pretended to drop off to sleep.

12

At the end of March 1915, the 3rd Battalion was ordered to a support trench a few hundred yards back from the front line. They had marched to this location through the centre of Ypres, or 'Wipers' as it was called by the troops. George considered it a pleasant little town, not unlike Abergavenny, with a large stone building, the Cloth Hall, in the centre. The battalion marched past this building to the cheers of many people that George thought must have interrupted their day to welcome and encourage the Welsh troops.

As they neared these front-line trenches, George experienced mixed emotions. He felt apprehensive about what they might face when they came within the range of the German guns. The troops had been able to hear them for a while, but as they got nearer they became more nervous as they realised they could be hit by one of the shells the German gunners were sending over. George's conflicting emotion was that he felt exhilaration at finally facing the enemy with little between them now except for a few hundred yards of cratered ground. George remained quiet as they moved towards the trench. While some showed nervousness at what lay ahead of them by talking incessantly, others remained silent.

The men had become accepting of the unrelenting bombardment that had kept them awake when they were meant to rest. They realised that a shell could land anywhere in the trench system and cause large loss of life. Some seemed able to put this constant threat behind them and were oblivious to the danger while others became increasingly nervous.

After four days in the trenches, Captain Gattick, a smartly dressed officer with a thin scar across his left cheek, moved along the trench. He stopped and touched the brim of his cap as he came up to George and said, "Corporal."

George was taken by surprise as he had never spoken to the captain before. He stood to attention and gave his best salute. "Yes, sir!"

The captain said, in what George considered a very posh voice, "I want you to take another man with you and escort a German prisoner back to the command post and wait with him until Major Reynolds comes to collect him for interrogation. Understood?"

"Clearly sir," replied George, very formally.

Brinley was just about to burst out laughing, when George turned to him and said, "Private Evans, if you could come with me, please."

Brinley said, under his breath as the two moved away, "you could have left me there. I was just getting comfortable and about to brew a mug of tea."

"Stop your moaning and shift," George shouted back to Brinley, who turned to pick up his rifle. Brinley then began to make his way quickly along the trench system to catch up with Captain Gattick and George.

After they had gone a few hundred yards through the connecting trenches, they climbed up an incline and out of the trench system. They then crossed to a few tents that had been laid out in a square. The captain entered the nearest and beckoned to the two Welsh soldiers to follow him. They passed a guard that had been posted outside one of the tents. Inside were two other armed privates but George could see no one else.

The captain pointed behind George and Brinley and said, "here he is. Take good care of him. He might be valuable. He's got to go to Brigade H.Q. at Shell Trap Farm."

The two soldiers looked at each other, as neither knew where Brigade H.Q. was. George was about to ask where the H.Q. was when the captain, who could see their bemused expressions spoke, "ask someone if you don't know. Anyway, I'm pretty sure it's signposted to the west of here."

Both men looked back to find the man the captain had referred to. A bedraggled figure sat on the floor of the tent. George beckoned with his rifle and the German soldier immediately stood up. He was splattered with mud across his face and clothes. His tunic was torn on one shoulder, and he had a bloodstained bandage around his right-hand knuckles. He seemed comparatively unconcerned at his captivity, and he stood quietly awaiting instructions. He was about George's height, dark-haired with sparkling eyes. The small group moved off through the tents, always with one of them in front of the prisoner and one behind. They soon moved onto a cobbled lane.

George shouted ahead to Brinley, "you forget what a field looks like. It's funny to see green grass without shell holes and not covered in mud, eh Brinley?"

Brinley turned to reply to George and immediately stumbled on an uneven section of the cobbles. "Uh, yea, reminds me of the fields between the Bont and Treafon a bit."

The prisoner gave a laugh at Brinley's stumble and was rewarded with a push in the back.

After a while, they came to a series of army signposts, which indicated Brigade H.Q. across a field. George climbed over a low wall and stood on guard as the prisoner and Brinley crossed the wall. The prisoner was clearly experiencing difficulty in walking, but neither of the guards showed much sympathy.

After about twenty minutes, they could see activity around a partly ruined farmhouse and crossed to it. They spoke to a guard posted outside the farm and explained that they were bringing a prisoner to be interrogated. They then spoke to a captain outside one of the tents that had been erected alongside the farmhouse, who indicated a small room at the back of the farmhouse where the prisoner could be locked in and guarded until the major from intelligence appeared. George unceremoniously pushed the German soldier into the room by prodding him with the end of his rifle. The prisoner, who was now very unsteady on his feet after the trek across the countryside, fell forward.

George closed and locked the old wooden door and after checking that there were no officers in sight, took out a cigarette and offered one to Brinley.

Brinley said, "you were a bit rough with him, weren't you? The bloke is obviously injured."

George scowled at the closed door and said, "boches, you've got to show them who's boss, so they know their place."

Brinley gave a wry grin at George's newly found toughness.

They both chatted for a while and then sat on the grass to wait for the major. After a while, the captain they had spoken to outside the tent came across and both George and Brinley stood and saluted.

The captain said, "sorry gents, we've just had a communication to say that the major who was supposed to collect the 'hun' you are guarding is not going to be able to come here until tomorrow. You will have to stay. We've already informed your unit, so they know you haven't run off anywhere. You can collect food at the cookhouse, just at the back of this row of tents, but please make sure one of you stays to guard the prisoner at all times."

With that, the captain walked off and George and Brinley sat back down on the grass, happy to be away from the frontline trenches for a few more hours.

George said, "a lot of officers here, I bet the grub is pretty good."

Brinley nodded and replied, "I hope so."

Within half an hour, the clouds began to gather, and it started to rain. The two soldiers looked at each other and thought of the miserable night they would spend out in the open guarding this prisoner and getting soaking wet.

George said, "hey come on, nothing stopping us guarding him from inside this room, is there?"

Brinley considered whether that was feasible.

George stood up and unlocked the door. He looked into the room where the German soldier had curled up on a pile of hay on the floor.

Brinley entered the room, looking as if he really shouldn't be there.

George turned to Brinley and said, "what the bloody hell is wrong with you? Why should we stand outside in the rain while this scruffy boche sleeps in the dry." Both soldiers stared at the German, who stared back at them with little interest or concern.

They made themselves comfortable on the hay, and George went off to collect some food from the cookhouse, leaving Brinley in charge of the prisoner. George came back looking very disappointed. "Usual slop. I couldn't see if the officers were given anything different, as there wasn't anyone around at the time. It's like a stew, but it's full of bones and fat."

Brinley left to get his food and to collect some for the prisoner. George was left on guard.

After a few minutes George jumped as the prisoner said, "so I get some grub as well?" in a strange accent, which seemed to be a mixture of German and cockney.

George looked at him for a while and replied, "that came as a bit of a shock. I didn't know you could speak English."

The prisoner smiled. "Lived just off the Old Kent Road. I was a waiter at the Langham Hotel in London for nearly ten years. Went back to Germany after being sacked because I was German," and after a few seconds, "so loop the loop wasn't so good." He waited and as he could see that George didn't understand, he said, "soup, mate."

George looked dumbstruck and then said, "ah, yea."

The prisoner said, "any chance of an oily rag, mate?"

George stayed silent but looked quizzically at the German.

The prisoner gave a brief laugh. "A fag."

George passed over one of his cigarettes and lit it.

George said, "what's your name?"

The prisoner replied, "Otto, Otto Gusman. You have an unusual accent. What part of Britain are you from?"

George said, "both me and Brinley, we're from South Wales - a small place called Treafon."

Otto immediately shook his head. "You lot down there. You don't like us Jews. There's been a lot of trouble in South Wales for Jews like me in the last couple of years. One of the men I worked with in London had to leave South Wales after the tailor's shop he worked in was attacked and burnt down. His wife and children were threatened in the street." He looked sullen and didn't speak for a while. He then looked up "mind you, no different to the way us Jews was treated in London. It's why you got to live in areas with other Jews - protection and all that."

George said, "yea, there's been trouble, but I've got no problem with Jews. I know a few in our town." He began to feel a little guilty, remembering the Jewish riots in Treafon, and the brick he threw through Elstayn's window. He carried on, "so how did you end up a prisoner?"

Otto replied, "I was in a party of troops who were trying to repair the barbed wire outside the trench in the dark a few nights ago. I got separated from the rest of them as I stayed to finish the job. I bumped into some of your lot who were out on patrol." He looked down at his hand. "One of them took a shot at me. I let off a shot myself and after they took the gun off me, they roughed me up for shooting at 'em."

George and Otto continued chatting for quite a while and eventually Brinley returned, shocked to see the two of them chatting away like two long-lost friends, laughing and joking.

Brinley passed a plate of food to Otto and sat down. After the initial shock, he started to chat to him. "Our lot bloody hate Germans.

83

How is it you seem ok? I don't understand. Are you one of the good ones?"

George shook his head at what he thought was a stupid question.

Otto laughed. "How many Germans do you know?" He looked directly at Brinley and said, "I think I know more Brits than you know Germans, and one thing I can tell you is there's no bloody difference between a Brit and a German." He stopped to take a drag on his cigarette and then said, "there's a bigger difference between a soldier and an officer in both armies than there is between British and German soldiers."

George stared at Otto. "You one of them communists, are you?"

Otto looked down at his feet and failed to answer.

Otto eventually looked into the distance. "There's loads of Jews fighting on both sides, but we Germans are going to win because God is on our side. Look at this."

He stood up and for one minute, George thought he was going to drop his trousers when he pulled his belt buckle forward. He read "Gott mit uns, it means God is with us."

George said, "that's a load of cow dung. You can put anything you like on a belt buckle, doesn't mean it's true."

Otto sat back down. "Well, that's what all German soldiers believe, anyway."

George said, "which God, Jewish, Christian, Mohammedan?"

George began to feel tired and was ready to arrange with Brinley, who should take first turn at guarding Otto, when Otto said, with a broad smile, "you two have a sleep, I'll take first guard."

Brinley replied, "no, it's no trouble."

George looked at Brinley. "Fucking idiot."

Otto laughed, and said, "you seem like two tidy blokes. I'll let you into a little secret." He tapped the side of his nose and stayed quiet for a while for effect.

Eventually George said, "well, what's the secret?"

Otto looked down at his feet. "We, the Germans that is, will win this war and not because it says so on a belt buckle." He hesitated and then continued, "about two weeks ago I was helping to carry pipes up to the front line. I gave the officer in charge of us a fag and just asked in passing what the pipes were for." He let that sink in and delayed answering his own question again for effect. By now Otto had the two Welsh soldier's full attention. He continued "I expected a straightforward answer, like water pipes to drain the trenches or something like that, when he said 'gas.' I asked him what he meant, and he said that they had machines that could produce a gas, which could be pumped down the pipes and directed towards your trenches. He said that the troops opposite would just die in droves when the gas reached them - like a secret weapon, you know." He pointed at George and Brinley. "Before the next attack, they would direct the gas towards you and then attack. Your lot would either be blinded, choked or dead"

Brinley looked bemused. "Gas, what will that do?"

Otto said, "don't know but the officer told me this secret weapon might be enough to win the war in the next few weeks."

George shook his head, not really understanding the significance of what Otto had told them but was shocked by the fact that Otto had said it would quickly win the war. The term 'secret weapon' worried him.

The three of them talked on for a while longer and then George noticed that Otto was beginning to drop off to sleep and that Brinley seemed to be struggling to stay awake. George sat and watched the two of them sleeping and his mind wandered. He thought about what Otto had said about the gas attack and thought that the British troops had nothing to protect them against gas. It wasn't like a tin helmet that could stop a bullet. Then he thought what a pleasant bloke Otto

85

was - for a German anyway. He thought, that's twice I've had a chat with Jews, Otto and Isaac and they were both tidy, nothing like some people said. George thought, what a crazy world, where you might hate a British officer, but actually like a German Jewish soldier. A funny old world. After a few hours, George shook Brinley awake and told him it was his turn to stand guard.

Morning came and George went off to get some breakfast and brought a ration of food back for Otto.

Otto looked at the food on the plate and said, "good to know that you lot are being fed the same rubbish that we are."

At about mid-day the major arrived to collect Otto, with two armed privates. George asked if he could speak to the major and went around to the back of the building with the major following.

He said, "Otto, the German in there, told us that they are going to attack us with gas the next time they come. Thought you ought to know."

The major answered, in a very arrogant manner, "hmm, yes, he would say that. We have taken a few prisoners who all tell the same story. We at H.Q. think their troops have all been given the same story, so if they get captured like this blighter, they say things to frighten the men. I wouldn't go repeating this to anyone, otherwise people might think you were spreading sedition; know what I mean. Keep it to yourself, man, otherwise it could be a court martial." He stopped and gave a knowing look. "Understand what I'm saying?"

George nodded and said no more; thinking this is a waste of time. The major and the two privates came in and indicated for Otto to get to his feet. George and Brinley went outside to make a bit of room. The major came out with Otto, with his hands tied behind his back.

As they moved off, George shouted, "good luck Otto," to the German soldier. Otto shrugged in response. The major scowled at George and gave him a withering look. George and Brinley turned to head back to their unit, discussing on their way what Otto had told

86

them and the officer's attitude to the news.

13

In early April, the battalion returned to billets near a village called Westoutre. After they had caught up on their sleep and spent a few evenings at the only estaminet in the village, the men were becoming restless. One afternoon, several were kicking a makeshift football around one of the fields whilst the rest of the company were sitting in groups or lying against a grass bank. The day was dry but cold and most of the men had their greatcoats drawn around them. They roused themselves when a small army truck pulled around the corner. After verifying that the men were part of the 3rd Battalion Monmouthshire Regiment, they unloaded sacks of mail. The mail hadn't caught up with them for weeks as they had been shunted around parts of the front line and the close support area and they had been billeted in different villages.

George sat reading one of the two letters that he had been given, while Brinley and Rhys sat reading theirs. George read Maud's letter, which was mainly about various families in Treafon; some of whom were embroiled in domestic battles while others had new babies arriving. She said that Willie was still not well and that she had to take him to the doctor's surgery on two occasions. Both Willie and Joan sent their love and she was showing them a picture of their father everyday so that they would remember him and know who he was when he came home. She then put a 'PS' on the bottom to say that Joan was now walking.

All pretty boring stuff, George thought. The second letter was from his younger brother Ben. George read the first few lines, which explained that Ben was continuing to work underground but that he was thinking of joining up as many of his workmates had done. He said that he would let George know when he had made his mind up. He read on and had to re-read a section where Ben explained that Thomas was now a stretcher bearer in the R.A.M.C., the Royal Army Medical Corps. He was undergoing training and would soon be sent to the Western Front. Ben finished by asking George to keep a look out for Thomas. He also said that he had been over to see Esther and she had told him that she had received a letter from Evan. He was in France, and he had been wounded. He had now recovered and had been moved into a detachment driving lorries behind the front line.

George sat quietly for a while, trying to gather his thoughts. He was confused. Thomas was not carrying a rifle, but he was helping the army's cause. George couldn't work out whether Thomas' decision was enough to warrant him not being called a coward. He wondered why Thomas went to such lengths to avoid joining the regular army. After all, Evan was in the regular army, but he was now driving lorries. He walked off on his own despite Rhys shouting to him that the Cambrian Inn had closed after damage done during a fight between those advocating peace and those who believed in the war.

Rhys shouted, "what the hell's going on? They smash a pub up in the name of peace. They should be out here fighting Germans and using their energy for that."

George nodded agreement and walked off into an area of long grass to dwell on his own thoughts.

Following an inspection by a high-ranking general, the men were put onto a fleet of London buses as before and driven through Ypres. The town had suffered some shell damage but the large building, the Cloth Hall, stood proud in the centre of the town. Here they got off and marched to Polygon Wood to relieve a French unit. To call it a wood really stretched the imagination as Polygon Wood was no more than a series of wooden stumps sticking out of the ground, and the land around the stumps a churned up mix of mud and pieces of tree root together with the discarded remains of army equipment. George had no doubt that, in time, the stumps would disappear as the Germans continued to shell the area. As the Welsh battalion moved aside to allow the French troops to come out, George used his best French to shout, "bonne rest, Frenchies."

Most of the French troops looked tired and ignored George as they shuffled past. However, one came up to George and leaning over quietly said, "Polygon Wood est merde."

George replied, "yea, yea, I'm sure," not having a clue what the French soldier meant.

Ten days later, they were back in billets after having been relieved by the King's Own Regiment a few days before. George felt that a routine had been set up, with them spending four or five days in the front line, and then four or five days in billets. However, he did think that the German shelling had increased. Where they had been in relatively quiet parts of the front line, they now seemed to be in an area where the shelling was worse.

An obvious salient had been created east of Ypres. The 3rd Battalion Monmouthshires seemed to be at the furthest point - further forward than any other detachment. Shells were coming over at a faster rate and more bodies seemed to be passing on stretchers as they moved the casualties out of the trench. George reckoned that they would be relieved the following day as it was 20th April and they had been in the front line for three days.

The next day came and there was no sign of relief. The shelling became more intense and certainly more frequent, and there seemed to be more 'Jack Johnsons' coming over, a large high explosive shell which could leave a huge crater. Despite ducking every time one went off, George realised that it was pointless as the noise meant the shell had already exploded, but he couldn't control the automatic response of his brain to the explosion.

The following day, the explosions became even more frequent, and resting and sleeping were not an option. Men looked tired and frightened, as some thought that an attack might be imminent. George became more frightened, though he desperately tried not to show it and found himself shouting louder than usual and laughing manically in front of the other men, in an act of nervous bravado. He looked at the faces of the men around him who all had dark rings around their eyes from a lack of sleep. They looked a sorry bunch with streaks of grime running down their faces where they had attempted to wash with the water from their water bottles. They all had drawn expressions because of weight loss from a lack of adequate food. Despite the exhaustion showing on their faces, they still carried out their tasks carefully and efficiently; they knew their lives might depend on it.

The evening of 22nd April followed a beautiful spring day. The men had become a little more relaxed in the sunshine. Most of the men had discarded their greatcoats and carried out their duties in their shirtsleeves. Some men in the company suddenly returned after collecting ammunition from a support trench. They seemed very excited and one, Private Alfie Jones, from 'the Bont', just over the valley from Treafon, was keen to tell the other men what they had heard.

He shouted out "hey, you lot, we've just been chatting to a Canadian soldier who said that an hour or two ago a French Battalion to their left suddenly upped and ran out of their trenches and then ran back to the support and reserve trenches. He said that there were men falling down, covering their eyes and holding their heads. They could then smell a funny smell and they noticed a yellow mist over the trench." He held his hand up and waved it slowly and theatrically to describe what he was saying. He continued, "some of the Canadians had to put handkerchiefs over their mouths."

Alfie now had the full attention of his audience and he stopped for dramatic effect. Then he stepped back and bug-eyed he said, in a loud voice, "gas," and then "that's what they are saying - a secret weapon. The French troops all ran away, and the Germans poured into the French trenches. The Canadian said that it was only the Germans' fear of the gas itself that stopped them from taking over the whole of the front line."

George was listening from his position on the firing step of the trench with interest, thinking back to Otto's explanation and the officer's response in saying the German was more or less talking nonsense. He thought, so Otto was right; it's the soldiers that know what's going on and the officers that haven't got a clue.

A few days later, they heard that the 1st Canadian Division had also been attacked with gas and the men in George's battalion became panicked by the rumours. Captain Gattick appeared in George's section of the trench and asked George to bring together as many men as possible so that he could speak to them. George left a skeleton section of the company on the firing steps to guard the trench and keep lookout, and he called the rest of the men together.

Captain Gattick shouted to the men at the back to check that he could be heard and began, "listen up men, I hope you can hear me? If you can't, ask the others what I have said afterwards. It is important news. It seems the boches are using chlorine gas on parts of the front line. We need to be prepared for this as they might do the same to our part of the line." He stopped, and then continued in what George thought was a posh accent, "if this is to happen, if you think you are being attacked by gas, you will probably see a yellowish cloud. Before it gets to you, put a wet handkerchief or cloth over your mouth and nose. If you can't find any water to wet the cloth, piss on it." George laughed out loud and had to pretend to cough. It was one of the funniest things he had ever heard. To hear an officer saying, in a very posh voice, that the men would have to piss on a rag, and then put it over their mouths.

George lent over to the soldier next to him and whispered out of the side of his mouth, "very fucking technical. He'll be telling us to piss on our food next, to stop the gas contaminating it." Both had to pretend to cough to stop themselves convulsing in laughter.

14

George leaned back against one of the wooden supports that went around the door that opened into a small shelter at the back of the trench. His eyes started to close, but at that moment, someone brushed against him and that brought him awake again.

The battalion was at the easternmost point of the Ypres salient and so would be the first troops to face a German attack.

The first gas attack had come a week before and had left a gaping hole in the Allied line, as French troops ran from the effects of this new and deadly weapon. The Germans had followed this up with a further gas attack two days later against positions held by the Canadians. The salient was shrinking as troops were pulled back to shorten the front line and fill the gaps. However, the Germans, who seemed fairly reluctant to attack in large numbers, had failed to take full advantage of the results of the gas attacks. During these two days, George had been able to smell the remains of the chlorine gas in the air. While it had not done serious damage to the men in the Monmouthshire Regiment, it had resulted in minor ailments. Some of the men had vomited and many were suffering from eye complaints where they found it difficult to focus. Many prayed that the Germans would not launch a major attack until they had recovered.

George had kept a scarf around his mouth in case any of the gas lingered in the trench, or the Germans produced a surprise gas attack. At one point, he had gone to the support trench and noticed a line of Allied soldiers being led back behind the trench system. All of them were clearly blinded and were holding on to each other in a long chain to guide their way back to safety. This new development was making the men nervous as they felt unprepared for this new type of warfare. George looked at the men that he could see. No one was speaking. They just stood or sat where they were, in absolute exhaustion. They had now been in the front line for twelve days without a break. Their eyes clearly showed their exhaustion through lack of sleep and the effects of the chlorine gas. Their drawn expressions were accentuated by the red rims around their eyes. George thought that if the Germans wanted to attack now, they could just walk all over their position with little opposition. As he was not on the firing step, he could relax a little, and after five or ten minutes, he drifted off to sleep.

He woke later, not sure how long he had slept with something pulling at his greatcoat. He lifted one eyelid and looked down. He found it difficult to see as it was now dark, but as he looked down, a large dirty brown rat had started to climb up his coat, gnawing and pulling at the fabric. He jumped up quickly, brushing the animal down to the ground shouting, "I hate these fucking things. They give me the creeps." He shook himself and looked around to see the men on the firing step looking down at him and smiling ruefully. He noticed that the rat stayed where it was for a while; unconcerned by the presence of humans. Eventually, it scurried off through the puddles at the bottom of the trench.

Within an hour, George was back on the firing step, trying to focus on the ground in front of the trench but also trying not to rise too far above the parapet in case of snipers. In the last hour, he had sat down to a meal of cold maconochie; a soup containing sliced turnips, carrots and two dried biscuits which he learned to keep in his mouth for as long as possible to add a bit of moisture which might allow him to bite through them. These so-called biscuits could only really be eaten if you dropped them in warm tea to soften them. He had tried to bite them dry at first and had chipped a tooth.

George was a few yards along from Rhys, but it was impossible to communicate, as the shelling had become heavier, more frequent and deafening. George was keeping his head down as a great deal of shrapnel was flying about. On the odd occasion that he caught Rhys' eye, he simply pulled a face and rolled his eyes up to the heavens. Rhys knew exactly what he meant, shook his head and pursed his lips in a sign of defiance at the German shelling.

As dawn rose on the 3rd Battalion's thirteenth day in the front line, the men on the firing step were relieved by another contingent of the battalion. George stepped down into the bottom of the trench and turned to speak to Rhys. "Thank God for that, a short rest and some…"

He got no further as a huge shell landed nearby. The force pushed him backwards onto the ground and he stayed down for a minute or so to try to overcome the concussive effects of the blast. He eventually got up onto his knees and turned, but his friend was inert and seemingly lifeless. George was stunned for a second but then went over to Rhys and turned him over. One side of Rhys' head had disappeared completely, and a narrow fountain of blood spurted onto George's coat. George tried to place his hand over the source of the blood and to call for stretcher bearers, but in his heart, he knew it was too late. After what seemed ages, stretcher bearers arrived and worked on Rhys, but only for a very short while, as they could tell they were too late to do any good. George slumped back against the trench wall as the stretcher bearers lifted the lifeless body and carried it away. An hour later, George had not moved even a fraction and the stretcher bearers had long gone. When George appeared to recover a little, he noticed that Brinley had come to sit next to him. He turned and spoke quietly, "how long have you been there?"

Brinley said, "about half an hour."

"You heard about Rhys?" George said quietly.

Brinley nodded and no more was said. Nothing could be added that had any meaning or made any sense.

George shrugged, stood up and walked along the trench aimlessly, as if he could walk back to the previous day and all would be well.

Three days later, the battalion had orders to evacuate their part of the front line. Later, when George thought back to this time, he could not remember anything of their last three days in the forward trench, despite it being one of heavy fighting, heavy shelling and heavy casualties.

The evacuation had to be handled carefully to avoid the enemy getting wind of it. They would try to take full advantage of it and shell the trench to cause chaos. The company was split into two sections, with one section holding the line while the other retired through communicating trenches. Then the remaining section was split into two with the same manoeuvre as previously until all were back safely.

Eventually, the company was back at the Potijze line east of Ypres. Any thoughts of any movement back to the rear for rest and relaxation were quickly dispelled the following day when they were ordered up to relieve the King's Royal Rifle Corps in the front line, albeit a new front line. The 3rd Monmouthshires stayed in the front line for a further three days before they themselves were relieved by the King's Own Yorkshire Light Infantry. George was in a daze the whole time. He found he couldn't sleep, as the nightmare vision of Rhys' facial expression in death kept coming back to him. He found it difficult to concentrate and several times he failed to respond immediately to orders given by an officer. He noticed his hands shook and he had developed a nervous twitch in one eye that he couldn't control. Ivor Hancock, one of the men who had been in the company with George since Abergavenny, came across to him asking, "you alright George? You don't seem yourself."

George became angry with the question from Hancock as he wanted to be left alone with the horrific images in his head. Those images were reality and everything else was fantasy. He scowled at Hancock and said, "what? What's it got to do with you?"

Hancock moved off and left George to his nightmares.

The shelling was a little less severe that day but there was little respite, as two days later it increased again. The 3rd Monmouthshires were back in the front line. Along with the KOYLI, they were guarding a section between the Ypres-Roulers railway line and the Menin Road. They had been ordered to hold this section of the line until reinforcements could be brought up. George heard that Ivor Hancock had been killed that afternoon along with five members of a machine gun company and two officers, and he immediately felt guilty at his sharp response the previous day. He had never been so exhausted in his life, but as he looked along the line of men, they all looked very determined, despite being ready to collapse with tiredness. It was a strange feeling. Despite exhaustion, George preferred to be doing something. When he wasn't doing anything, he thought of the horrors he had seen - bodies strewn about and men crying in pain; a living hell.

The men had commented that there seemed to be a big difference between the frequency of the firing of the German guns and the British guns. The Germans had brought their guns up onto the Frezenburg Ridge after the gas attack and that meant they were nearer and more accurately pounding the Allied front-line trench. The heavy bombardment had started at 5.30 am and it was now 8.15am. The men had had no breakfast and were hanging on to sanity by a very thin cord. Stretcher bearers were running backwards and forwards through the trench. It all seemed very chaotic.

Ten minutes later, the whole company was ordered onto their firing steps and George realised why when the German shelling began to ease. In the distance, he could see small figures in grey moving towards them, every so often crouching to fire at the British defensive position. Apart from Otto, these were the first Germans he had actually seen, and unlike Otto, they were armed. He could see the puffs of smoke in amongst the grey figures caused by Allied mortars and he was encouraged when he could see a few of the grey figures falling to the ground and not moving. Shortly after this, he could see the remaining Germans falling back to their own lines.

It suddenly occurred to him that this was the first time either side had attacked while he was in the frontline. The rest of the time, the two sides had sat back and shelled each other.

Thirty minutes later, the Germans attacked again, and though they got nearer to the Allied trenches, they again retreated following a period of accurate Allied fire. George turned around to cheer at the

German retreat, when all of a sudden, a shell landed a few feet away. Although George managed to stay on his feet after the initial cloud drifted away, all he could see was a huge crater where the trench had been. A thought entered his head that at that moment that was where Brinley had been standing when he last saw him. Apart from an army boot and what looked like a hand, there was little evidence of any human beings having been in that area. Robert Owen, a private from Newport who had ended up joining the 3rd Monmouthshire's, stood alongside George and both were dumbstruck. Owen eventually said, "there must have been five or six men there, and now….," after a bemused silence, "nothing."

George could not speak but realised that they had to get back to the firing step to stem any further attacks from the Germans. An hour later, Captain Gattick came along the trench, telling the remaining men that they would have to evacuate. They began to move back with a degree of covering fire, but George could hear the ratatat of a German machine gun in the distance.

As the men moved back along the length of the trench, Captain Gattick stepped up onto the firing step to encourage the men to move more quickly. As he did so, he was hit by a bullet which struck his temple, and he slumped sideways. Two of the men went across to see what they could do for the stricken captain but one of them turned and shook his head to indicate that Captain Gattick's brave life had come to an end. Such things as this in peacetime would be devastating but in the cauldron of front-line warfare it was common-place. The preservation of life became the main aim. Most of the men had stopped as if statues at the shock of the loss of this brave officer and it was George who shouted to shake them out of their trance-like state. They quickly remembered the danger they were in and scurried from the scene.

As the men got to a bend in the communicating trench, they had to negotiate a slight rise in the ground. George and several other members of the company saw their route blocked by a collapse in the trench. George, having no other option, led the men out of the trench onto the ground above, which was more exposed to enemy fire. He looked around to check their position and as he did, he was hit by a wave of air knocking him backwards. He lay on his back for some time, but he found he couldn't move his arms or his legs. He could see some men crouching and some running, seeking to move beyond the range of the guns and the snipers and reach safety.

The German spotters had guessed at why so many men were having to leave the trench system at this point and their guns concentrated fire on that section of ground. Some of the retreating men were dropping into shell craters, and then after they felt safe to make an escape, they would look over the edge of the crater, rise and attempt to run back to the support trenches. Some of these men fell, as they were struck by bullets, or pieces of shrapnel. It was a scene that George could not comprehend - living humans one minute, pieces of dead flesh the next. He thought of the hell he had heard about in the chapels back home, and how that description could be applied to the scene around him.

He slowly moved his head back and forth and noticed many groups of stretcher bearers running in all directions, every so often stopping and kneeling to help a casualty or to place them onto a stretcher and then rushing off. He tried to tell himself that he needed to escape this death trap, but his body wouldn't respond. All the time shells continued to fall, and George could feel the vibrations of their exploding through his whole body. He could also see rifle and machine-gun bullets zipping through the air above him. Every so often a stretcher bearer would fall, but miraculously another would materialise to take his place. George could not help thinking about his brother doing this at some place in Belgium or France. He wondered how he could have ever thought that he was a coward. These men seemed oblivious to danger; their first thoughts always on the soldiers they were tending to or were carrying off the battlefield.

George's thoughts became confused and, for the first time in his life, he felt he might die at this point. When he worked underground, there was always danger, but he never felt he might die. In this hellish place, his feelings were different. He tried to remain conscious, as he felt his life might slip away into death if he lost consciousness. After a while, George could no longer fight the feeling. His concentration faded and though his head throbbed, he could not stop himself drifting off into unconsciousness.

The next time George was aware of anything, he was looking up into the face of a nurse. He had been told by other men that nurses who had come over from Britain and the colonies were stunningly beautiful and heaven sent. Well, he thought, this one must have been on a different boat. The stern and pointed features of the older nurse were looking down into George's face, as if studying a famous painting. She said, with a look of concern, "and how are you feeling, young man?"

George was just about to say, 'fucking awful', when he found that his mouth was too dry to speak. He tried to mouth something, but nothing came out.

The nurse lifted his head a little and tried to pour a small amount of water into his mouth. He winced at the pain of even the slightest movement.

She said, "you've had a bit of a bad time, but you'll be alright now," and after what seemed a long hesitation she added under her breath, "I think." She tried to feed a little water onto George's lips by wetting a small piece of cloth and letting it drip into his mouth.

After a while, with the nurse still stood there, George said, "what happened to me, and where am I?"

The nurse replied, "well, according to the notes that came with you, you were taken to a dressing station and a Casualty Clearing Station, and because you hadn't come around, they feared that your head wound was sufficiently serious to send you to a Base Hospital. So, you are here, under observation, in Boulogne."

George, thinking out loud, said, "Boulogne, that's by the sea, isn't it?" and after a few seconds, "how long have I been unconscious?"

The nurse picked up a set of papers at the foot of George's bed and said, "well, you arrived at the dressing station on 8th May and today is 12th May - so four days."

George just lay and gently shook his head but stopped almost immediately, as the pain was too great. Within seconds, he was unconscious again.

15

George woke the following morning feeling as if his head was going to explode. He started calling for the nurse, who rushed quickly to his bedside to see what was wrong. George, with a pained expression said, "nurse, you are going to have to give me something for this fu…," he stopped himself and then continued "headache."

The nurse didn't reply but rushed off. George was afraid she hadn't heard him but a few minutes later she returned with another nurse who carried a tray with a hypodermic needle. The nurse injected into George's arm, and he gave a whelp.

The nurse chuckled briefly, and so did the man in the next bed.

The nurse said, "come on now, let's be a brave boy."

George didn't answer for fear of delving into expletives but sunk back onto the pillow.

The nurse turned to leave saying, "doctor will be along shortly."

For the first time, George was conscious enough to feel a large plaster at the back of his head and a bandage wrapped around his forehead. He turned his head sideways, but he had to close his eyes as the movement caused intense pain. He glimpsed a dark-haired man in the next bed with a shoulder and arm wrapped in a bandage.

George quietly said "shwmae."

The man turned his head and said, in what George thought was a Northern accent, "hello pal, don't know what you just said but you don't look foreign, except perhaps with a feather in your bandage you might be a red Indian." After a few seconds he added, "Rob Arkwright, Kings Own Yorkshire Light Infantry."

George introduced himself. "George Williams, 3rd Battalion Monmouthshire Regiment."

Arkwright said, "you were next to us in the trenches, a territorial regiment, but you lot fought well, fair play."

George said, "you a professional?"

Arkwright replied, "yep, certainly am. Sergeant, been in eight years."

George asked, "when did you come in?" and then added "here to the hospital?"

Arkwright replied, "yesterday. Machine-gun bullets in my arm and shoulder. Doctor said he took out two. Just hope I'll be able to use the arm after it heals. I always wanted to work with horses on a farm perhaps, after I got out of the army. What about you?"

George said, "well the nurse said I was taken to a dressing station on 8th May. To be honest, I don't remember anything for quite a while."

Arkwright said, "Well, today is the 14th, so you've been out of action for six days."

George looked puzzled. "What happened after the 8th, on the front line, I mean?"

Arkwright replied, "we retreated back to a new line east of Ypres and dug in. The Germans had opened up the front line after the gas attack. A lot of my mates were gassed and taken out of the line. Don't know what happened to them. The Germans seemed a bit slow to take advantage, so we dug in on the new line and held them. Your lot were brought back to that line about the 8th; so that would have been about when you copped it."

George looked blankly at Arkwright as he couldn't remember anything.

Arkwright continued, "I think your lot were taken out of the line a few days later, but I've no idea what happened to them after that."

George mumbled "ta," but fell back into a troubled slumber.

By the following day, George was sitting up in bed and chatting with Arkwright about their different wartime experiences and their lives back home. George's head felt a little better, but the headaches were coming and going. The nurse arrived with a smartly dressed man with a white coat over his army uniform. George assumed this was the doctor. The man came up to the side of the bed and introduced himself as Doctor Ames. He looked at George from all angles and turning to the nurse, asked her to take the bandage off. She scurried off to find another nurse to help. The nurse, with little sympathy, undid the bandage and then yanked at the plaster underneath. George yelled at the pain caused as the congealed blood separated.

With George's head still throbbing in pain, Doctor Ames inspected the wound carefully and said, "hmm," several times, and then, "nurse, could you put on a new plaster and bandage it back up." When he was alone with George he said, "well, the wound looks clean enough, it's healing. It looks as if a bullet or a piece of shrapnel has grazed your skull. I don't think there's a fracture, but we'll keep checking it. Any confusion you are experiencing is probably concussion. I'm pretty sure you'll be right as rain in a while."

George sheepishly asked, "will I be sent home?"

The doctor rubbed his chin and replied, "no, I don't think so. We'll patch you up and then you can go back. I'm sure that's what you'd want?"

George wasn't so sure. Back at the beginning of the war, he wouldn't have hesitated. Now as his attitude hardened, he wasn't so sure.

As the days went by, he felt better, and the pain and the headaches were less severe. He took to walking out onto the veranda at the front of the hospital where he could sit on a bench, sometimes with other walking wounded, sometimes on his own. He looked across the landscape in front of the hospital, which had a view out to sea. He thought how peaceful it looked. He could see the blue of the water and the white lines where the waves were breaking. Seagulls were swooping over the grass in front of the hospital, and no-one would guess that perhaps seventy miles away men were dying in their hundreds every day in scenes that might be seen in a slaughterhouse. Here you could hear birds chirping away and bees and butterflies criss-crossing the grass area in front of the veranda, and squirrels climbing the trees.

He enjoyed his chats with Arkwright, and he built up a very real friendship. This made it worse one day when he went back in from the veranda only to find Arkwright's bed being made up by two nurses and no sign of the soldier.

George asked what had happened to him. One of the nurses replied, "he's been shipped back to Blighty. He needed surgery on his arm, so they decided to move him."

George was disappointed at the removal of his new friend, and he became even more depressed when he began to remember the events before he was wounded. With no one to talk to, he found he had more time to think, and he became more withdrawn. He remembered Rhys' horrible death in the trench, and he couldn't erase the vision of his friend with half of his head blown away. Then, Captain Gattick, who George thought was indestructible, was taken by a solitary bullet. Finally, Brinley being killed as they retreated.

He thought how misguided his idea of warfare had been. None of the glory of running at the enemy and feeling the moment of victory as they ran away. The reality was that he had barely seen any enemy and he had hardly moved from the frontline position he had first arrived at and unfortunately any movement had then been to retreat. George thought that perhaps his father and Thomas had been right. War was awful, and if you'd never experienced it, you wouldn't understand the terror and the loss. He thought how all the time they practiced with rifles, not once thinking that a rifle would do you no good against indiscriminate shelling or gas.

He wondered whether O.H. and Thomas knew what it was going to be like. Did they have some premonition? Had he been naïve?

These thoughts had a real impact on George as he felt guilty that he should still be alive, and his friends and the officer were dead. He had seen so much death and he was worried that he was becoming immune to it.

After a few days, the bed next to him was filled by a soldier whose head was completely encased in bandages. He couldn't move or speak, so George continued to feel lonely and was beginning to hope he would be sent back to the front line.

The following day, a private came onto the ward with a sack of mail. He shouted out a list of names, and then George's name. He put his hand up to acknowledge his presence.

The private brought over three letters. George was pleased to have any contact with the outside world and was filled with anticipation as he began to open the first letter, particularly as he didn't at first recognise the handwriting on the front of two of the letters. He opened the first letter, which was from his brother, Ben.

Dear George,

Love to you from all the family. We are all well here, and I am working very long hours trying to provide you lot out there with coal.

I have finally made up my mind to join the army. I am going to the recruiting station this weekend with Albert Morris. We hope to be in the same regiment. Hope you are well? We don't hear much about where you are and what is going on, but I hope that is a good sign. Esther got a letter from Evan who is in France. He is well and in good spirits. Someone told me where he was, but I can't tell you as I can't spell the name of the French town. Keep a look out for me when I get out to France or Belgium, however I might not want to speak to you as I might be a General by then.

Your ever-loving brother

Ben.

George went on to open the second letter. He was surprised it was from Elizabeth, Thomas' wife.

Dear George,

Hope you are well? I am fine here, though I worry about all of you doing your bit for the country out there.

I have been up to Treafon a few times and stayed with your mother and father. I went down to see Maud, Willie and Joan. I won't say too much about my visit and what we talked about as she said that she is going to write to you, and you would be bored reading the same things twice. I have received letters from Thomas who I'm afraid seems to be having a tough time in France. He says he's seen some horrific things which he couldn't describe to me in a letter or probably not even tell me when he sees me either. He said that many men would be returning home after this war with injured bodies and minds. This experience had made him all the more determined that he had made the right decision not to fight. I know that parts of his letters are censored but I get the impression that Thomas was struggling with what he was expected to do.

George thought most of the letter was pretty mundane, but after reading the next section, he didn't really know what to think and had to immediately re-read it, though it still seemed odd to him. Elizabeth continued,

I miss you as well as Thomas and think of you both constantly. I am desperately lonely here in Caerphilly and feel guilty for telling you when I know what you are going through out there.

I have few friends and as you know I am generally a shy person and find it difficult to make friends. I can only tell you this in a letter, as I would not have the confidence to tell you in person.

107

People here think that Thomas is in France fighting and I don't dissuade them from that. I'm sure he is brave and doing what he can to help save lives. He is stubborn and will always do what he wants, and rarely asks me my opinion.

Enough of that for now. Try to write if you can.

Love,

Elizabeth

George was confused by what seemed a very candid letter. He decided to read it again and took Elizabeth's letter and the unopened letter out onto the veranda. He placed Elizabeth's and Ben's letters in his pocket and opened the other letter. He recognised his mother's handwriting straight away.

Dear George

I am writing to you as Maud is not able to at present.

George thought this very strange but continued reading.

Sadly, I have to tell you that two days ago Willie died of consumption.

George looked up from the letter, not sure he could carry on reading. He re-read the opening sentence in case he was mistaken. He was trance-like but found the strength to continue.

He had become ill over ten days ago and after the doctor had been called, he was taken to the cottage hospital and put into isolation. Maud came up with Joan to tell me and I went down to stay with her. Maud found *his death very difficult to deal with as you would expect, but doubly difficult because she could not visit the poor mite. He became very ill, and the doctor came down to the house on 5th May to say he had passed away during the night. Maud took to her bed soon after and O.H. organised the funeral and spoke at the graveside. I didn't go to the cemetery, but I have spoken to some of the deacons in the chapel and they said that O.H. spoke beautifully about a grandson that he loved. I am so sorry to be communicating this desperately sad news to you. I realise how difficult it is for you being so far away and how difficult it will be for you to cope with the experiences of war as well as this very sad loss, but you must take strength from the fact that he is in heaven with the Lord and his angels. He was such a loving little boy, and we all miss him so much. Stay strong for all of us and try to write to Maud when you get time.*

Your loving mother.

Ann

George slumped back on the bench and the letter fell into his lap. He stared into space and the tears fell onto the paper. He fell forward, holding his head in his hands and sobbed. He thought how much he had loved Willie. He was, as his mother had said, such a loving little boy. George was in despair. He shook his head in the hope that this was a nightmare which he would soon wake from. He had lost some of his closest friends, and now he had lost his son. He wondered why he should continue to live when all around seemed to be dying. He found it hard to believe that all this was really happening, and it made it more difficult not having anyone else nearby to share his grief.

He carried the letter, which had brought the sad news, with him at all times. He walked with it, and he lay with it as if he could not bear to let it go. He couldn't eat, and he couldn't sleep. However, after the nurse had returned to collect his dishes following his meal, only to find it hadn't been touched, he passed her the letter in response to her concerns. He couldn't bring himself to explain to her and thought it would be less painful for her to read about the dreadful news.

He was still in deep despair a few days later. He had taken to finding the loneliest spots in the grounds of the hospital, where he could just sit without anyone talking to him about things that didn't matter. He couldn't settle to do anything. When he was walking, he wanted to sit and when he sat down, he then immediately wanted to walk. Having found it difficult to sleep he would walk around and around the hospital to tire himself out in the hope that he might sleep. The nurses often commented to him about the distances he was walking. The doctors and nurses now all knew about the loss of George's son. George was feeling a deep sense of guilt that he had survived, and others had died, and he became desperate to go back to the front, to his comrades and his friends. Above all, he wanted to be active, as active as he could be. He wanted to be so tired he would collapse with exhaustion. He was sure that this was the only way he could rid himself of the desperation he felt. He feared the nights when he would lie and think of his son and his friends, who he would never see again.

One day, an army chaplain arrived. When George asked whether the visit was a random one, the chaplain said that Doctor Ames had suggested that he might visit him, as he seemed to be very depressed. The chaplain was well meaning and stayed for some considerable time, asking George about his home life and his wartime experiences. However, George thought that he had got the wrong end of the stick when he mentioned that his father was a lay preacher. The chaplain seemed to assume that George was a firm believer and when he asked George to join him in a prayer, he closed his eyes to humour the chaplain, but he felt that his loss had completely eradicated any belief in a religion he might have had.

George rejoiced when Doctor Ames, the doctor who had first seen him when he was brought in, told him that transport would be arranged to take him back to his unit the following day.

16

George would like to have said that his return would seem as if he had never been away, but it wasn't. His close friends had gone. There were still some friends or perhaps he would call them acquaintances from Treafon, such as William Marsden, the West countryman who George would sometimes drink with in the Castle Vaults and John Walters who worked in the same pit as George, but there were many new recruits from all over Britain who joined the men from all parts of Monmouthshire. Most surprisingly, George learned that the three Monmouthshire battalions had been amalgamated into one because they had lost so many men in the 2nd Battle of Ypres. William Marsden told him that an officer had explained to him that when they had completed a roll call in May at the end of the battle, one hundred and thirty-four men remained out of a total of one thousand and twenty. George shook his head in disbelief. The casualty figures made it worse for George, as he felt even more guilty for surviving when others had died.

He said, "well, no-one can ever say that the Monmouthshires didn't do their bit. Their sacrifice was as great as any regiment that had been mentioned for their bravery."

A private from Blaenavon, Private Robinson listened to George and whistled in the air. "George, you should have been a fucking preacher, the way you use them words, a fucking preacher, I say."

George laughed, mainly at what his father might say to that opinion.

Marsden added, "we also got us a new officer, Captain Jessop and a new lieutenant, Lieutenant Irwin-Brown, a right toff, and very wet behind the ears, as they say. He went out on patrol with a few of the lads and got 'em all lost. Corporal Foster had to bring 'em back. Didn't have a clue where he was. Might as well have been in Aberbargoed for all he knew."

The following day, Captain Jessop came into the quarter-master store that had been set up in a farmyard. The men were replacing damaged and lost equipment before their next posting. Jessop asked one of the privates which of the men was Corporal Williams. After he had been pointed out, Jessop came across to him. He spoke with a Northern accent and had an air of authority. The men had already found out that Jessop had been in action several times and was clearly experienced and respected.

He came across to George and said, "Sergeant Williams, you spent a length of time in hospital, I hear."

George was just about to correct the captain when he continued, "anyway, good to have you back and pleased to be gaining a man who's had battle experience. Good news is you've got yourself a promotion, as you might have guessed. You are now a sergeant, and you will move to company C. I will look to you and your experience to help some of the new men find their feet, particularly if we are called back into action, as we might well be."

George replied, "thank you sir, it's an honour and I will try to do my best by you."

Jessop turned back to George and said, "yes, very good. Collect your stripes, and I will look forward to seeing you in action, if only on the parade ground, for the moment."

"Yes sir," replied George, appreciating that the extra money would come in handy.

George thought that life outside the trenches was almost more difficult for him than when they were on the frontline. When danger was ever present, the men were focussed and thought of little else than getting through that day. During rest periods, after a few days, the men became restless. Their days were filled by parades, inspections, lectures, exercises, demonstrations, physical training, and bayonet and trench mortar practices. They quickly became bored with this, and the sergeants and corporals would have to think up activities to keep their minds occupied.

112

The group of N.C.O.s sat on a grass bank surrounded by perhaps a hundred cheering and screaming men. They had decided to hold a boxing contest to pass the time. Ten men had entered for the prestige of being the battalion champion and gaining a small purse of winnings. These had been whittled down to the last two men, who were now fighting it out inside a single rope ring.

Tom Jones Draft was fighting Billie Wilson. Tom Jones was a bit of a legend as he had been kept back in England in a reserve detachment after he had joined up. However, he was impatient for action and deserted his detachment to make his own way to France. When the authorities caught up with him, they decided that his motives were honourable, and that he wasn't trying to avoid the fighting but quite the opposite. No further action was taken, and they let him stay. He joined the battalion in the front line and became a popular member of George's company. He was a burly man of over six feet tall and was overpowering Billie Wilson, a dock worker from Newport. Wilson had been hit several times and the fight would probably have been stopped if it had been a proper contest, but the referee, a sergeant in A Company thought he might have been lynched if he stopped the fight prematurely. After over half an hour of punishing boxing, the two men were beginning to tire and suddenly, with one huge uppercut, Jones floored Wilson. Jones' supporters cheered as the Wilson supporters urged him to get up from the floor. He stood up but his legs failed him, and he immediately fell back down, shaking his head.

George had put money on Tom Jones Draft to win and he pushed through the crowd of men to collect his winnings. The contest had briefly stemmed the boredom of the rest area and George had frequently said that war was "mainly boredom, interrupted by a few hours of sheer terror." He didn't claim the comment, but he couldn't remember where he had heard it.

Following re-equipment the regiment became a pioneer detachment, working behind the lines doing a range of jobs including repairing the railway lines that brought troops to the front, unloading

113

stores, repairing trenches and bridges which had been constructed over some of the streams, filling in craters and strangest of all being asked to repair a woman's farmhouse, only to find that on completion the woman was evicted, and the farm taken over as a brigade H.Q. Some of the men felt very guilty but they were just following orders.

George tried to use this time to help his body and mind recover. He had a little more money in his pocket, partly from his time in hospital when he couldn't spend anything and partly from his promotion.

At times, he would go off with William Marsden and John Walters and a couple of the lads from Pontypool and Newport to a local estaminet. The first time he went he tried the local wine, which he found was rough, and nothing like his taste for beer at home. However, he persevered and as it was very cheap, after a few glasses he found he was not capable of telling the difference and he could certainly get drunk for less money. It was obvious from the number of girls who sat on the stairs at the side of the small bar, and those who circulated around the tables that the estaminet was also a brothel.

On his second visit a few days later, he quickly became intoxicated and despite warnings from some around the table about the dangers of venereal disease, George decided to try the delights offered by the girls. He moved slowly towards the bar, leaning on each of the tables as there was a danger he might topple over. When he eventually got to the bar, he peered over the counter towards the old crone who seated herself there. She stared back at him, waiting for him to speak. The realisation came to him that he would not be able to make himself understood in either French or English as he was totally incapable of speech, and so he spun his body around to the side and pointed towards the girl who he thought looked the prettiest.

The crone called out "Odile," and one of the girls rose and walked towards George. He took her arm and with the full attention of the table of his mates, he crossed the floor and began to ascend the stairs. He waved to the table where his mates sat, with a stupid grin on his face and some of his mates cheered him on while others shook their heads.

They reached a small landing area with rooms off to both sides. Odile led the way and showed him into one of the rooms where a washstand stood in the corner and a large double bed took up almost the whole of the rest of the room. Odile pointed towards the washstand, but George couldn't understand whether she expected him to wash or that she intended to wash. After taking a cloth and washing between her legs, she quickly went behind a screen that George had not noticed in the corner of the room and came back from the screen in just her underwear. George struggled to undo the buttons on his shirt and Odile had to help him.

She then stood and brushed the palm of one hand with a finger of the other hand in the universal sign of a request for money. George brought out the coins he had in his pocket, but Odile shook her head. George smiled as he thought the scene was beginning to seem like one from a silent film he had seen recently. Everything seemed to be done through sign language without a word being spoken. He then brought out several notes from a back pocket and Odile reached across and took all but one of them.

All then seemed well, and George quickly dropped his trousers at the side of the bed and squeezed himself under the distinctly grubby looking quilt. Odile undressed while under the quilt and threw her underwear onto the floor alongside the bed. She quickly turned and pulled George on top of her. He moved to kiss her, but she pulled away and shook her head. George knew exactly what he was expected to do next but unfortunately his body seemed to be failing him. He lay on top of her for quite a while, then he pushed the quilt aside to look at her body to try to arouse himself to some sort of action. He stared at the triangle of dark curly hair between her legs and became a little aroused but then noticed a very severe and angry looking scar just above the triangle, which quickly dampened his ardour. He also noticed that close up Odile was neither as pretty nor as young as he thought when downstairs.

She became agitated, and though he could not understand what she was saying, he guessed she was telling him to get on with it. It seemed the harder he tried, the less success he got. He simply could not get an erection, and eventually he slumped onto the side of the bed. Suddenly, he felt a desperate need to sleep and he closed his eyes. Odile got up and walked around the room, jabbering in a language he could not comprehend. She seemed very agitated, but then he must have slipped into a deep sleep.

The next thing he remembered was that he could feel himself being shaken, and then two burly men shouted at him and grabbed him by the arms. He tried to push them away, but they dragged him out of the bed and carried him to the top of the stairs, still naked. At that point he was half pushed, and half thrown down the stairs and Odile followed him, throwing down his clothes, which landed on top of him. He slumped back in absolute exhaustion on the floor of the bar while the clientele were in uproar, cheering and laughing.

George's mates carried him out of the estaminet and tried to dress him outside. The night was freezing cold, and they made every effort to try to get his clothes back on. Though they managed to get most of his clothes back on, they failed to get his boots on, and he was forced to walk back to camp in his stockinged feet with his boots tied around his neck. The following morning, which fortunately was the second day of his leave and did not involve any army activity, he stayed in bed trying to shake off the hangover, which he thought was as bad as the head wound he had received a few months before. When he did eventually get up, he couldn't understand why his feet had stuck to the blankets. It was only when he managed to pull the blankets off that he could see that his feet had been bleeding and consequently they had stuck to the blankets. When he did get his boots back on, the pain shot through his feet, and it would take several days before the effects of his barefoot walk would wear off.

He sat down on some bales of hay outside the farm buildings where his company were billeted, and William Marsden came across to speak to him.

George said, "what the bloody hell happened to me last night, and why didn't you do a better job of looking after me?"

Marsden said, "you're an awkward bugger and when you make your mind up that you are going to do something there's no stopping you; and to be honest it was probably a good thing you were in the state that you were, as the girl indicated that you weren't up to the job."

Marsden laughed at the image he had of George and the girl the previous evening. "She showed everyone in the bar that you weren't capable by crooking her little finger. That got a good laugh. At least it means that you are not taking an unwanted present back home to your missus."

George, now completely sober, could see the sense in what William Marsden was saying.

He thought for a while and then turned to his friend and said, "you know, if I go to do that another time..."

Marsden said, "yes?"

George continued, "knock me out!"

They both laughed and went off to find some food.

Two weeks later Captain Jessop came to find George and said, "Sergeant Williams, I want you to get twenty men from the company together as we have been requested to be part of a contingent to be inspected by the King at Abeele, in two days' time."

Two days later, in the early morning light, two trucks pulled into the farmyard and the twenty men, George and Captain Jessop, got in. They had already been inspected by their major before leaving and they had been jeered at by the other men because they looked so shiny and smart. George could hear someone shouting out "tart's handbag," as they got into the truck, and he smiled to himself. Halfway to Abeele, George's truck suddenly stopped. The engine had cut out and the driver got out to open the bonnet. He pointed out to

George a trickle of oil coming from the bottom of the engine. The driver got underneath the engine compartment but shouted up that he couldn't reach the oil leak to place something into the gap to stop it. George reluctantly got underneath the lorry with the driver. He could hear Captain Jessop becoming more agitated with impatience as he tried to reach the damaged part of the engine. "Hurry up Sergeant, otherwise we will miss the royal inspection."

George was thinking of a response but decided to keep quiet. He could see a gash in the metal where the truck had struck a rock; which had pierced the sump. The oil continued to drip onto George's tunic and over his face. Eventually, he managed to secure a piece of metal over the damaged part and squeezed a rag into the gap around the repair where the leak was. He then took a cannister from the back of the truck and poured more oil into the engine. It seemed to be just enough to get them to Abeele. Captain Jessop told George to get into the back of the truck and not to touch anyone. The soldiers in the back of the truck smiled at George's isolation but said nothing. When they got to Abeele, the contingent of men joined the others on the parade ground. George went off to get cleaned up, but he could see his uniform had been badly stained. He was told by Captain Jessop to make himself scarce and was forced to stand and watch the parade from a distance. When the men got back to where the trucks were parked after the parade, they formed up ready to climb aboard. Captain Jessop spoke up. "Men, we only have one truck. The other has gone off to be repaired and is now out of action. However, Sergeant Williams is going off to some of the local farms to organise transport for you."

George rose his eyebrows at this. Half of the men climbed aboard the one truck, smiling and waving at the other half of the men. George turned to a private who was standing disconsolately alongside him. "Come on Watkins, let's go and see what we can find."

After an hour or two, he managed to find a farm wagon, which would just about take the remaining ten men, if two of them squashed up to the farmer on the board at the front. However, the farmer refused to move until he had been paid. George brought out the money he had on him, and the farmer leaned over and scooped it up. They trundled slowly back to camp, arriving hours after the first truck. It was dark and raining as George made his way back to his billet to sleep. He passed William Marsden on the way, who asked innocently "good parade?"

George scowled at him and said, "fucking great day - got covered in oil mending the truck after it had broken down, missed the parade because I was too dirty and had to give this bloody Belgian farmer all my money to get back to camp. Another day like that I can do without, thank you very much."

William Marsden stood in silence, wishing he had never asked, and George stamped off.

George felt as if there was a heavy weight on his shoulders all the time; except when he was drinking. He was beginning to feel that the only time he felt normal was when he was drinking. Drink was the only thing that relaxed him. He approached his work with a mania that bemused the other men. He wanted to be active all the time. He couldn't sit down and rest as to do so left his mind relaxed and empty and then he would begin to think about Willie. God how he missed him, even though he was not at home and not in places where Willie would normally be, he still thought of him all the time. To relax was to open his mind to the horrors he had seen in battle, heads blown apart or blown off; friends dying and others around him in pain. He found it difficult to speak to people as he didn't have time for them. He was reluctant to get to know people too well as they might not be there the next day; just as Rhys and Brinley had been taken away. He was thoroughly miserable. People avoided him as he was no fun to be with. He did his work, he ate, and he tried to sleep, though he dreaded going to bed. Unless he was exhausted, he would lie awake and think of the horrors he had experienced. When he slept, he would suddenly wake and for a while, not know where he was. Sometimes, he would shout out in his sleep – or so his comrades told him. Occasionally, he had jumped out of bed and tried to crawl under it to protect himself.

119

His only saving grace was that others did the same from time to time and consequently people ignored this irrational behaviour - to an extent it was accepted as normal.

In that way, George was able to become a good sergeant and well respected. He never got close to anyone, and he never had favourites. He seemed to dislike everyone to the same degree. His troops respected his experience and wouldn't question his commands - they thought he must know what he was doing. Soldiers and other N.C.O.s dared not cross him. He was aggressive and angry all the time, angry at himself primarily but also angry with the world. Men killing men, and enemy soldiers attacking Allied trenches meant that he couldn't go home to see his wife and family - and go to speak to a long dead son.

In November 1915, the whole regiment was moved to Elverdinghe, north of Ypres to help guard the Yser Canal, which had effectively become the new front line.

17

The two privates who had been standing next to George had to turn away for fear of bursting out laughing. George lifted his head out of the mud and turned to them to see if they were laughing. He shouted, "if you are fucking laughing, I'll put a bullet in both of you."

"No sarge, we're really not," said one of them, spluttering and trying desperately to keep himself under control.

George was covered from head to foot in mud. He had pushed the two privates out of the way to show them how the trench should be repaired. He had tried to hold up a wooden support while pushing his shovel underneath to drag out the debris when his feet went from under him, and he fell forwards into the mud at the bottom of the trench. He didn't mind hard work. He was used to it underground but working in these conditions was nearly impossible. The trench had filled with water, which had turned to mud as troops trudged backwards and forwards along it. The outflow from the trench to the Yser Canal had become blocked by debris thrown up by shellfire, and the rainwater had simply collected in the trench bottom.

He stood up and confronted the two privates, daring them to laugh. He spoke between his teeth, trying to control his temper and his frustration, "anyway that's how you do it," he shouted at them.

With that, he moved over to one side to allow the men to continue with their work. The battalion was ordered to repair the trenches along the Yser Canal to the north of Ypres. The battalion still had four companies. B and D companies would relieve A and C companies every six days. This seemed to work, as every company would spend a short time in the frontline trenches knowing they would be relieved in six days for rest and recuperation. They had started out in billets in the grounds of the local chateau. When that was heavily shelled, they moved into billets known as Dumbarton Dugouts on the west bank of the canal. The men became exhausted quickly as the work on repairing the trenches after the 2nd Battle of Ypres was difficult and exhausting in the very boggy ground.

The following day, George returned to the trench they had been working on with four privates, ready to start on the next section of the trench repair.

George turned the corner of the communicating trench and stopped. "Oh God, look at the bloody mess." He stood still with his hands on his hips.

The privates looked around him to see what George was looking at. The scene in front of them brought very glum looks from all of them. The trench had been hit by at least one shell, if not more. That had caused the sidewall to collapse and allowed the floodwater from the next trench to flow into the trench they now stood in. The men were faced with over three feet of water, which was impossible to work in. It had taken two weeks' work to repair the trench and now all that work was wasted.

It was now the end of November 1915 and with a winter to come, the trench would be flooded with even more rainwater. George set the men to work on cutting a channel to try to feed the water into an unused stretch of trench. He looked back to observe the work; to check that the men began the work knowing what to do. He had four gangs of men on different parts of the trench system and was ready to leave these to go and check on another group. As he looked back, he noticed one of the men climbing the side of the trench to avoid getting wet. Just as George was about to warn the soldier about going up too high for fear of snipers, he heard a dull thud and the soldier fell backwards.

George waded through the water to try to get to him. He was beaten to it by one of the other privates, who turned to George with a look of shock, and said, "he's gone sarge." George manically pushed his way to the prone body, grabbing the nearest soldier to the body and throwing him out of the way. He grabbed the dead soldier by the lapels and pulled him up and then threw the body back. He released the body and then began thumping him hard on the chest shouting, "you stupid fucker! I told you a hundred times to keep your head down and now you are fucking dead - you stupid bloody trooper." It was as if the loss released something in him which he could not control. The other soldiers stood back, not really knowing what to do. George got a grip on himself and slowly calmed down. He could see a neat bullet hole about the size of a shilling piece in the man's forehead and dreaded to look at the back of his head and the exit wound. George turned to one of the other privates and said, "go and find stretcher bearers, and tell them not to rush."

The private bustled off. "Yes sarge."

Events such as this just added to George's depression. He reported the incident to Lieutenant Irwin-Brown and the lieutenant asked how long the man had been with the company in Belgium.

George replied, "he's been here ten days."

The lieutenant said that he would write the necessary letter informing the next of kin, as the captain was snowed under with letter writing to the families of casualties.

A month later, in December 1915, George sat with a group of N.C.O.s and privates in the dark, in a wooded area about two hundred yards from the canal. They gathered around a tin bowl into which many of the men had scooped their ration of bully beef. Someone had then found a candle and had placed it and lit it on top of the mound. One of the men then started to sing a carol. George recognised the voice of a man from Treafon who had been in the Treafon Male Voice choir. He had a powerful tenor voice, but this time sang softly, which carried on the evening air. He made the carol seem soulful, and some of the men joined in quietly - mouthing the familiar words. Some were afraid to sing louder as it could spoil the effect of the tenor's rendition. They became inert and thoughtful. George could hear some snuffling back their emotions. Home was a long way off in time and distance. It was 24th December and Company C was lucky enough to have been relieved on 21st December. They would have three more days of rest before they went back into the front line. The candle was allowed to burn and then blown out. Then some of the bully beef was ladled into the men's bowls. Many of the men refused it as they noticed a thick layer of candle grease lying on the top. One old wag said, "go on eat it - think of it as icing."

One of the privates replied, "yea, but you wouldn't have icing on bully beef."

The old wag laughed and replied, "you would if you wanted to take the taste away."

The men chuckled. The joke had broken the sad spell and after a short while, they moved back to their billets to bed down for the night.

George felt even more depressed than usual. He had been away from home for sixteen months. Christmas brought back feelings of home, which he tried to push away, but failed. Maud would be there with Joan and no doubt would be thinking of Willie. George remembered previous Christmas celebrations. Yes, he would probably be drunk for some of the time, that was just the way of it, but he would find time to play with Willie. Joan would have been too little to play with, but he would've found time to be with Willie and taken him for walks in the park; where the little boy would chat away.

George thought these were special times, and he could feel tears rolling down his cheeks, as he realised that he would not experience these times again. He thought that he had missed his chance of compassionate leave after Willie had died, when he was in hospital recovering from his wound. He could have been home with Maud, helping her and trying to support her. According to his mother, she had taken it badly. He would have liked to have been home for Willie's funeral as difficult as it would have been, just to say goodbye to his son properly. He had sent two letters to Maud since Willie's death. Neither was longer than one side of writing paper, as he simply didn't know what to say. It had taken him weeks to send the first letter and to decide what to put in it. He would sit in front of the piece of paper, and then would leave it. In the months that had gone by, Maud had not written to him - possibly for the same reason. He had received several letters from his mother, and each repeated that Maud was taking Willie's death very hard. He had written back to his mother relating the fact that he had sent letters to Maud but had received no reply.

Two days after Christmas, they went back into the front line. They were next to a French detachment and George could hear some of the men call across "Bonne Fetes." George didn't have a clue what that meant but he made a promise to try to remember it and repeat it the next time he saw a Frenchman.

Suddenly, the shelling seemed to increase. Captain Jessop appeared and called to George across the trench. "Sergeant Williams, I want you to pass the information down the line that a gas attack is expected. We think that they will shell us first, release the gas and then attack with troops after that. Pass the information to the men."

George saluted smartly and replied, "yes sir, will do, sir." He quickly called three of the corporals together and told them to pass the information down the line to the men. They scurried off to carry out his orders.

The shelling continued for a while and then they began to smell the gas. George shouted, "gas, cover your eyes and mouth as best you can."

The men began to soak rags in water which had collected at the bottom of the trench; being careful not to get the dirty water into their mouths. The yellow mist enveloped the trench. The men had difficulty trying to keep their attention on the front of the trench where an attack would come and, at the same time, try to prevent the effects of the gas. It was difficult to see through the greeny yellow fog of the gas. George squinted to both sides and noticed men falling backwards; some screaming or crying out. He called out, "stretcher bearers," who duly arrived. Immediately, he thought of his brother again. He shook his head to try to clear everything from it except the

125

job in hand; looking to his front to warn of an impending attack as well as trying to keep his men safe from the effects of the gas. He noticed one private chatting away to the man next to him with the rag around his chin. He shouted, "Private Roberts, for fucks sake shut your gob, pull your scarf over your mouth and look to your front! You're a soldier, not a fucking fish wife."

He could see some of the men laugh at the private's expense, who shouted back "yes sarge, sorry sarge."

George shouted back, "don't speak, just do it."

The private went to say "ye….," and then kept quiet.

George smiled to himself.

George could hear the British guns, which made a different sound from the German guns, and he thought to himself - that's the first time the British guns seem to be outdoing the boches. Good for them. The German attack never came, and George wondered if the heavy shelling had deterred the Germans from trying to attack.

He had spoken to one of the artillerymen who had told him, "we need more shells and fewer duds. As it stands, we have to ration our firing." Perhaps the message had gotten through to the top brass.

18

A few days later, George was sat finishing his meal of bully beef and a solitary potato. He had just picked out the potato as he could see a maggot crawling out of it. He cut out the section with the maggot and threw it over the top of the trench. Turning to the private next to him he said, "that could do more damage to the Germans than a grenade if they got hold of it." The private grinned just as Lieutenant Irwin-Brown arrived to his left.

He said very properly, "Sergeant Williams. Could you get some chaps together to escort two engineers who are going out to repair the telephone line that connects the next trench system with this one, and H.Q. It's obviously got damaged in the shelling. I'd like you to get two or three men and bring them to Hyde Park Corner. That's where they can begin to feed the cable out. Our job is to make sure that they are safe while they carry out their work. See you there in an hour. By then, it should be completely dark."

As the lieutenant left, George turned to the private and said, "thought for a minute we was going to be invited to a dance!" In a mocking posh voice he said, "if you could get some chaps together," he stopped for effect and then continued, still in his mock posh voice "and we'll have a little claret and perhaps a snorter of whisky, eh what." George was a polished mimic and often entertained his fellow troops in this way.

An hour later, George waited, leaning against the trench wall with two young privates, one of whom had only been with the battalion for two days. He looked very nervous - George could see his hand shaking as it held his rifle. He crossed to the soldier and patted him on the back. The soldier smiled in a very forced way. George grinned as he looked at the men around him and their blackened faces - they reminded him of his time with the minstrel band. George had checked that the men had taped up any parts of their equipment that might reflect light or give off a metallic sound which could be picked up by the enemy, as well as removing the straps on their rifles in case they got caught on something while they were out of the trench. At that moment, the lieutenant appeared with the two engineers; who had also blacked up and were carrying a large reel of cable.

The lieutenant stood to one side and when it was obvious that he was not going to be the first to climb out of the trench, George looked up to the heavens and said quietly, "well, this is what we get paid the big bucks for." With that, he climbed out of the trench and went straight into a crouching position. He was quickly followed by the two privates, the two engineers and then lastly the lieutenant. George whispered, "keep your heads down; don't make it easy for the snipers. Keep absolutely quiet."

The news of their departure had been passed along to their own sentries. They moved off to the right-hand side of the trench, looking around, ever watchful, with the two engineers spooling out the cable behind them. George sidled up to the lieutenant and whispered, "why are we not taking this along the trench system between us and the King's Own?"

The lieutenant whispered back, "because the frontline to our right swings backwards in a ninety-degree angle. The trench has collapsed at the point where the trench turns between us and the King's Own. We have to take the cable around the collapsed section for about two hundred yards."

The ground they crossed was just a mass of craters and they knew that they had to try and make their way in the darkness around the rims of the craters without slipping down into them. This brought its own perils as it meant that they were silhouetted against the horizon. Any movement was being watched for by German spotters in their trench and snipers who could be anywhere.

As they made their way forward in the darkness, George could hear one of the privates slip and slide into a shell crater. He realised that he had wandered off a very narrow pathway. He stopped and whispered, "are you ok?"

The whispered reply came back, "sorry sarge, I slipped and now my trousers are covered in shit."

George dropped his head down to his chest to stop himself from laughing out loud. He whispered, "I'll get the butler to wash 'em when we get back."

The party reached the King's Own trench, and the lieutenant was heard to whisper the password 'Tunbridge Wells', Monmouthshires here with your new cable, just on our way down."

A voice came from the trench. "Tunbridge Wells, it's ok, we've been expecting you."

George thought, thank God for that. Didn't fancy a British bullet in my arse. The men slid down into the trench one by one, and the engineers continued to work their way back through the trench still spooling out the cable. They were met by a King's Own sergeant who said, "we've just brewed up. Glad you got our invitation and were able to make it."

George laughed but the lieutenant kept a straight face. It confirmed what George thought. The man had no sense of humour. After the welcome cup of tea, the men collected their rifles and started to climb back out of the trench. George asked, "where are the two engineers?"

Lieutenant Irwin-Brown said, "they are not coming back. They have to connect the cable to the existing system, and after that they will make their own way back from the King's Own trenches, around the back," indicating with his hand a route around the back of the Allied positions.

George said, "why can't we go back that way?"

Irwin-Brown replied, "if we went back through their trenches, we would be three or four miles from our own trenches."

George added, "can't you get trucks to take us back from there?"

Irwin-Brown, sensing George's impatience said, "I asked, there are no trucks available." He stopped then added, "so we do it this way, if that's ok with you sergeant?" in a very sarcastic tone.

George tut-tutted under his breath, and thought, typical, men's lives are worth less than re-routing a couple of trucks. He began to climb out of the trench. The four men crouched down and began to make their way back to their own trench. When they had gone thirty or forty yards, the sky suddenly lit up with two Verey flares, almost directly over where they were. They immediately dropped to the ground. George could hear a scuffle behind him, and he managed to catch a glimpse of the nervous young private half crouching and half running off to the left. He managed to catch the lieutenant's attention and pointed towards where the private had dropped into a large crater. The lieutenant whispered, "follow him."

George and the other private slid off to the lip of the crater and then dropped into it, quickly followed by the lieutenant. All four men lay back against the side of the crater. Two more Verey flares went up and they could hear the ratatat of a German machine gun firing over the top of the crater. The men could see the tracer bullets lit up against the light of the flare just above them. The lieutenant said, "that was close. Thank goodness we followed that man into the crater."

George looked across at the two privates and whispered, "you two, ok?"

Two whispered replies came back, "yea, sarge."

As George looked across to the other side of the crater, he noticed the Verey flares had lit up the skull of a dead British soldier staring back at them. He said, probably too loudly, "urgh, he wasn't so lucky."

The men remained at the crater's edge for over forty minutes. The firing above them seemed to have stopped and there were no more Verey flares. George looked across at Irwin-Brown. "Shall we make a run for it, or should I say, a crawl for it?"

The lieutenant nodded.

George indicated to the two privates that they were ready to move out of the crater. They reached the top and stayed in a crouch position just below the lip of the crater. George started to move off when Irwin-Brown said, "that's the wrong way."

George stopped and crawled back. "It's this way," pointing to the left.

The lieutenant said, "I think you'll find it's this way," pointing in the opposite direction, to the right.

They both looked around them and neither man could identify anything that looked remotely familiar to them. George said, "where's your compass?"

The lieutenant, looking rather sheepish said, "I didn't bother bringing it. I thought this trek would be easy."

George looked at him. "For fuck's sake. Easy? Nothing is easy here."

"Well, I'm sure it's this way," the lieutenant said confidently, pointing again to the right.

George went right up to the officer and whispered quietly "well you're the boss, but if you get it wrong - and you've done that once before - you could get us all killed or captured, so you'd better get it right."

The lieutenant suddenly looked less sure. After a moment's thought, he started to lead off in the direction he had indicated. After they had gone a few yards, they could hear movement in front of them and all four dropped flat to the floor. George slowly lifted his head and whispered back, "boches in front - play dead!"

All four soldiers dropped their faces into the mud, just as a party of six German soldiers crawled past them, moving from left to right, dragging something behind them. After they had gone, George crawled back to the lieutenant and said, "that doesn't help us as we don't know whether they were moving towards our trench or going back to their own trench."

The nervous private suddenly said, "yes it does, didn't you see what they were dragging?"

George said, "no, I had my face down in the mud."

The private said, "it was an Allied soldier. You could see his regimental badge just catching in the light. One of the Canadians, I think. I'm sure he was unconscious." After a second, he added, "so they wouldn't be dragging him back to the British trenches, would they?"

The lieutenant said, "makes sense, well done lad."

George, looking very pleased with himself said, "so, I think I win that bet, sir. It's this way," indicating to the left, making sure that the officer knew who had been correct.

The four then crawled off to the left and after a few hundred yards they could identify the posts and the barbed wire arrangements that they were used to seeing in front of their own trench.

Irwin-Brown shouted down the password, "Harrogate, Monmouthshires coming back in."

A voice shouted back, "Harrogate, where have you been.? We were just about to give up on you."

A relieved group slid down into the trench. George said, "well, I'm glad to be back on home soil, so to speak." He looked at the sergeant who was there to meet them and said, "only our officers could make up passwords with two of the poshest places in the whole of Great Britain."

The sergeant laughed and said, "yea, why not Gilfach Goch?"

19

Captain Jessop, Lieutenant Irwin-Brown and three of the sergeants in the two companies had spread themselves out along the communicating trench as the men moved back to the support trenches behind. As they came out of the trench system, they formed up and began the march back towards the chateau. The word had gone around that the men were to be taken to a rest area. There was much chatter, and spirits were high. On reaching the chateau, Captain Jessop ordered the men to form up in an orderly fashion, ready to get into a row of trucks that had just appeared and were turning into the grounds of the large manor house.

A quiet afternoon suddenly changed into mayhem when the Germans began to shell the chateau grounds. With shells dropping around them, the men stood their ground and waited for orders.

Captain Jessop bellowed out, "take cover!" As there was little cover, the men ran in all directions in panic, some into areas where shells were falling. A 'woolly bear', a high explosive shell, burst over the top of the chateau, blowing off part of the roof, causing masonry to fall onto some of the men - burying them. Others who had begun to move away from the chateau now went back to help pull out their comrades from under the masonry.

George could hear a droning sound, and suddenly saw light being reflected off something just beyond the chateau. He shaded his eyes and looked up, noticing the outline of an aircraft with British markings circling the chateau. He immediately wondered what he was doing there. He thought he would be better off clearing out of the way while this shelling was going on. It was very rare to see aircraft activity when areas were being shelled. George was suddenly surprised by the force of a particularly powerful explosion, as the earth around him shook violently. It felt as if there had been an earthquake. It seemed to raise his whole body off the ground and then to throw him back down again with immense power. He felt winded and had difficulty drawing breath. Suddenly, he realised he could not hear anything. There was intense vibration and a whole section of the chateau collapsed onto the ground - burying men.

George could see other men running towards the debris, pulling soldiers out and throwing bricks and chunks of plaster out of the way. He tried to lift himself up to go and help, but his legs went from under him, and he fell forwards. He was told later that a seventeen inch shell had hit the grounds of the chateau from a German naval gun based in the Forest of Houthulst.

George couldn't feel his legs. He squeezed his right arm down to his side and as he brought it back up, he could see it was covered in blood. He immediately thought - not again! This was quickly followed by concern that he might lose his leg. He lay on his stomach for some time. He didn't lose consciousness and was able to watch the men's attempts to recover casualties.

The shelling subsided a little. He noticed that some of the bodies were taken to one side and any material available placed over their faces. Others were taken to an area near to where some of the undamaged trucks were parked. The drivers had moved the undamaged trucks away from those on fire and groups of men were employed in lifting the wounded onto these trucks. Two privates with red cross armbands came across to George, and one put a tourniquet around the top of his leg to stem the blood flow.

George then shouted at them, "I'm ok, now go and see to the others." One of the privates spoke to him, but he indicated that he could not hear him and eventually he left him and went to help pull men from the damaged building. He could see Corporal Owens come across to him.

Owens said, "you ok sarge?" George could not hear the question, but he could lip read what he said.

George nodded and said to Owens, "look they are going to take me off to a dressing station pretty soon. Can you tell Captain Jessop

134

that there was something odd about the whole incident. I don't know if you noticed but when the shells were landing, there was an aircraft circling the chateau. It had British markings but surely if a British aircraft had been shelled it would have buggered off, to protect the aircraft and the pilot. Ask the captain to look into it, will you?"

It felt strange speaking and not hearing yourself.

Owens nodded.

With that, two men came across and lifted George into the back of a truck. The truck left with the wounded, some walking wounded and some badly injured. George thought, well at least this time I get to the dressing station while I'm conscious.

20

George had been taken care of at the dressing station, where nurses and doctors had managed to stem the bleeding and had dressed his wounds. He was then taken back to a Casualty Clearing Station. To get to the Casualty Clearing Station, the ambulance had to pass through Ypres. As it made progress through the town, George could see around the canvas cover at the back of the truck that the town had been devastated. The large building in the centre of the town, the Cloth Hall was in ruins, a very different look from that seen when they had arrived, some months earlier. The attractive stone-built dwellings and larger functional buildings they passed now lay in ruins.

A doctor, who looked worse than some of the wounded, came to speak to him the morning after he had arrived at the station. He asked, "are you comfortable here?"

At first George was surprised that he had heard the question, then he realised with grateful thanks that his hearing had returned; though he still had ringing in his ears. He thought it an unusual question and replied, "yes, perfectly." He smiled as he thought what the doctor might have replied had he said "no, not really."

The doctor continued, "that's good, because you'll be here for a few days. We plan to get you shipped back to blighty, but the recent attacks have given us more casualties than we can cope with, and it may be some time before we can get you back there."

George, though concerned about the seriousness of his wounds, was pleased that he would be going nearer to home. He asked, "how serious is my leg wound? Will I be able to walk again?"

The doctor rubbed the fingers of one hand across his lower lip and replied, "I think so. I'm not an expert and you'll need a specialist to look at it. From what I can see, you had lost a lot of blood, but that was put right at the dressing station. You've damaged some of the muscles in your thigh. The numb feeling you are experiencing is because the nerves have been damaged. In time, I'm sure the feeling in your leg will return and I think you have every chance of a full recovery. It may leave you with a limp. I'm really not sure. I'm not sure how long the recovery will take, but you may be back in the front line before the end of the war." With that, he left.

George shook his head and muttered to himself "that's all they think about, patch us up and get us back to the frontline - bloody cannon fodder."

The following day, a nurse came into the tented ward and told George he had visitors. In walked William Marsden, John Walters and Corporal Owens.

They sat at the bottom of the bed and George asked, "who's fighting the war if the three of you are here?"

The three men chuckled, and Marsden said, "hey, a few days ago I spoke to Captain Jessop. He said that you had spotted a lone aeroplane with British markings, when the chateau was attacked. Well, he went to H.Q. to check why it was there and why it stayed after the Germans began shelling. Seems they have no record of a plane in that area at the time. General feeling at H.Q. is that it might well have been a German plane with British markings, a sort of spy plane. Apparently, it's happened before. Sneaky bastards."

George said, "so, it was acting as a spotter for the artillery?"

The three men nodded. Walters said, "Jessop also said that the Germans had noticed the line of trucks moving up the road to collect the battalion and H.Q. thought that they guessed why a line of trucks would be moving up a road towards the front line together - so that probably persuaded them to have a bash at the trucks or the grounds of the chateau, as they guessed there would be men there."

"Who'd have thought, eh? Our top brass have got to be learning from all these things, otherwise we stand to lose a lot more men," said George.

John Walters looked glum and said, "lost a lot of men at the

137

chateau, thirty-nine dead and over a hundred wounded. Some of them had only arrived as reinforcements the week before."

George looked up. "I'm one of those statistics, John."

They asked George about his leg and said they were a little disappointed to be losing an experienced sergeant and a friend. A nurse came in and realising that there were too many visitors crowded around one bed, began to shoo them out. As they were leaving, Corporal Owens asked if George would be returning to Belgium.

George assumed he meant to re-join them and was touched that they seemed to genuinely miss him. He laughed and said, "I hope not. I won't have to look at your ugly mugs anymore." They waved and left.

A week later George was on a hospital train, heading to Dunkirk. Two days later he was in hospital in Reading.

In early April 1916, George was sat on a bench alongside a grass area just outside the hospital building. Doctor Phillips appeared and stood next to the bench. He looked down at George and said, "the nurse told me you were out here, taking the sun. How is the leg today?"

George replied, "fine sir, getting better by the day. The therapy is really helping."

The doctor said, "well, it's been nearly three months, and it seems a good deal better than it was. Well done, Williams."

"Yes sir, thanks for all you've done." He looked up at the doctor, knowing the answer to the next question could determine his future. "Any news on when I can leave and what will be happening to me?"

Doctor Phillips said, "regimental adjutant is due to visit the hospital next week. You need to ask him."

With that, the doctor left, and George grabbed his stick from the back of the bench and levered himself up. He slowly and carefully made his way to a sunroom at the one end of the hospital. Here he had his therapy classes where he was embroidering an army belt. He found this relaxing. It seemed to take his mind off the war, his family and his future - there was regular banter with the other wounded soldiers.

Two weeks later, George was on a train making his way to South Wales. He had spoken to the officer who had visited the hospital a few weeks before. The officer said he would return the following week and inform George whether he had found out any information regarding his future posting. When George had his next meeting with the officer, he had said that his release from hospital would depend upon Doctor Phillips, but after his release he would be due three weeks 'permissionaire'. Following that, he was to be posted to Tonfanau Army Camp in North Wales, where he would take up a post as P.T. Instructor for the troops based there; the Royal Artillery.

George had found it impossible to stifle a laugh. The officer had looked up and then noticed the walking stick which George was leaning on. He looked back down at the paper in front of him and read it more closely. He said, "the letter actually says P.T. Instructor Organiser, so?" He stopped and thought for a moment. Not knowing how to continue, he eventually said in a gruff voice, "well, I'm sure they'll tell you all about it when you get there." He could see George's quizzical look and added "or the army have cocked up. Either way, that's where you have to report to after leave." The officer could offer no more, so said, "if that'll be all?"

George replied "sir," and saluted, realising it was pointless to press the officer any further.

HOME

21

As George continued on his journey home, he became extremely apprehensive at the thought of seeing his family for the first time in nearly two years. He was looking forward to seeing Joan, and to see how much she had grown, but he wasn't so sure about the rest. He thought how difficult it would be meeting Maud after all this time and everything that had happened. He had his demons, which seemed to have taken up permanent residence in his head, but Maud would have her demons too. No doubt O.H would berate him for going to war and he expected the circumstances within his home town to be much changed as it tried to cope with the strictures of wartime. He was wearing himself out thinking and trying to plan what he would say to Maud. It would have been so much easier if she had written - it would have broken the ice.

He was tired and even though his body had recovered during his time in hospital, the wound to his leg meant that he was not able to have any real exercise apart from walking. This caused him pain if too strenuous, leaving him unfit and lethargic. The motion of the train and the monotonous clicking and clattering it made as it passed over the points didn't help. After an hour or so, he fell asleep.

George wondered what was happening when a railway official began shaking him. "Sorry sir, but I thought, judging by your accent, you might well be looking to get off somewhere around here."

George had fallen into a deep sleep and found it difficult to come to his senses. "Where am I?"

The guard stood upright. "Just coming into Cardiff station, sir."

George pulled a face. "Oh blast! I was supposed to get off at Newport."

The train pulled into the platform and George got off with his kitbag. As the train pulled off again, he approached a railway official who was just leaving one of the offices. He tried to shake off the drowsiness and said, "excuse me, I need to get to Treafon. I missed my stop at Newport. Any idea what I can do?"

The official pulled a sad face. "Sorry sir, you'd have to go back to Newport or up to Rhymney or Pontllanfraith. There are no more trains from here tonight to any of those places. You'll have to bed down on a bench here and catch the early train in the morning."

George said, "bugger. It's bloody freezing. Which trains are leaving here tonight?"

The official said, "one moment, sir," and went back into the office. He returned a short while later saying, "well, there's a train to Swansea in half an hour, one to Pontypridd in fifty minutes and one up to Caerphilly in fifteen minutes. That's about it, sir."

After thanking the official, George dragged his kit bag across to a bench. After considering his options, he suddenly remembered Thomas lived in Caerphilly. He decided he would take the Caerphilly train and try to find Thomas' house, as he had been there twice before. He could then stay there, and then he could go on to Rhymney in the morning and get a lift over the mountain from there to Treafon. He was annoyed with himself for falling asleep or not asking the railway guard to wake him at Newport.

He muttered to himself, "bloody valleys. Once you are in one, it's the devil's own job to get into the next one."

He collected his ticket and boarded the train when it came in. It was only a half hour to Caerphilly. When he left the railway station, he looked around for landmarks in the town to help him find Thomas' house. It suddenly dawned on him that Thomas would not be there but having made the journey, he decided to see if Elizabeth was at home. He felt stupid for not remembering that Thomas would not be at home, but he put it down to his extreme weariness. He noticed a chapel and then a pub that brought a brief recollection. Turning a corner, he spotted a row of villa style houses with small front gardens that he recognised, and he knew that Thomas lived at

142

number eight. He knocked at the door and was dubious that anyone would answer, as it was all in darkness. After a minute or so, he could hear someone inside and the door opened. At first Elizabeth stood staring out without saying a word. George wondered if she had guests, or if the time was inconvenient.

He said, "I fell asleep on the train and missed my stop. I didn't know what else to do." He stood looking helpless and followed up with, "if it's awkward I can find somewhere else."

Elizabeth took a step outside and with a look of surprise, she said, "George, I couldn't see you properly in the shadow. How absolutely wonderful!" With that, she threw her arms around him and kissed him firmly on the lips.

George was more than a little taken aback, but he thought the kiss a pleasant surprise.

Elizabeth noticed his stick and asked, "can you manage the step into the house?"

George replied confidently, "not a problem."

He followed her in, along a passageway and into a kitchen at the back. The rest of the house was in darkness.

He said, "I wasn't sure if anyone was in - it was all in darkness."

Elizabeth stopped and looked back at him. She said, "I tend to only light a fire in here - coal is difficult to get, and expensive. It's easier and cheaper, but it's cosy enough. Please put your bag down and come and sit near the fire. You look frozen. Cup of tea?"

George said, "a cup of tea would be great. I haven't had anything since I left Reading."

Elizabeth started to get a small plate of food for him, and he leaned forward to warm himself at the fire.

They sat opposite each other and chatted for a long while. George asked about Thomas and how he was coping in France.

Elizabeth replied with a sad face, "to tell you the truth, he's not. His letters have become more and more a tale of woe. He describes some of the cases he has dealt with. The letters are censored from time to time but the sections that are not would suggest that what he has to do is giving him nightmares. He has never experienced anything like the conditions he is living and working in now to prepare him for it.'

Elizabeth looked up at George. "He was a solicitor's clerk, for heaven's sake. How does that prepare you for war?" She was getting more upset as she spoke.

George looked across at this beautiful woman and noticed tears running down her face. He knew that he didn't cope very well with women who were upset or emotional - he never knew what to do.

He thought quickly and said, "I feel like a drink. Have you got any brandy or whisky?" Immediately he said it, he realised he was in a very religious household and that the question was a stupid one.

To his surprise Elizabeth said, "there is a pub on the corner if that's any help?"

George immediately got up and went back out along the passage and out of the front door without speaking. He quickly found the pub, as it was the only building in the area with a visible light. He went in and he could see that the owner was clearing up and just about ready to close and that there were only a few old men sat around a table in the corner still there. The barman stopped collecting glasses and spoke firmly, "we're closing."

George said "it's ok, I'm not stopping. I wondered if you had a bottle of whisky or brandy to sell?"

The barman stood upright at George's request and passed back behind the bar. He collected a bottle of whisky from under the counter and George handed over a note. George had given a sharp intake of breath at the price the publican asked, and left clutching the bottle tightly, having handed over two weeks' earnings for it. He kept saying to himself, don't think about it, we both need this - I had saved up money for my leave, and I am on leave.

He got back to the house, where Elizabeth had already placed two glasses on the table in front of them. She had lit a candle which she had placed on the table. George didn't ask whether she wanted a drink of whisky. He simply poured and assumed that was what the glass was meant for. The flicker of the light produced strange shadows on the wall of the kitchen, creating surreal images as they moved. George looked across at Elizabeth and wanted to laugh as the light which shone from below her gave her a weird and slightly scary look. A little like the images he had seen on the magic lantern productions where they had tried to create representations of the devil or witches. He thought that if that were the case, Elizabeth would look like one of the most beautiful witches he had ever seen. He looked at her and said, "don't worry, this will be our secret. Thomas will know nothing about this."

Elizabeth giggled, as if they were committing a mortal sin.

22

George poured small measures of whisky into each of the glasses and lifted his to sip the amber liquid. It quickly burned the back of his throat but, he thought, in a pleasant way. Elizabeth lifted her glass and hesitated. George wondered if this was the first time she had tasted whisky. She took a gulp, probably larger than she should have, and immediately had to take a large intake of breath. Her eyes widened and she sat completely still for some time seemingly not able to speak. She eventually got up and moved towards a bowl that stood on a small table which had a jug alongside it.

Elizabeth stood facing the wall, spluttering and coughing. She poured a large measure of water from the jug and drank it to ease the burning sensation in the back of her throat.

George couldn't help but laugh. Elizabeth tried to laugh but continued to cough and splutter. George, pointing at the water jug, said, "might be an idea to pour some of that into the whisky before you drink anymore."

Elizabeth didn't answer. She didn't pour any water into the whisky glass, but the next sip she took was a smaller one. Even this caused her to look wide-eyed until the warming effect travelled down her throat.

George relaxed and said, "I haven't seen you or Thomas since Esther's wedding nearly two years ago."

Elizabeth looked down at the ground and said, "I haven't seen Thomas in that time also. I get anxious sometimes because I find it hard to remember what he looked like," she stopped and corrected herself "looks like." She continued, "is that awful?"

George didn't answer her question, but said, "he writes though, doesn't he?"

Elizabeth replied, "not as frequently as he used to. I think he's afraid of causing me too much worry and perhaps he's thinking about repeating the same awful things all the time." They both stayed silent for a time and took a few more sips of the whisky. Elizabeth looked up at George and asked, "is it as dreadful out there as people say?" and then quickly, "sorry, you're on leave. I shouldn't ask you to relate the horrible things you have seen."

George said, "it's ok, it'll take a long time for me to get some of the things I've seen out of my head. Whatever Thomas wrote and told you is probably true," he stopped briefly, and then shook his head and continued, "and we need to be cheering each other up, which isn't going to be helped by me talking about it."

Elizabeth suddenly remembered, and offered, "I'm so sorry George, I forgot to offer my condolences to you about Willie dying. I get so wrapped up with my own worries I forget about other people's. I went up to the funeral. O.H. said some lovely things at the service, and he was such a lovely little boy. We will all miss him so much. The day was so unbearably sad. Maud was struggling to hold things together, but you could see it will haunt her for the rest of her life, as you'd expect."

George stood up and moved towards the bowl which was on a table against the kitchen wall. He looked away from Elizabeth, and made as if to wash out his glass, but it was really to wipe away his tears. He put his handkerchief back in his pocket and quickly knocked back the whisky that was in his glass, and as he turned around, he noticed Elizabeth doing the same. He immediately poured them both another glass.

Elizabeth said, "I really shouldn't you know," and after a brief silence she added, "do you know I've never drunk alcohol before," and she giggled.

George now relaxed, said, "me neither," and they both laughed. George smiled and asked, "what happened when Thomas went off to the war?"

Elizabeth thought for a second and said, "a few weeks after war was declared, we went up to town to do some shopping. I went into a shop to buy some material and Thomas stayed outside. He had seen a friend coming towards him in the distance and he said he wanted to speak to him. I was only in the shop for a few minutes and when I came out Thomas was stood there on his own looking down. I looked down to see what he was looking at, and I noticed he was holding a white feather in his hand, and he looked pale, shaken. I was used to the confident Thomas we all knew, but this really seemed to affect him. When I got to him, he said that a young girl had come up to him to ask him for directions to the railway station. When he gave her directions, she then asked if he intended to join up. When he told her he wouldn't be going to war, she grasped his hand in quite an affectionate way and then she drew away. When he looked down, he noticed she had placed a white feather in the palm of his hand. He threw the feather away and shook his head as if to shake off the effect of meeting the girl but, that night he just sat in his armchair in the lounge. "

Elizabeth was silent for a moment as she thought back to the earlier events. "He didn't want to speak. He was just lost in his own thoughts. The following morning when I woke up, I found Thomas sitting out in the garden, which he rarely did. He shouted back to me that he was going out for a walk. I didn't think he was at all himself and so I decided to follow him to check he was alright. I couldn't find him at first, and just as I was ready to come home, I could hear shouting coming from the castle grounds. As I crossed the road, I could see a recruiting stand with a few men in army uniforms shouting out to a crowd of people and I could see Thomas was stood listening to them. I wondered at that time whether he might change his mind and join up. I went home and he followed about half an hour later. He went to sit in the garden as he had done earlier in the day."

Elizabeth stood and moved towards the wall out of the light of the candle. "When I went out to him, he said straight away that he had decided to join the R.A.M.C. as a stretcher bearer. That was it. He took no notice of anything I said that day. He's a stubborn man, as

148

you know. He couldn't be persuaded from it and the next week he kissed me goodbye and off he went to Kent to join the R.A.M.C. They obviously accepted him, and he did his training and the next letter I got from him he was in France."

Elizabeth, having regained her composure went back to her seat. She looked down at the ground with a very sad expression.

George said, "all I will say is that what you see when you are out there would affect any man. It's a living hell, and I'm not saying it to frighten you, and I know you don't want to hear that, but I am just preparing you for the time when he does come home." He stopped to take a further sip of the whisky and he noticed that Elizabeth had continued to hold the glass tightly in both hands while he had been speaking and had emptied it. He continued "you will need to be patient."

She reached across and poured herself another drink and topped up George's glass. He thought that it was her way of anaesthetising herself against what George was saying.

He looked across at Elizabeth, "the one thing I will tell you is that the stretcher bearers are some of the bravest men who are serving out there. I have watched them collecting the dead and the wounded; almost forgetting they are on a battlefield. At the height of battle, the Germans can't possibly see who they are firing at, and the stretcher bearers are often outside the trenches in the most vulnerable positions. You watch them and when someone calls out 'stretcher bearer', they move to where they are needed, with no thought of their own safety. They are so well respected amongst the men, and they have saved so many lives."

Elizabeth listened to George speaking and then started to weep.

She said, "it's very strange. Thomas is a very introverted person. He rarely tells me that he loves me or that he has any feelings for me - yet now that he is away, I feel so lonely without him. I feel awful. I am so selfish. I often feel sorry for myself while Thomas is out there risking his life every day. I am such a bad person - so spoilt." She started to sob deeply, and George could feel himself beginning to get upset for her. He stood up and went across to put his arm around her; to comfort her.

She sobbed into his shoulder for a few minutes and then she seemed to quieten down. She suddenly looked up and through glazed eyes she said, "love me George, just for a minute."

George, despite the whisky, was taken aback and started to pull away but she held him ever more tightly. She reached around his neck and pulled him to her to kiss him. George pulled back to look at this stunningly beautiful woman and finally gave in and allowed himself to kiss her.

They stayed in the embrace for a few minutes and then Elizabeth stood up and holding George's hand, she pulled him towards the passageway and the stairs. She seemed to suddenly remember George's wound and asked, "are you alright climbing the stairs?"

George said, "I'll be fine," thinking that a coach and horses would have difficulty stopping him now. Then he suddenly had a sober moment and thought about what he was about to do. He began to speak, and it was as if Elizabeth knew what he was about to say. She looked back and put her finger to her lips and continued to guide him towards the stairs. He continued to try to resist and then she stopped at the foot of the stairs.

She said, "am I so ugly that you don't want to love me, if only for a short while?"

George couldn't find a suitable reply, so he leaned forward to kiss her passionately.

23

When they got to the bedroom, George unbuttoned his shirt and went to pull down his trousers, but the effect of the whisky caused him to stumble back onto the bed. Elizabeth went to the bottom of the bed and when she was sure she had George's attention, she began to unbutton her blouse. She stopped and took the clips from her hair, shaking out her blonde curls, which fell about her shoulders. Her cheeks glowed and she gave a wicked smile. Still standing at the foot of the bed and obviously emboldened by the whisky, she uncovered her large breasts and held them up for him to see.

George was mesmerised by the contrast of her pale skin and the large erect dark nipples, which she began to fondle. She smiled, confident that her display was having the desired effect. Elizabeth undid her skirt and let it slip to the floor. He quickly pulled down his trousers and slid down his underpants and lay back resting his head on the wooden headboard. By now Elizabeth was completely undressed and George could see the triangle of dark blonde pubic hair between her thighs. She climbed over the low bottom of the bed and crawled up to where George was lying. She rested her head between his thighs and took his erection in her mouth.

George was in ecstasy and found it difficult to believe that this seemingly demure woman could behave like this. He didn't want to debate it with himself, he just wanted to enjoy her. He kept wondering if the experience was as wonderful as it seemed or was it the effect of the whisky. To make love to someone as beautiful as Elizabeth was like making love to some unobtainable famous actress or singer, someone that George could worship from afar, never once believing that he would end up in bed with her.

Quite quickly he entered her and after a few thrusts he came. He felt guilty as he had intended to pull out of her, but she pulled him towards her and nuzzled his ear, whispering how much she missed this and how good it felt. She continued to cover him with kisses for a while and then she turned, pulled him into her back and quite quickly she drifted off into a sound sleep. George fell asleep almost straight after her.

As they hadn't closed the curtains, the morning light shone very brightly into the bedroom when George woke. He wondered at first how long they had slept as he knew they had gone to bed in the early hours of the morning, and now he had no idea of the time. He got up and looked out of the window at the blue sky and suddenly fell back onto the bed remembering where he was and what had happened. In the sober morning light, George's thoughts were completely confused. He remembered with clarity the act of making love to Elizabeth but in the next split second he felt desperately guilty that he had just made love to his brother's wife. He turned to look down at Elizabeth, whose face projected the innocence of an angel with her blonde hair spread across her pillow. He realised that the experience of pleasure was beating down his feelings of guilt. He now knew what was meant by irresistible.

After a few minutes, Elizabeth began to stir. She opened her eyes and there was an immediate recognition of what had happened. George wondered what her response would be in the cool light of day. Was it going to be tears and worry and guilt and oh my god what will we do now?

However, Elizabeth lay silent for a while and then turned towards George and with a slight grin, she pulled him towards her. She giggled, just as she had done after drinking the whisky, and George wondered if she was still slightly intoxicated. She began to kiss him passionately and he quickly lost control. He climbed on top of her and slowly made passionate love to her, all the time nuzzling her nipples with his tongue and caressing her wonderful breasts. She was equally enthusiastic, to George's surprise, but the whole experience was far more satisfying than it had been the previous night. George, who was now more sober than he had been before, remembered to pull out of her before he came. The first thing Elizabeth said as they began to

152

get out of bed was, "thank you for doing that. I wouldn't want to present Thomas with a small bundle when he got back from France."

As he had been away for nearly two years, that might be a difficult thing to explain. George wondered had she remembered what had happened when they made love the night before.

He couldn't believe how Elizabeth seemed to treat the whole thing in such a matter of fact manner. Her reaction was totally unexpected. George thought that he was displaying more guilt than she was.

They got dressed and George washed his face in the bowl of water, which he found on a table against one wall. He then went downstairs to allow Elizabeth to dress. She came downstairs and continued to chat as she made George some breakfast and a cup of tea, and then she went to put on her coat, to walk with him to the railway station. As they walked through the town, she insisted on putting her arm through his and when he went to pull away, she stopped and looked at him.

She said, "you are my brother-in-law and I'm allowed to walk arm in arm with you, you are a close relative."

George didn't want to argue, but he did continue to look around him in case there was anyone there who knew him. However, Elizabeth didn't seem bothered and there was far more likelihood that she would see someone she knew than George, so why should he feel bothered.

When they got to the station, George collected his ticket and as the train for Rhymney pulled in, Elizabeth grabbed him and pulled him towards her, kissing him passionately on the lips. She said with a hopeful look in her eyes, "you will come and see me again, won't you?"

George's head began to spin, and he nodded quickly. How differently Elizabeth was behaving from the woman he thought he knew. He couldn't help but wonder how many people were watching him kiss this beautiful woman, and that they didn't know that he had just made love to her - twice.

He smiled to himself, waved and blew a kiss to Elizabeth and then he went to sit down in the railway carriage.

He churned over what had happened in the last twenty-four hours and shook his head. He thought, you just can't figure women out. You don't know how they are going to react or behave in any set of circumstances. He nodded off to sleep, knowing that Rhymney was at the end of the line and that he couldn't possibly miss his stop.

24

George managed to get a lift from Rhymney station in a grocer's van, delivering to several shops in Treafon. He was dropped at the top of the town and the van driver gave a wave as he pulled away. George stood and looked around at the town and thought that the fabric of the town had changed little from the time when he had left nearly two years before. He noticed that some of the shops seemed to have changed ownership and he also noticed that some of the Jewish names seemed to have disappeared. He noticed several union flags, particularly around the Town Hall and other large buildings as if the town had been expected to display its patriotism at this difficult time.

However, there were very few people about. As he walked down to his home in New Road, he passed a few people who nodded to him, more to the uniform than to him, as these were people he didn't recognise. He had noticed there were far more women than men, but that was to be expected in wartime. He walked slowly as he was reluctant to face Maud. He wondered whether that was guilt from what had occurred a few hours before or because he didn't know what sort of reception he would receive. Normally, he would have been looking forward to going home, but a combination of the recent tragic events and the interlude with Elizabeth had made him apprehensive.

He pushed open the gate and looked up to see next door's upstairs curtains moving. Ma Thomas would know he was home before Maud. He didn't have a key so tapped at the door, and it was immediately opened by Maud. She looked at him for a second and then fairly unenthusiastically came forward and gave him a kiss on his cheek and went back to her cooking. She said quietly, "I wasn't expecting you," as if George had just got back from his work at the colliery rather than two years at war.

George said, "I only knew a day or so ago, there wasn't time to write."

She must have suddenly remembered George's wounding and asked, "how's the leg?" and noticing the stick she continued, "is the stick permanent or will the leg get better?"

George replied "no, it's getting better all the time, just stiffens up a bit from time to time."

Maud said, "sorry I didn't write, just wasn't the um…" and then the sentence tailed off.

George said, "that's fine, you had a lot to do."

They both avoided the one topic that neither wanted to talk about.

Maud said, "I haven't got much food in, as I didn't know you were coming home. We'll just have to share what's here." She added, "Joan is playing out the back if you want to go and see her?"

George felt he was being dismissed and so went to find Joan. He got up, collected his stick, and went out to the garden through the back door. He could see Joan playing with her dolls on the grass. She was four when he had left for the army, and she was now six. He was surprised by how much she had grown. He moved towards her and in response she cowered back against the garden wall, clearly afraid of this strange man. She suddenly darted past him and ran, crying into the house. He could hear her saying to Maud, "there's a man with a big stick in the garden. I think he's going to beat me."

As George went back into the house, he could see Maud had moved from her cooking and was nursing a tearful Joan on her lap on the chair by the fire. Joan pulled Maud's arm over the bottom of her face so only her eyes were visible. Maud laughed and turning to Joan she said, "this is your daddy - he's been away at the war since you were little, and now he's back."

Joan looked up at her mother and replied, "he's not my daddy. He's come to steal me away and give me to another mam." She watched him out of the corner of her eye warily.

156

Maud said, "let me give you a big cwtch, to show you how much we both love you."

After a long while, Joan sat on the chair on her own, allowing Maud to get on with the cooking. She wouldn't take her eyes off this strange man sat opposite her, watching his every move, and hugging a ragged doll as protection, very wary of what he might do. However, it helped that George was able to hide the stick, which was soon forgotten about.

They sat down to eat, and George noticed that Maud had given him by far the bigger portion of food and had hardly anything to eat herself. He thought he would go out the following day and buy provisions, and then he remembered he had spent any spare money he had on the bottle of whisky.

After Maud had put Joan to bed, she sat and asked about his experiences during the last few months and whether he had heard from any members of the family. George had to be careful how he answered. He could not betray anything that Elizabeth had told him as he had not mentioned meeting her for fear Maud would become suspicious. Maud showed little interest in any mention of Belgium or what happened there but showed more interest when George discussed the members of the family.

Maud explained that she had seen his mother and father recently and that they were both well. She said that all members of her family were well, though her brother-in-law, Alfred, who had been fighting in France had been captured during a battle she couldn't remember the name of and was now a P.O.W. Ben was still training in Wiltshire and was expected to be sent out to France any day.

George could put it off no longer. He looked down and quietly said, "I can't stop thinking of Willie. Are you able to tell me what happened?"

Maud suddenly gave a deep sigh and stood up, looking away from George at the scullery wall. She collected a jug and a glass of water and took a long drink. It was some time before she was able to

157

explain.

She sat opposite George, looking down at the floor. She started to relate the events hesitantly. "He was having coughing fits more regularly, where he didn't seem to be able to stop. He was spending more time in bed, and he didn't have the energy to get up. After a week of this, I called the doctor. He was very nice. He said he thought Willie's condition was worse and he was fearful of consumption. The next day Willie coughed all day, he was having trouble breathing and he said his chest was hurting. The following day the doctor called again, and he said he thought Willie ought to go into hospital. They collected him in an ambulance."

She stopped to collect her thoughts and George could see tears collecting in the corners of her eyes, as she knew what she would have to relate next.

Maud continued, "I went up to tell your mother and father, and your mother came down to stay to look after Joan while I went to the hospital. When I got there, the nurse said that Willie was resting quietly, but I wouldn't be able to see him as he had been put on an isolation ward. I went up to the cottage hospital every day to see how he was."

"Then one day, about two weeks later, the nurse came out to speak to me and said that he had spent a very restless night as he couldn't stop coughing and it had made him very weak. I came home and in the early part of the evening, the doctor called. It was the nice doctor I had spoken to before. He told me to sit down and then he went next door to bring in Mrs Thomas. I thought that was strange, and guessed he had bad news for me, but I tried hard not to think the worst. Then he told me that..."

Maud started to sob bitterly and found she couldn't say the words that Willie had died. She realised she didn't have to, as George already knew, so she skipped over that part. She continued after she had calmed a little, "they let me see his little body through a glass panel, and...," she broke down again.

158

George crossed the room with difficulty and put his arm around her. It took her a long time to calm herself, and George thought it best to change the subject.

He started to explain that he would have to visit Rhys Jones' wife and Brinley Evans' wife to pay his respects, and then he realised he was not really changing the subject. Death seemed to be ever present at this time; for them and for many other families. He thought, how depressing life could be, death at home, and death when you are on the front line. He decided he had little else to say that would be of any comfort and so, in sadness, trudged his way up the stairs to bed.

When he woke in the morning, he noticed that the other side of the bed had not been slept in and he wondered where Maud had slept. As he entered the kitchen, he noticed a pile of blankets spread around the chair next to the fire and realised she had slept there.

He said, "look cariad, you can't sleep down here and then do a day's work - that's madness."

She said, "I didn't want to disturb you. I could see you were tired after your journey, so I thought it was easier to sleep down here." She immediately set to make a cup of tea for George.

George wondered whether the thought of sleeping in the same bed with him after two years of sleeping on her own was just too much for her. He noticed Joan hiding behind the chair in the corner, glancing at him through the slats at the back of the chair as if she had been imprisoned. He smiled at her and thought it was best if he left her alone to get used to him slowly over the next few days, before he disappeared again.

Maud brought the cups of tea to the table, sat and asked, "when do you have to go back?"

George said, "I have to go to a camp in North Wales, as a, don't laugh, P.T. Instructor."

Maud pulled a face and said, "with a stick?"

George shrugged his shoulders and replied, "you have to go where they tell you."

"So, no more front line. They're putting you out to pasture, like they used to do with the pit ponies after they were no longer useful." She gave a brief laugh, as if it was of no consequence to hurt George as she herself had been hurt.

George, feeling deflated replied, "thanks for the vote of confidence."

Maud asked, "how long is your leave?"

George replied, "I've got a 'permissionaire' of just short of three weeks."

He thought he detected a look of despair in Maud's eyes, and he wondered whether that was at the length of time he would be at home.

25

George sat at a table in the corner of the Castle Vaults. He looked around carefully at the men sat at the other tables. He didn't recognise anyone. It was a Saturday night and George counted ten people there. He thought, on any Saturday night before the war, this place would have been full. He finished his glass of ale and walked back up to the bar. He pushed his glass across to Maldwyn and said, "another one please Maldwyn," and as he pulled a few coins from his pocket, "well, your ugly face managed to frighten off all the locals."

Maldwyn looked up, "I don't notice anymore. It's been like this for so long." He pulled the pint and then said rhetorically, "You were with Rhys and Brinley when they copped it weren't you, George? Sad, sad, so many good men gone, and probably more before this is over."

George said, "the sad thing is that like you get used to the quietness of the pub, we also get used to those good men dying unnecessarily," and after a moment's hesitation, "life goes on."

Maldwyn gave out a sigh.

George collected his beer and pushed a few coins across to the barman. He said, "have one yourself, Maldwyn."

"Ta," replied the barman.

George could have carried on the conversation with Maldwyn as he seemed keen to talk, but the last thing George wanted was to be reminded of the war. He was planning to visit Rhys' and Brinley's homes in the next two days and that would be enough. George wasn't enjoying his own company, and all the local old men wanted to talk about was the war. The few people he had spoken to since he had come home wanted to tell him what a terrible time they were having in the town with a lack of food and how they were expected to work long hours. George wanted to describe to them in detail what the front line was like, but he thought he would be wasting his time, as nobody could possibly understand what it was like without having been there.

He constantly felt guilty about his brief liaison with Elizabeth and wondered how he would be able to face his elder brother. He found great difficulty in speaking to Maud, who was so badly stricken with grief for Willie that his presence seemed an imposition and his daughter was frightened of him and wouldn't come near him. He was still in some pain with the wound in his leg and he felt guilty that he survived when good men like Rhys and Brinley had died. He really was not looking forward to visiting their wives, who he knew would look at him with a controlled anger that their men, who they thought were better men, had died that he might live. Oh God, he felt so depressed.

The following day, while Maud took Joan to chapel, he went for a walk up into the mountains around Treafon to try to clear his head. It was a warm and sunny day, and he found the climb up the side of the mountain to be hard work. He eventually got to the top of the mountain, but his leg began to give him pain and he was out of breath. That would never have happened when he was working underground or after the first few months of joining up. Then he was fit and would have had the stamina to climb the mountainside without a problem. That is what a few months in hospital would do to you. Lying about in a hospital bed is no good for your health. He smiled at his own joke and sat on the grass, with a view overlooking the valley.

The town was shrouded in smoke from the brick works and the iron works and dust from the colliery, The ironworks was now smaller than it had been when he was a boy but could still pump out a fair amount of ugly smoke. Smoke also drifted over from the next valley where there were large works, which overshadowed those in Treafon. Despite the physical nature of the work in this part of Wales, many people would develop problems with their breathing due to the foul air. George wondered if men from the South Wales valleys might fare better against the evil gas that the Germans were spreading because their lungs were better adapted to breathing this polluted air.

162

He looked beyond the town itself to the countryside and the woodland that surrounded it. He was attracted to the idea of working the farmland on the outskirts of the town, as the clean air would be a very suitable place to bring up children. Then he wondered if that was just a reaction to Willie's death. How wonderful it seemed for children to grow up around animals. After the war, might he be a farmer? He chuckled at the thought of it, as he knew nothing about farming or farm animals. Even the pit ponies shied away from him when he was underground.

His thoughts were muddled and confused. He kept coming back to thoughts of his family. He considered how he could have helped Maud cope with the grief of losing Willie and that he could have supported her with all her tasks if he had been at home. He was confused at how willing Elizabeth had been to go to bed with him. Was it the whisky or would she have been as keen without the help of alcohol. She had been very keen the next morning when the effects of the alcohol were beginning to wear off. She just seemed desperately lonely.

Would Thomas survive the war doing the dangerous work he was doing and doing it without the help of a gun to defend himself? He was filled with admiration for his brother and thought how unfair people were in branding him a coward when stretcher bearers were so brave. Ben would soon be in the thick of it, with all the dangers that entailed. How could he have thought that war was glorious and exciting?

George stood up and started to walk down off the mountain, not having resolved anything more than when he came up, but it was a wonderful hour, just to be in the sun, with this view over the parts of South Wales he had grown up in, and that he loved.

The next day, he was standing in the bedroom trying to elicit some advice from Maud. Joan sat on the bottom of her parent's bed, closer than at any time since he had come home on leave. For this, he was hopeful she might be beginning to accept him. He said, "Maud, I need your advice. I have to go to Rhys' house to see his wife. Should I go in uniform or wear ordinary clothes?"

Maud was reticent to offer advice. "I don't know, it's no good asking me." She paused and then said, "they'll perhaps get a bit more upset if you go in uniform as it will remind them of the last time they saw their husbands. You have to go in what you feel most comfortable."

"That settles it. I'll go in ordinary clothes."

George dressed in trousers and his newest working shirt, despite them both being very creased from being in a chest of drawers for nearly two years. When he put them on he looked ridiculous as he realised how much weight he had lost, despite having spent the last few months in hospital with better food than he got while in Belgium. He quickly took off his civilian clothes and put on his army uniform, cursing quietly, "damn it, I didn't want to be doing this."

George and Maud lived on a long ribbon of terraced houses which ran along the bottom of the valley. He knew that Rhys lived in one of the rows of terraced houses that ran behind each other on the side of the mountain leading out of Treafon. George looked up at the area as he walked towards it. He thought it looked like the rows of troopers who would line up on parade one behind the other. Rhys' house was in the top row and George thought this must be devilishly cold in the winter, as it was such an exposed spot.

Having walked for about thirty minutes, he knocked at the door of the terraced house. It was answered by a lad of about nine or ten, who said "yes?" and after a sideways glance at George's stripes "Sergeant."

George smiled and asked, "your mum in?"

The lad ran down the passageway, shouting "mam, there's a soldier to see you."

After a short while, a woman of about thirty-five came to the door. She looked quizzically at George and said, "George Williams, isn't it?"

164

George nodded, thinking at least she knows who I am.

She moved aside and ushered him into the front room, which traditionally was kept for guests if you had a small enough family and could afford to leave it unoccupied. The room was sparsely furnished, but was clean, light and airy.

George offered her the parcel he had been carrying. He said, "some cabbages, from the garden."

Rhys' wife thanked him and placed the parcel on the floor. She introduced herself. "Rachel, I know Maud, well vaguely. We both go to the same chapel."

George hadn't really planned what he was going to say, so he started, "I thought while I was on leave I would come up and pay my respects." He began to stumble over his words. "I, uh, was with Rhys when he was uh, you know."

Rachel looked down, sad for a moment. "I don't want to know the details, but was he brave? You know, at the end?"

George stretching the truth said, "he was always brave. He was always the first over the top and he was great with the young lads, you know - keeping their spirits up and telling jokes and all that."

Rachel smiled and after a moment said, "they bury them out there, don't they? They don't bring the ..." she stopped, looked down and after a few seconds she continued, "they don't bury them here."

George said, "no, they decided that they would do that for everyone, so you wouldn't have some coming back and some being buried out there." He hesitated and said, "and I think in a funny sort of way it's the right thing to do. They gave their lives for the land where they are buried, and they are out there with the lads that fought with them. If they gave me a choice, that's what I would want." He gave a wry smile, "but not just yet." Then he realised the comment was probably in bad taste and so he just sat quietly.

As Rachel seemed to have nothing to say, he added, "it's just tough on the families back here as they have nowhere to visit and pay their respects. They do say they are going to build memorials after the war where people can put their flowers and wreaths, and these will have the men's names on them, so we don't forget them," he added "not that we would."

Rachel started to fill up and was clearly upset, but before she started to speak, the door opened and a girl of about fourteen came in with a tray with two cups of tea on it. The two of them were then left alone and as neither knew what to say next, they pretended to sip their tea, though it was far too hot to drink.

George asked if Rachel was coping with the money situation, and thankfully she said she was, as George would not have been able to help if she was in any difficulty. He said he would try and pop some vegetables up from time to time.

Rachel asked, "how long is your leave? When do you go back?"

George explained, "I was wounded," he pointed to the stick, "and so they are moving me to what I think is a training camp in North Wales."

Rachel didn't know what to say and so George added, "no more ducking German bullets and shells." He smiled to lighten the mood.

Rachel suddenly remembered that George had fairly recently lost a son and felt uncomfortable that she had not offered her condolences sooner. She said, "you well know what it is to lose a dear one and perhaps it's worse for you as little ones have their whole lives in front of them."

George felt choked and couldn't answer. He merely nodded in response.

George felt he could not attempt to lighten the mood again and so after a few awkward minutes, he made his excuses and left. Rachel stood on the doorstep and thanked him for taking the trouble to visit.

He stood out in the street after the front door had closed and gave a deep sigh. He had planned to go to see Brinley's wife the following day, but he would now try to get it over with in one day. Brinley had lived at the other end of town and by the time George got to the house he hoped he would be offered a cup of tea here as well, as his leg ached, and he was out of breath.

He knocked at the door and for a while, there was no answer. He was just about to give up when he heard shouting from inside and a tall man came to the door with trousers and waistcoat on but no shirt. He was strongly muscled, and he stood there with his arms folded, accentuating the size of his arms and chest. George thought him probably a miner as he could see the tell-tale blackness ground under his fingernails. The man gruffly said, "yes, what do you want?"

George said, "I was hoping to see Mrs Evans. I was in Belgium with Brinley." After a second's hesitation he added, "when he was killed."

The man turned and bellowed back into the house. "Margaret, bloke here says he was in the war with Brinley. Do you want to speak to him?"

George could hear someone coming to the door muttering, "what the hell does he want now?"

Brinley's wife came to the door and looked George up and down and begrudgingly said, "suppose you'd better come in."

George was ushered into a kitchen where it was difficult to see beyond the grey washing hanging from the ceiling to dry. Nobody spoke and in the small space, the large man stood over George in an intimidating fashion; still with his arms folded. George said, "I was with Brinley when he was killed." Neither Brinley's wife nor the large man acknowledged George's comment, so he carried on. "So, I thought I would come up and pay my respects."

Still, neither of them spoke. Eventually, the large man spoke up. "Hope he didn't owe you any money cos Margaret and me have got fuck all?"

George was more than a little taken aback by the question and looked bemused. He replied, "no, he didn't owe me any money."

The large man said, "did he have any money on him when he died?"

The woman quickly said, "he had a watch with him and a case for his ciggy's. It might have been silver."

George looked non-plussed and clearly irritated said, "we were in the middle of a battle. I didn't have time or any wish to go through a dead man's pockets!" George didn't want to explain that after the shell had burst there was not a sign of Brinley. The army would send back anything he had on him at the time of his death.

It then appeared that Brinley's wife had thought of something. She suddenly stood up and said, "you're a soldier, a sergeant, yea? Brinley was what, a corporal? So does he get extra pension for being killed because he was a corporal?"

George thought for a second. "Yes, he will have more pension for being a corporal, but I would have thought the War Office would work that out when they contact you. Have they contacted you?"

Margaret said "yes, we had a letter, just thought I could write and ask them for more if they had perhaps forgotten he was a corporal, cos me and Archie are really struggling. We can't go out like we used to; money is tight."

George said, "Archie?" and Margaret pointed towards the large man.

George was just about to ask if Archie was a relative when Margaret said, "we'd like to get married, and there's not much money coming in. Archie works in the brickworks, after he got the push from the pit, but he might have to give that up as he's got a bad back."

George had to try desperately to stop rolling his eyes, as Archie might notice. Despite his bad back, he seemed perfectly capable of giving George a pasting.

Margaret said, "suppose you want a cup of tea? What you got in that bag?"

George held on tightly to the bag which held the vegetables he was going to offer to Brinley's wife. He said, "some vegetables I just bought in town for our supper, and no I won't trouble you for tea, I have to be getting home."

"Suit yourself," was Margaret's reply.

George quickly got up and moved towards the front door. He made his way out and turned to say goodbye, but when he looked back, the door had already been closed.

George stood in the street, baffled by two completely different responses to his visit. Dazed by this experience, he was almost knocked down by a coal cart coming up the street behind him. He continued to shake his head in amazement as he headed home.

26

George could see that Maud was fully occupied with hanging out the washing and he noticed another pile ready to be washed. She didn't see him leave the house with his coat and scarf over his arm.

He trudged up the steep road to the cemetery and as he arrived at the cemetery gate, he looked around. He thought that they could not have picked a bleaker spot to site a cemetery, as it had been situated at the top of the ridge to serve the two towns either side of the mountain. This was one of the most exposed spots in the area, where you would have the devil's own job to find a shady nook for a loved one's last resting place. The image was not helped by the dense cloud and the constant drizzle. The whole scene was grey - even the stunted trees and grass were grey. He passed the fenced off cholera cemetery which had been in use some sixty years before. He noticed sadly that one of the gravestones stated that a victim of that dreadful disease had died at four years of age. He felt sympathy for the child's parents.

Maud had told him where Willie's grave was in the very large cemetery. He didn't think that she was suspicious of his questions as he felt he wanted to go alone. He didn't know why, but he didn't want Maud to go to the cemetery with him out of duty. He knew she went to the grave on her own and he wanted to do the same - to be alone with his son. It took him a while to locate the grave but eventually he found the small mound of earth and the wooden cross with 'William Owen Williams', written in clear letters, and underneath 1908-1915.

George stood for some moments, looking down at the simple cross. Then, emotion got the better of him and he started to cry, and without looking around to see if anyone else was nearby, he began to bawl uncontrollably. He slid down to his knees and then almost lay alongside the small mound of earth. He pulled out his handkerchief and blew his nose.

He said, "Son, I'm so sorry I wasn't here for you when you were so ill. I would give my own life to know that you were at peace now. We all miss you so much. Everybody in the family loved you so much - you were such a happy boy."

He found he couldn't say any more and turned to kneel alongside the grave. He ran a series of memories of Willie through his mind while he sat silently.

Looking up at the heavens he said, "why did you have to take him? You have had plenty of chances to take me instead and nobody would have cared. Willie was a good boy. He loved life and he would have been a good man. Why did he have to go? It's shits like me that deserve to die."

His head dropped. "It makes no sense. Does it make no sense to me because I have difficulty believing in you? Does it make more sense to someone like O.H. because he is a believer? Try to help me understand. Try to give me a sign that will help me understand why you would take my boy but leave sinners like me here." He looked up again. "Did you know that I would sleep with my sister-in-law and so you decided to punish me before I did it? Uh, is that it, is that it?" he shouted out.

He composed himself and looked around but thankfully there was no one to hear him. He sat in silence, thinking of the loss of his son, who he would miss so badly. He thought of the times when he would be working in the garden, or re-building a wall, or painting the house. Willie would sit and watch him. He loved to be near his dad, and he would chat away, and now that would never happen again. He vowed to spend more time with Joan and to be part of her life.

He shouted, "when will this war be over so we can get on with our lives?"

George found it difficult to drag himself away from the grave. He had found it difficult to muster up enough courage to visit the grave, now he found it difficult to leave. Eventually, he trudged back down to the house.

When he got home, Maud was washing the dishes and Joan was playing on the floor in front of the fire.

Without looking around, Maud asked, "where have you been?"

George replied, "oh, just out for a walk."

"You didn't say you were going out."

George noticed that Maud had turned around and glanced down at his mud-stained clothes. He hesitated, "ah, no, I didn't think it was important."

Maud dried her hands and looked directly at him. It was as if by looking into his red-rimmed eyes she knew straight away where he had been. She looked away but said nothing and walked out of the kitchen as if she couldn't bear to ask him or to have her thoughts confirmed.

George's gaze followed her out of the room, and he took a few minutes to compose himself. It was as if both knew of George's visit to Willie's graveside, but neither could admit it, because it would involve talking about the sad event once again. George went out to the back door as Maud came in carrying the wash basket of dried clothes. He reached across and took the basket and placed it on the floor and then held her and kissed her.

He moved back from her as she looked at him in surprise. He said, "come on, let's go out for a walk."

Maud looked shocked but said nothing. The atmosphere seemed to suddenly brighten.

The three of them walked around the block of houses and alongside the river to a bench. George sat with Joan on his lap, pleased that she seemed finally to accept him. He felt contented that they were a family again, and he felt that even Willie was with them in spirit. Joan had jumped off George's lap and was making a pyramid of stones she had collected from the gravel path. Maud sat next to him with her eyes closed, enjoying this quiet time to relax; if only for

172

a few moments.

After a while, Maud looked across at him. "You went to see Willie?"

George looked down. "Yes, I did."

No more was said.

A few days later, as he passed the Drill Hall, he noticed activity inside, and he could hear muffled shouted commands. He entered and watched as a group of young soldiers marched up and down the hall. He was really surprised at how young they looked. After about twenty minutes, they were dismissed, and George was just about to leave when an elderly sergeant major approached him.

He said, "hello, can I help you?"

George said, "just came in to watch. I was here in the territorials drilling like these in 1914. Where's Sergeant Major Turner?"

"In France somewhere, left here in 1915, not heard anything since, hope no news is good news, eh?" He continued, "so you served. You were wounded?" and then added, "I noticed the stick."

George said, "yes, home on leave for…" he was about to say three weeks, and then said, "well, I've got just over a week left."

Before George could say any more, the sergeant major said, "you're not going back to the front like that?" pointing to his leg.

George said, "no, I've been posted to a training camp in North Wales," and then "P.T. Instructor."

The sergeant major looked at him as if he was making a joke.

George said, "the army eh, they've got some strange ideas."

The sergeant major asked, "where were you?"

George replied, "Belgium - the 2nd Battle of Ypres."

The sergeant major pulled a face. He said, "just heard this week, I've lost a close mate in the Middle East. It's hard to take."

George replied, "yea, same here. Spending time visiting the families of my dead mates. The world is not a nice place at the moment."

Suddenly the Sergeant Major thought. "Any chance you can come and speak to the men?" he then lifted his eyebrows and corrected himself, "boys. Perhaps on Thursday, or before you go to your next posting. I'd really appreciate it, and I'm sure they would benefit from hearing about the war from somebody who's seen it first-hand."

George said, "yes, no problem. Hope I don't put them off going."

The Sergeant Major shook hands and said, "Sergeant Major Brooks. See you on Thursday, and thanks. Oh, and can you come in uniform, about seven thirty, ok?"

George said, "look forward to it, seven thirty Thursday it is."

On the Thursday night, the boys had just finished drilling when the Sergeant Major came across to George. Seeing him in uniform, he saluted him instead of shaking hands, as he had done previously. George realised that he had not introduced himself last time. He stood to attention and announced, "Sergeant Williams, Monmouthshire Battalion. At least it was when I left."

Brooks turned to the boys and asked them to gather around George and sit on the floor. George took his place and sat on the edge of a piece of staging at the end of the hall. He said that he would first explain what had happened at the 2nd Battle of Ypres, and where the Monmouthshires were during the battle and then he would talk a little about life in the trenches and then they would be free to ask him questions.

George explained what had happened at the battle and the difficulties they could expect to experience when they went to the front. The boys listened carefully and quietly and then he asked if there were any questions.

A ginger haired boy who George thought looked about twelve or thirteen stated, "I think I can say that we all think you boys did a wonderful job out there. We can't wait to get out there and kill as many hun as we can."

George looked down at the ground and smiled in embarrassment. "Look, I don't want to dampen your enthusiasm, but I felt the same as you when I first went out but when you get there…"

George could hear a rumble of disapproval from the boys in front of him. "Look around and think to yourself, how would I feel if the boy sat next to me now was uh, well, didn't come back." George then said, "look, the most important thing is that you stay alive. So, look after yourself and your mates if you can and listen to what the experienced men out there tell you. We've had some boys who come out thinking they know it all and then they make mistakes because they don't listen and… well, you can guess the rest."

The Sergeant Major, who had stood at the back, started to seem a little unsettled. He stepped forward and said, loudly, "next question, I think."

One young man put his hand up and asked, "what's the beer like out there and are there any women - you know what I mean?" This brought a laugh and a look of admonishment from the Sergeant Major.

George said, "the beer's rubbish, many men drink the local wine now because it's cheaper. I wouldn't know anything about the women, I'm a happily married man." Though at the same time he was thinking about how miserable his life was at the moment with Maud, and he was thinking of the girl Odile that he went upstairs with at the estaminet. He continued, "if you do go out to France or Belgium leave the women alone otherwise you could be bringing something back that will put paid to your chances with a nice Welsh girl - you know what I mean!" nodding to the boy who had asked the question.

The Sergeant Major smiled in approval of George's comments.

Another boy asked, "what was it like being shelled all the time?"

George didn't want to frighten them anymore, as he thought he

175

would incur the disapproval of the Sergeant Major, so he said, "you get used to it, like everything else."

There were many more questions about trench life and whether the Germans were coping with the war better than the Allies were. The evening finished with a question from a faired haired soldier at the back, who looked a thoughtful type. He said, "you mentioned about your mates getting killed or wounded. From the beginning of the war, most regiments were 'pals' regiments, so there was more chance of someone you knew or someone you had grown up with or worked with getting killed. Do you think that was a stupid idea?"

George paused and then said, "thankfully, I'm just a poor old sergeant. It's the generals and the politicians who make those sorts of decisions. They are the ones who see the bigger picture. You have to assume they had thought about it and made the right decision." In reality George knew that the men at the front always said that the army decided to have 'pals' battalions because it was easier to gain recruits when you were shamed into it by your mates, and he wondered whether the politicians cared about the relationships between men in one battalion. He continued "with the number of casualties, regiments are taking men from several battalions and mixing them up together, as they have with the Monmouthshire Regiment, so the men are now with other men from different areas." He paused and then said, "so the pals battalions are dying out." He thought about the words he had used and added "I didn't mean they are dying; I meant the battalions of pals are changing. What I really mean is ....." He stopped and didn't know what to say that would correct his mistake so he scratched his head and said, "well, you can tell why I'm a soldier and not a teacher. This talking lark is harder than you think."

The boys all laughed.

George thought that his little talk to these boys was a harder task than he first thought. They asked more perceptive questions than he was able to answer, and he had also tried to be diplomatic in his

176

answers. He stood up to indicate the talk was at an end. The young soldiers remained sitting, thinking about George's answers, and chatting amongst themselves. The Sergeant Major got up on stage and asked for a round of applause before dismissing them. As George went across to say goodbye to Sergeant Major Brooks, many of them came across to thank him as they left.

Brooks thanked George and he said, "that was very enlightening. I was too old to fight in a war zone. I didn't even make it to the Boer War or Omdurman, so it was really helpful for them to hear it from you. How bad is it out there, really?"

George hesitated for a second and said, "think of all you hear and read, multiply that by a hundred and that is nearly as bad as it is."

Brooks blew out through his teeth, and said, "pray it ends soon, before this lot have to go out. They are so young. Conscription means there's going to be a lot of young men going out who don't want to go. In a war as bad as this, should we be sending them? This is our nation's future."

George turned to leave the hall, thinking of Thomas and O.H. and whether they might have been right to oppose the war. This prompted him to think of his parents and he realised he would have to pay them a visit before his leave ended, otherwise he knew he would be in the dog-house for being home and not seeing them. He had put off the visit until now as he knew O.H. would preach to him that he should have been more like Thomas and refused to fight. He was just too weary to debate the issue with his father.

He spoke to Maud and they both agreed to go up to see George's mother and father on the following Saturday.

27

George tapped at the front door, and it was quickly answered by his mother. Her eyes sparkled at the sight of her son's family.

"Oh, how wonderful to see you all." She brushed past George to pick Joan up, giving her a kiss. They all followed her into the kitchen where O.H. sat at the kitchen table with a cup of tea in front of him.

George was a little surprised to see his father less than completely dressed in his shirtsleeves. O.H. rose to greet them, shaking hands formally with George, and nodding in his direction "son."

They all sat at the kitchen table with cups of tea in front of them and shared their knowledge of how each family member was coping in the difficult times they faced. Joan became a little restless after a while and Ann took her out to play in the back garden. Maud, sensing a silent tension between the two men, decided to follow her mother-in-law and daughter out to the back of the house.

O.H. looked up and said, "you ok? I heard you were wounded. Is it healing?"

George replied, "yes, it's getting easier." He pointed towards the stick resting on the back of the chair. "That helps."

O.H. shook his head. "I read about the Battle at Ypres, a bloody affair, many casualties. Lots of families will have lost their loved ones."

George nodded in agreement with all those sentiments.

O.H. looked directly into his eyes. "Do you now regret going?"

George fully expected this question to come sooner or later. He sighed deeply and looked down at the table. "We are stopping the German advance. I don't pretend it's not a living hell when you are out there - because it is. You cannot imagine how awful. The areas where the fighting is taking place are the most god-awful places on earth."

He paused, and then gathered his thoughts. Putting his hands together on the table in front of him, in almost a parody of prayer, he said, "but the men fighting there believe that they are stopping an evil power from spreading its influence and control into the rest of Belgium, France and in time Britain. You have to believe that otherwise you would wonder why you are in such an awful place, and why you are seeing such dreadful sights."

George started to relate the story of Otto, the German prisoner he was assigned to guard. He laughed ironically. "He showed me his belt buckle, which all German soldiers wear. It has 'Gott mit uns' on it. God is with us, or something like that. How can they believe that God is on their side when they commit the atrocities they do?"

O.H. guffawed and sat back saying, "when the reality is that God is on neither side of those who carry the weapons of war." He paused and then continued, "and who is to say that atrocities are not committed on both sides? I daresay you only hear of those committed by Germans." There was silence for a few seconds and then O.H. looked George in the eye, "you don't have to be there. You can give up at any time."

George, beginning to tire of the conversation, said, "not if you believe in what you are doing." He looked O.H. in the eye. "You go to chapel because you believe. You don't change your mind halfway through and say being a Christian is probably wrong. I think I will try and follow the preachings of Mohammed for a while. The same is true of the men out there. They believe in what they are doing, on both sides." He stopped and then after a short silence, "and that is why it continues."

O.H. remained silent for a few seconds and then said, "and what of the men who die or are terribly crippled? I see some of them in town, the ones who have come back with arms and legs blown off. Can it be worth it?"

George looked O.H. in the eyes. "I have been lucky. My wounds

179

will heal. I stood next to two of my closest friends who were killed. I can comment as one of those who has seen the cruelty of war close up." He waited for his statement to sink in and then added, "but I still believed in what I was doing; and still do."

O.H. shook his head and for a while seemed to be reluctant to continue the discussion. George sat up straight in his chair. "It is a classless war in some respects. All classes are losing men. I saw an officer killed when he stood as far away as you are from me. I know it is a popular thing to say that the wealthy classes are sending working class men to die at the front, but take it from me, as many officers are killed as ordinary soldiers. It's said at the front that the Germans target the officers in order to make ordinary soldiers leaderless." Before O.H. could say anymore George continued, "this German soldier, Otto, that we had to guard overnight told us the Germans were facing the same hardships as us and that they are losing ordinary soldiers and officers; so for them, it's a classless war as well. I tell you this, you don't have feelings of gaining any glory from fighting. It is a bloody and de-humanising life in the trenches, with the constant rain, the rats, the awful food and the terror of battle. The men want it to end, but they continue to fight because they fear a German victory more."

O.H. began to shake his head once more, but before he could speak George said, "you said before the war that we shouldn't fight and I have to give it to you that perhaps if many people, particularly people in power such as the politicians and the army leaders, on both sides, knew what it was going to be like they might have worked harder to maintain the peace. It is the politicians I blame. I think both sides thought it would be a short war with some casualties, but with nothing like as many as there have been, and that the deaths would bring them to the table to negotiate a peace settlement."

George felt quite clear and confident in elaborating on the things he had spent a great deal of time thinking about during his many weeks in hospital. "In a perverse way, the more casualties there are, the further away the chance of the two sides negotiating a peace - as they feel that they cannot give anything away to the other side because so many men have been lost on their own side. I remember meeting people just before the fighting started that were impatient to get out to France and Belgium because they were afraid the war would be over before they got there. I was one of those. Remember the call 'it'll all be over by Christmas?' Here we are two years later, and peace is no nearer. Neither side will give way. Having sacrificed so many men, they have to have victory to justify it. Unfortunately, many more will die before there is an end to it."

George thought he might have rendered O.H. silent as he had been as honest as he could be about the war and its implications. It took away any debating points his father might have thought of. He had assumed beforehand that O.H. would be in a preaching mood invoking the verses of the Bible, and that he would be telling him, in no uncertain terms, that he had been wrong to go to war. However, George thought O.H. looked weary. He had seen the effect the war had had on his own family with himself, Ben, Thomas and Evan all away from their own families and all being involved in some capacity in this senseless war. He seemed depressed by all the hardships and the brutal killing that war brought. George thought that he would agree with him.

O.H. lifted his hands and was about to speak, but just at that moment Ann, Maud and baby Joan came in from the back garden. Ann could see that the two men had been talking and guessed quickly what the discussion had been about.

In turn, she looked at both men and spoke loudly, "enough now. No more talk of war in front of the little one." She continued, "did you know Thomas has come home?" looking at George.

He was taken aback but could not admit that he had seen Elizabeth just two weeks before.

Maud said, "was he injured? Why is he home?"

Ann said, "we received a letter from Elizabeth yesterday. All she said was that Thomas was suffering from some sort of nervous illness.

He had spent some time in a hospital in London and then had suddenly appeared at the house a few days ago. She didn't go into any details but said that he remained in bed and that she was attending to him."

George thought that Thomas must have turned up at the house not long after he had left to catch the train home, thanking God it was not the morning he had woken up in Elizabeth's bed. He remained silent. Ann, Maud and O.H. spent some time surmising what might be wrong with Thomas, but all became distracted as Joan fell forwards going over a step from the passageway into the kitchen and banged her head. The conversation regarding Thomas tailed off as they ran to tend to Joan, and George was very glad of that.

The following day, Maud presented George with a boiled egg for his breakfast. He thanked her and announced that as his leave was coming to an end, he would like them to spend a little time together as a family, and that they should go out together. Maud turned around from her bowl of water, her hands covered in soapsuds, with her mouth open.

George said, "careful, you're dripping all over the floor."

She said, "did you just say you wanted us all to go out," and after a moment's hesitation, "together?"

George moved forward and eased her out of the way. "I'll finish these dishes. Go and put your coat on and get a coat for Joan."

George finished the washing up and started to put all the cleaning items away; except that he wasn't really sure where they went. Maud came back into the kitchen with her outdoor coat on, smiling at George who stood in the middle of the floor with dusters and polish in one hand and a wooden spoon and rolling pin in the other hand, not knowing which cupboard they went in. She took the items from him and said, "go on, get your coat on, before it gets dark."

They both laughed, as it was only just after lunchtime. Joan came into the kitchen with her coat on, looking bemused. "Are we really going out today?"

George picked her up in his arms and gave her a kiss on the cheek. She pulled a face and said, "you haven't shaved Daddy, your face is scratchy."

Maud said, "can't stop now to do that or we'll never get out."

Maud lay down on the grass in the town park with a sense of satisfaction, watching George chase Joan around a flower bed. Joan was laughing and loving spending time with her father. She smiled to herself and thought, I wonder what has brought about this change in him?

As George sat down, she turned to him. "You ok?" meaning in more senses than just at that moment.

George said, "I want something nice to think about when I am back in uniform; knowing it's not always going to be like it is."

Maud leaned over and gave George a quick kiss. It was noticed straight away by Joan, who began to run around shouting "I saw Mummy kiss Daddy. I saw Mummy kiss Daddy!" over and over again.

CAMP

28

George had gone for a walk along the edge of some low level cliffs. He looked out to where he assumed the sea was, though he could see nothing through the heavy mist. He was being careful to stay on the pathway and not stray near the edge. He could see about twenty yards in any direction. The mist was swirling, and it felt cold and damp. George wondered what the winter was going to be like in this god-forsaken place if the end of the summer was like this. Two days after he had arrived, the sky had been clear and that had allowed him to get his bearings, but since then it had been wet with thick, dense cloud every day. The weather and the terrain, which seemed less welcoming and more desolate by the day, added to his loneliness and despair.

It was September 1916, and he had been at Tonfanau Camp for two weeks. The Somme offensive had been going on for two months, and there were reports from France of very heavy casualties; perhaps the heaviest of the war.

He had received his first letter from Maud, in which she said she had been speaking to various people in town while shopping and some said the Monmouthshire Regiment had been disbanded, and were now part of the Welsh Regiment, but that he would probably know that. She had heard that they had been moved into France and some thought that they were fighting on the Somme. This news made George feel even more dispirited. He wasn't sure whether he was dispirited because his regiment and probably many of his old comrades were fighting this terrible battle or because he wasn't there with them.

He had travelled up from Treafon on the train and it seemed that the further north he went, the more remote the area appeared to be and the more rugged the terrain. He had seen few houses and those he did see appeared to be isolated farmhouses. After a long journey, he stepped down from the train as the only person to disembark at Tonfanau. It was no more than a short platform with a small wooden lapboard waiting room and an even smaller office. He dragged his kit bag along the platform and as he looked at an area behind the waiting room, he could see the rows of huts which made up the camp. It had been built on a flat piece of land between the mountains and the sea and covered a surprisingly large area. He was in danger of ruining the kit bag if he continued to drag it and as he couldn't be bothered to haul it any distance as it was so heavy; he decided to leave it in the waiting room and come back for it later - hopefully with some sort of cart.

George was welcomed in the camp's main administrative office by Captain Parker, who was second in command at the camp to Major Fisher. Both were Royal Artillery officers. Captain Parker said he would arrange for George's kit bag to be collected and delivered to his dormitory.

George was then taken to the N.C.O.'s Mess, which was little more than a hut with a corrugated metal roof and a wooden floor. George looked up as he became distracted by the rain beating down on the metal roof. There were two other sergeants and four corporals there. George was told that there was also a sergeant-major, who was at that time out drilling the men. Two of the corporals stood up and introduced themselves to George as being P.T. Instructors. He realised that he would be working closely with the two gentlemen stood in front of him. They both looked young, keen and fit, certainly fitter than George, who still continued to use a stick.

The two corporals explained that the previous Sergeant Instructor had been posted to the front line some four weeks before and they had arranged a programme of physical training for the men between themselves. George ascertained that this primarily involved marching drills, with intermittent sprints in vests and shorts, which they managed to borrow from two local football teams with the promise to return them after the war, and cross-country runs which in the local terrain were extremely gruelling as it was either rocky or mountainous, or both.

George explained his medical condition, and that this would make it difficult to partake in physical activities, and that he wasn't sure when or if he would be fully recovered. He felt that he had to add that he had no say in where he had been posted or in what role, and that he didn't see much sense in posting an injured man as a P.T. Instructor - that was the army's decision. The two men were sympathetic and wished George well in his recovery. They agreed that for the time being, the two corporals would take the sessions and George would plan rotas and try to make the exercise routines as interesting and varied as possible. He would also deal with any paperwork.

Corporal Rogers said he had spoken to several head-teachers in the local schools, and he had managed to acquire a small amount of exercise equipment and access to the school's facilities as long as they could get the men there. George said he would ask Major Fisher if he might have use of one of the camp's trucks to transport the men to the local schools.

Later that evening, George met Major Fisher to ask about the use of the trucks. He was told that he could use one of them, as long as it was not being used by the Royal Artillery. It was made clear that the camp was being run for the benefit of the armaments training of the Royal Artillery and they warranted top priority. Major Fisher explained that detachments of the Royal Artillery would be directed to the camp for training purposes for periods of perhaps five or six weeks at a time; so there would be different groups of artillerymen there for short periods of time throughout the year.

As George's tasks were limited in their scope and there was little else that he might contribute to the work of the P.T Instructors, he found himself with plenty of spare time on his hands. Groups of men might go on a three-hour run and George would be left to fill in his time, hence his many walks along the coastline and up into the mountains. Once he had drawn up the rota for the month, there was little that required his attention.

He found that his time at the camp was in marked contrast to his life on the front line. Gone were the terrors and the threat of German attacks, either by men, by aircraft, by shells, or by gas. The experience of the noise of the shelling continued, as the men of the Royal Artillery practised all day and every day, firing out to sea, with both live and dummy shells and they often practised loading and firing. They would fire at floating targets towed behind a small boat out at sea; but only if weather conditions permitted. George quickly got used to the sound of explosions and the comforting fact that these shells were very different to those fired at you while you tried to hide from them.

George was plagued by guilt. The long periods of spare time he had seemed to make it worse as his mind would often be dragged back to the Western Front and the many men that were still fighting there. He could picture the men he knew huddled beneath the trench parapet to escape the fury of the shells and bullets the Germans were sending over.

Although George was bored with the inactivity at first, as time went on, he became more accepting of his position and the circumstances in which he found himself. He thought that there was no point in his frustration and that he might as well get used to it. He began to appreciate the countryside, and he looked forward to his long walks.

He would stop and chat with any locals, and many would ask about the war and George's experiences and some would offer opinions which George politely nodded to realising that they were opinions based on no real understanding or appreciation of what the war was like. While some would engage in conversation, others would look blankly at him and move on, clearly not understanding a word he had said, as they only spoke and understood the Welsh language.

To vary his activities and in the hope that there might be some correspondence from home, he would walk down to the mail office every other day.

After he had been at the camp for a few weeks, he was surprised to receive a letter which simply had on the front of the envelope-

SGT. GEORGE WILLIAMS

TONFANAU CAMP

Nothing else. George looked at the envelope and was amazed that it had found him. He opened it up and realised it was from Elizabeth.

Dear George,

Hope you are well and that your wound is on the mend. It was (a few words had been written here and crossed out, but George could not decipher what they might have been) to have spent time with you a few weeks ago. I was sad as I waved you off at the station. I have been in touch with the family at Treafon, and they all seem well.

Thomas came home from the front just after you left. He was in a terrible state, his hands were shaking, and he insisted on sleeping on the floor as he said he found the bed too hard. He had been in a hospital in Gravesend, outside London but he would not tell me what had happened there or why he had been sent there. He said he couldn't remember. A few times I returned to where he was sat only to find him in tears. I would hold him, but he couldn't tell me what had upset him and why he was crying. I worry about him. He is not the same man that went away.

After he had been home a week, a letter came for him, which turned out to be his call-up papers. He was ordered to travel to a camp in Aldershot and report four days later. He made no effort to report to the camp and a week after that, a further letter arrived asking him to attend a tribunal in Caerphilly the following week. He was determined that he would not join the army and so he would have to attend the tribunal. He was really in no fit state to go and so two days before the tribunal, I persuaded him to come with me to the doctors to see if the tribunal appearance could be postponed or that the doctor could give him some sort of exemption paper. I had not been to this doctor before, but he proved to be very difficult. He insinuated that we were trying to get around Thomas' call up and that Thomas might be faking the symptoms. I lost my temper and that didn't help.

We went down to the tribunal, and I caught a glimpse of the three men who were to interview Thomas. I was immediately suspicious as one of them had a very military bearing with a fine moustache. I was not allowed to go into the tribunal with Thomas but when he came out one of the gentlemen (if you can call him that) came out and barked at me (as that is the only way I can describe it) that the request had been denied and that Thomas was to present himself at a barracks in Cardiff, two days after the tribunal. Thomas could not have presented himself even if he had wanted to. He was far too ill.

Four days after the tribunal, two police constables came to the house and said that Thomas had to go with them as he had been charged with desertion, and that he would have to attend a Court Martial hearing in Cardiff. Thomas had befriended a local man, Charles Edwards, a deacon in our chapel who agreed to try to see Thomas after the Court Martial, as I was too upset to go. Charles returned that evening to say he had missed Thomas' case, and when he got there, he had already been charged and found guilty of desertion and had been taken to Winchester Prison, to complete a sentence of six months.

Oh George, I am so worried about him. He is not well; his nerves are in shreds, and I don't know how he will cope with the hardships of prison life. I can't tell you anymore. It is all too upsetting. I feel so lonely here with no one to share these troubles.

Please try and write

Love Elizabeth

George re-read the letter and immediately got out a pen and paper to reply, feeling Elizabeth's anguish and despair in every word he read. He sat ready to offer a sympathetic hearing for her concerns, but he found that he couldn't put pen to paper. It was not that he wasn't sympathetic, but that he felt inadequate to supply the succour that she clearly needed - his reply might be misunderstood. He still felt very guilty for the time he had spent in her bed and was careful not to suggest that he might continue a relationship with her, despite her loneliness and the fact that she was so upset that her husband had been imprisoned. He also felt guilty that he felt he was continuing to betray Maud and Joan. After sitting for over two hours and having circled his room several times, George decided to leave the letter for a day or two until he could find the right words that might offer Elizabeth some comfort.

29

The following day was bright and sunny, though cold at first. His mother would probably refer to it as 'a real autumn day'. George cut himself some bread while in the canteen and put two small pieces of cheese and a thin slice of what is best described as 'fatty' ham into his lunch box. He placed the food and a water bottle into his haversack and collected his army cap, which he also put into the bag. He informed Sergeant Major Ross that he would be out for a few hours, and he lied that he would be investigating possible cross-country routes. The sergeant major gave a knowing smile and wished him a good day.

George walked along the coast road to Llwyngwril, where he dropped down to the beach. He looked back at the village and thought that the few rows of terraced houses looked more like Treafon. The area generally had more individual cottages spread out across the countryside, which were often no bigger than the terraced houses back home but there might not be a neighbour for a few miles, making life more isolated.

He stopped to look out to sea. The sun reflected off the surface of the water and was broken only by the sight of the waves as they gently broke along the shoreline. George stood in wonder at his surroundings, the sea, the cliffs, the shoreline and behind him the gently sloping hillside with the higher slopes of grass and bare rock in the distance. With the sun shining how different it looked from Treafon, and how different his impressions were from those when he had first arrived. The mist and fog at that time had simply hidden a gem. He thought the whole vista looked like a picture postcard he might buy to send home, but then as he turned around in a slow full circle, he realised that you could put nothing on a small piece of card that would do this any justice.

He then came back up onto the coast road and walked along the narrow grass verge to Fairbourne, to the sand covered point opposite Barmouth, where he found a fisherman sat in a rowing boat willing to take him across the estuary for a few coins. He was in awe of the fisherman's skill in navigating the small boat in the currents at the mouth of the estuary. He became a little nervous and deliberately distracted himself by looking in wonder at the structure of Barmouth railway bridge which crossed the estuary.

After landing and thanking the fisherman, George walked through the town. He sat on Barmouth beach eating his cheese, ham and bread and lost himself in thought. He noticed a few groups sat on the beach with a few children playing in the sand in the care of their mothers. He could only see one man who looked about seventy years of age, and he realised how unnatural the scene was. This brought back thoughts of the war being waged many miles away.

He forced himself to think of more pleasant things and smiled as he could visualise Joan playing on the sand, something she had never done as Treafon was too far inland to make such a journey possible. He felt that for the first time in his life he had time to himself. His mind wandered back to the times before the war, his work underground and the relaxing times he spent in the pubs of Treafon. He realised that he didn't really mind the work underground, the camaraderie of his fellow workers and the hard physical labour, which though it wore him out from time to time, was also quite rewarding. It brought him many friends and it had kept him fit and healthy. He thought about Maud and how she had kept the household together, not just while he was in Belgium but when he was at home. He had contributed little to the running of the house and he realised it was hardly surprising that Maud looked so tired and worn out.

When they were first married, Maud was a happy and cheerful person. She was very popular, and she always gave good advice to friends and family. She was attractive with an infectious personality, and she was great fun to be with. He realised that the housework she did and her efforts at feeding and looking after the children, and him, were wearing her down, so it was not surprising she was not as much fun as she had been. While he was on leave, he had spent a lot of time sitting in the kitchen chatting to Maud as she worked, cooked and cleaned. He had been lazy and had not offered to help but as he lay back on the sand, he realised that he still loved her.

The times he had gone up to the pubs of Treafon during his leave had not been the same. There were none of the men there he had been friendly with, and he had become bored with his own company. The time he had enjoyed most was the time spent at home with Maud and Joan, much more so than when he had been out in the evenings. He had enjoyed the family walks they had taken when both he and Maud had laughed at the things Joan said and did. He felt he had begun to appreciate the difficult life Maud had and he felt guilty that he seemed now to have so much time on his hands. The loss of Willie and the fact that Joan took so long to accept him after he had returned from the war made him appreciate his home life a little more. He wondered whether, after the war, he would be attracted back to the pubs and clubs of the town when the troops returned home. He didn't pursue this thought; he simply didn't know.

George decided to take a walk back through the town of Barmouth. He stopped at a small tea-room and enjoyed a cup of tea and a jam scone. He carried on walking past the shops in the town until he came to a pawn shop. He wasn't sure what had caused him to stop, but he noticed a lace collar in the window, which looked particularly attractive.

He went into the shop and behind the counter a small man in his seventies with a monocle asked him, "how can I help you, sir?"

George replied, "could I see the lace collar in the window, please?"

Without speaking, the man collected the collar from the window and laid it out in front of George.

He then seemed to suddenly remember something. He held his finger in the air and said, "one moment." He shuffled off into the back of the shop and brought out two other pieces of lace, which

194

turned out to be the matching cuffs which the shopkeeper said he had forgotten to put in the window and if George purchased the collar, he could have the cuffs for nothing.

George was looking carefully at the lace work when the shopkeeper said, "they are Belgian lace. They were brought in by a soldier who had come home on leave after fighting in Belgium, only to find that his wife had left him. A terrible state he was in. He said he had bought them for his wife's birthday, but now he wanted the money so he could go and get drunk." The shopkeeper shrugged.

George looked up at the shopkeeper and smiled. "Well, his misfortune will make this soldier and his wife very happy."

The shopkeeper smiled and nodded.

George handed over a few coins and the shopkeeper wrapped the lace carefully in tissue paper. George left the shop feeling very pleased with himself. Not only had he bought a present for Maud for Christmas, something he hadn't done for many years but it meant a little more that they were Belgian lace. George carried on down the street and noticed a toyshop with a small teddy bear in the window. George went in and came out tucking the teddy bear into his rucksack.

He walked back down to the beach area to look for someone with a rowing boat that could take him back across the estuary. He found someone sitting on the wall at the back of the beach. After agreeing a price, he followed the man down to his rowing boat and got in. The man was very chatty. Noticing George's uniform, he asked a myriad of questions about the war and what the fighting was like in France and Belgium, as he rowed. George had become apprehensive of the dangers of the return journey, as it negotiated the competing currents of the estuary. He gave the man a potted version of his experiences - as much to take his mind off the boat and the swirling water as to entertain the mariner.

When he got out of the boat, the man shook his hand and refused to take any money, which George was very glad of after buying his

195

presents. As he walked back down the coastline to the camp, George felt a warm glow after buying the presents for Maud and Joan, and he thought he would like to see their faces when he handed them over. His mood became a little darker when he remembered that he would not be getting any leave at Christmas, and he would have to post the presents down to the family.

For the next few months, George continued to enjoy his walks. He climbed Cader Idris early in the morning and stood in awe at the sunrise, which he thought looked like an oil painting. He walked to Aberdovey, along the beach for much of the way, and he never tired of the scenery and the vistas which opened up in front of him. The days through October were mostly wet but most of November and December were dry and sunny, though at times very cold. He wore his greatcoat more often and though it provided warmth, he looked forward to the Spring when he could discard the heavy weight of it.

He wrote to Maud regularly and got letters back, and that cheered him. He found he had a thirst for information from back home, and he enjoyed telling Maud what he had seen on his walks. Maud said that she was reading his letters to Joan. Well, most of them. His wife seemed to be genuinely interested, which was not the case when he was describing the scenes and events on the front line in Belgium. This gave him further satisfaction.

Then, one day in late December, he received a letter from Maud. He quickly opened it, hungry for news of Joan, and possibly a short note written by his daughter herself. However, when he opened it and read it, he slumped into a deep despair. Evan, Esther's husband, had been killed in France and Esther was now a widow. His death had been caused by a traffic accident when a truck he was driving had slumped into a crater, crushing the cab and Evan. George couldn't believe that Evan's death could be so pointless. Soldiers were being killed by shelling, snipers and gas almost on a daily basis, but in a road accident? It made no sense. George thought back to their wedding day. He had genuinely liked Evan and thought that he would make a good husband for Esther. He thought of his sister and how sad she

196

must feel. Now they would never be a family or have children. He could feel tears coming into the corners of his eyes. He thought that they had had no married life. They had got married so that Evan could go straight off to the war, and now he would never come back. George thought how desperately sad, how many more lives was this damnable war going to take.

George immediately took up his pen and paper, ready to write to Esther to offer his condolences. Within a very short space of time, he realised the same problem he had encountered when trying to write to Elizabeth. The words to adequately describe his emotions would simply not come. He did manage to write a short letter to Maud, and he said in that letter that he would write to Esther. As he wrote the words down, he knew he would have to be in the right frame of mind to write these sad letters.

George did eventually manage to write letters to both Elizabeth and Esther, and just before Christmas he received replies from both.

My big brother George,

Thank you very much for your letter and the kind sentiments you expressed. I am staying with mother and father until I feel ready to return to the house in Rhymney, whenever that might be.

I am obviously very sad after losing a loving husband. The depth of his love was apparent in the many letters he sent home during his time in France. He was constantly mentioning in the letters how much he was looking forward to returning home after the war and how we would start a family. That has now all gone. I realised during that time how much I loved him, and I will miss him dearly.

I think in normal times he would have made a wonderful husband. Now we will never know, except in my heart I know. I think he would have made a wonderful father to our children.

Evan's death leaves me feeling odd, as that is the only word I can use to describe my feelings. I never lived with Evan and so did not have the chance to live as other couples live, and as Evan is buried in France there was no funeral and though you cannot say you miss such an event as you might a wedding or a christening, I'm sure that a funeral does give a finality that must help you grieve. There is also nowhere that I can go where I know Evan will be, to leave flowers, or to talk to him. I do wonder at times if I was ever married at all, or did I just dream it?

I'm sure I will feel better in time, but at the moment I feel 'numb'.

Looking forward to seeing you again and hope that you are well.

Your loving sister

Esther

George also felt numb and though he was desperately sad for Esther the letter was very honest and was probably true to her feelings. He then began to read Elizabeth's letter.

My dearest George,

It is in a state of deepest loneliness and despair that I return your letter. I was so saddened to hear of Evan's death. I have written to Esther to offer my deep sympathy and I have every hope that she can continue to be the cheerful and happy soul she has always been, or at least that that will be the case in time.

I have not received a letter from Thomas for some weeks and I continue to have concern for his welfare. I wonder if he even remembers who I am?

Thomas left for France, and I felt so lonely, as you know. Then he came back briefly, even if he was much changed. Now he has been taken from me a second time, leaving me lonely once again.

I read this letter over and I realise I sound selfish, as if I am the one suffering, while I should be grateful. I still have Thomas, despite the

198

changes to his personality. I don't mean to sound selfish, and I am trying to continue life as normal, and I think of Thomas all the time.

I have made contact with the 'No Conscription Fellowship', and I have paid a subscription to receive their newsletter, 'the Tribune'. In one article a few weeks ago, a writer stated that the government were using something called 'the Cat and Mouse Act', which they used on the suffragettes. This is where they release prisoners after they have served their sentences, and immediately re-arrest them, court martial them and send them back to prison for a further period. If this is the case, Thomas may not be released from prison until after the war is over. What state will he be in by then?

Anyway, enough of my problems. How is life in Tonfanau? I hope things are going well and I am so pleased that at the moment you are not in any danger and hope that it stays that way.

Your very loving sister-in-law

Elizabeth

George had not heard of this 'Cat and Mouse Act', and it did give him food for thought. He wondered what Thomas had brought on himself, and what he would be like when he was eventually released, as Elizabeth says.

Esther had lost her husband but seemed determined to try to get over it and make a new life for herself, while Elizabeth, because Thomas was still alive, though in a much diminished state, was brought down by her concern and worry for his condition. At times, death brings a relief and an end, however final, while suffering merely brings continued anguish for that person's relatives. How strange life is.

Two days later, George received a letter from Maud.

George,

I am still recovering from receiving your Christmas present. What a shock that was. Joan loves her teddy bear and takes it to bed with her every night. I went up to the market to try to sell some of the vegetables from the garden to one of the market traders. I had a small amount of money for them and used it to buy material to make a dress. I have sewn the lace collar and cuffs onto the dress, and it looks wonderful. The problem is that the dress now is simply too nice to wear anywhere. Where will I go so that I can wear a dress with a real lace collar and cuffs. Thank you very much for both presents. We are both very pleased.

I have been to your parent's house to see Esther. She is bearing up very well considering her loss, and she is hoping to move back to her house in the future. All the family are well, and we are looking forward to seeing you on your next leave.

It was lovely to have you home for those few weeks at the end of the Summer. It was nice just to sit and talk to you and I really miss you.

Love

Maud.

George was quite shocked at what seemed to be a loving letter. Maud seemed to miss him as much as he missed her. It left him with a warm feeling, but it made him feel quite lonely.

Two days before Christmas Day George was approached by Captain Parker, who asked, "Sergeant Williams, will you be attending the Christmas party?"

George replied, "sorry sir, I know nothing about it."

The captain said, "we did it last year, and the men seemed to like it. The men give a concert on Christmas Eve, and anyone who can do anything, sing, play a musical instrument, tell a joke, recite a poem, gets up on stage and then we have a bit of a booze up after, but...."

he stopped and then said, "obviously, N.C.O.s, will have a separate party from the officers and the enlisted men will also have their own party."

George laughed, as there would be quite a few enlisted men, but there were only two officers, and maybe one or two others depending on which contingent were training that week, and then only four N.C.O.s. Some party that would be for the officers and N.C.Os. He decided to say nothing more.

Captain Parker said, "so, can you do anything that might entertain the troops?"

Nothing obvious came immediately to mind. After a little consideration he said, "well, I used to play a banjo in a minstrel band back home, but I uh…" He suddenly realised that he couldn't tell Captain Parker it had been smashed over his head while he was in a pub suffering from concussion, so he said, "I'm afraid I haven't brought it with me." He thought for a second. "I have been known to sing, but that's usually after I'm several sheets to the wind, so that won't be happening. Best I have a think and let you know."

Captain Parker thanked him and walked off.

George made his way into the N.C.O.'s Mess, sat down and said to Sergeant Major Ross, "I've just had a conversation with Captain Parker about the Christmas party."

Ross laughed. "Bloody shambles last year. We had one bloke dressed up as a woman who sauntered across the stage and caressed the curtain as he sang a love song to the private sat at a piano. He pulled a bit too heavily on the curtain and the bloody lot came down, exposing three other blokes behind the curtains, one in his underwear and two others completely naked who were getting changed." He laughed again. "Mind you, it was the highlight of the evening."

A few days later, as George was crossing an open space in front of the canteen, Captain Parker came up to him. "Good news, Williams, the major has been in touch with a theatrical group in Tywyn and they've got a banjo," and as he walked away, he shouted, "so you don't get away that easily."

George pulled a face.

Christmas Eve came and a nervous George mounted the stage to tumultuous applause. He was a little more ambivalent as the applause might not continue after his performance.

He had listened to the first half of the concert from a position backstage. The major recited Shakespeare which ended in silence and then a ripple of polite applause. He was followed by a comedian who managed to mess up his store of five jokes, not getting one of them right. Fortunately, these were followed by a local tenor from Tywyn - who was very good. George brushed past the tenor as he waited to go on stage. He listened to Captain Parker trying to persuade the tenor to go back on at the end of the concert. The tenor said he would for a bottle of whisky and the captain scuttled off to see what he could do.

George took the stage and sat on the only chair available. He began his rendition of musical hall songs, singing and playing the banjo at the same time. These brought a huge cheer and as he worked through the first four and got on to 'On the Good ship Venus', he cast care to the wind and thought, well they can court martial me if they like.

He came off the stage to a standing ovation, but he was forced back on by Captain Parker, who said, "a little crude, Williams, but they seem to like it."

He had only practiced the four songs and so wondered what he was going to do next. He gave a rendition of 'Home Sweet Home' but as he looked down at the front row, he could see two of the young soldiers with tears streaming down their faces. He decided to change the mood by singing the bawdy music-hall songs once again, but this time he encouraged the audience to sing along. There was such applause at the end that he had to go through the four for a third time. He came off the stage and stood for a few seconds, a bath of sweat. He put down the banjo, threw his arms in the air and shouted, "the new Dan Leno." This got a round of applause from the backstage team.

George went back onstage at the end of the concert as the performers took a last bow and the local tenor led them in the National anthems 'God Save the King', which was sung loudly and with gusto and 'Hen Wlad Fy Nhadau', which was sung by only a handful of Welshmen present but with equal gusto. George thought how odd it was that there were so few Welshmen to sing the Welsh National anthem despite this being in the heart of Wales.

George immediately retired to the N.C.O.'s Mess, where the six men there, as the present contingent of Royal Artillery had brought two cockney sergeants with them, partied until the early hours.

George relaxed, listening to the stories the cockney sergeants told and laughed along with the others. He thought that it was nice to be entertained, as he had entertained others earlier.

At one point, Sergeant Major Ross turned to George and said, "well, it seems the concert was a success, due in no small part to your talents. Well done, George, certainly far better than last year's fiasco and the horrible sight of the naked troopers." The sergeant major laughed at his own description.

At the end of the night, George went out to sit on the wall outside the N.C.O.'s Mess and smoke a cigarette. He looked up at a beautiful starry sky. It was a frosty night, and the stars were clear and bright. He began to hum a few Christmas carols to himself. How different this Christmas Eve was from the previous one, near the front line in Belgium, and even the one before that in Northampton, in a training camp. Two years ago, Christmas 1914, he hadn't experienced the horror of the war; it was still to come, and he was still enthusiastic. Then there was Christmas 1915, when the Monmouthshires had just been relieved from the front line, but he was very much in the thick of it. Now, Christmas 1916, he was away from danger, and he had to hope he wouldn't be put back into it. In two years, he had been to war, lost many friends and acquaintances, lost Willie and lost Evan.

Thomas was greatly changed by it, and he was just one of many who were from families completely transformed by the devastating conflict. He wondered out loud, 'where will I be on Christmas 1917? Will I be back home with the family, with Maud, Ben, Esther, my father and mother, Thomas, and my beautiful daughter, Joan?'

He felt tired and slowly made his way back to his dormitory.

30

By March 1917, George was becoming bored with his mundane life at Tonfanau Camp. Time seemed to pass slowly, and he felt guilty that other men were fighting the war for him while he was whiling away his days in safety. His wound was healing, and he no longer needed a stick for support. To assuage the boredom, he went on longer walks and began to take some of the P.T. sessions. He had always been an active man and he realised that he needed to be doing things to stave off his frustration and lethargy.

He discovered new routes around the locality and as he became recognised in the local villages, farmers and farm labourers would stop to chat if they had time. At the very least, they would acknowledge him.

On one such walk, George stopped alongside a farmer repairing a stretch of dry-stone wall. The big burly farmer with a slightly tanned face and a wide grin, with a mop of white hair shouted, "shwmae."

George nodded and replied, "shwmae."

The farmer took off his cap and began to scratch the top of his head with the peak. George noticed that there was a line separating the sunburnt skin on his forehead from the white skin which had been covered by his cap.

He spoke English with a slightly stilted accent. "You from the camp no doubt - judging by your uniform?"

George nodded.

It was a hot day and George took a swig from his water bottle, passing the bottle over to the farmer. The farmer took the bottle and after a pouring a small amount of water onto the palm of his hand, rubbed it over his face.

He looked at George and said, "Jac," obviously indicating his own name. He continued, "I've seen you passing here a few times these last months. You walk a lot?"

George said "George," also indicating it was his own name. "I try my best to stay fit," and after a short silence he said, "I was wounded and had a stick when I got here first but through exercise the leg's got better and I don't need a stick anymore. Anyway, its beautiful countryside and I like walking, perhaps not so much in the rain, but today's a beautiful day."

"You were at the front, were you?" Jac asked.

"Yes I was," replied George

George didn't elaborate and the farmer seemed to understand that by his brief answers, the soldier was not particularly keen to discuss his wartime experiences. The two men carried on chatting about the weather, the countryside and their families for some time until eventually George rose his hand and moved on.

A few weeks later, George turned into a lane alongside the section of wall where he had spoken to Jac previously and carried on until he came close to a farmhouse. George intended to pass through the farm to reach a gate which would take him onto the hillside but, a woman came out of the farmhouse and beckoned to him to follow her in. George shrugged and followed her in through the farmhouse half-door, noticing Jac and a small boy of about nine years of age sat at a table eating a sandwich and drinking a cup of tea. The woman pointed to a chair at the end of the table. George thought it odd that he was now sitting down in a farmhouse kitchen where still no one had spoken, but to the family, it seemed the most natural thing in the world. He sat and shortly a cup of tea and a ham sandwich was placed in front of him.

Jac smiled, and said, "saw you passing." Pointing at the boy sat at the table he said, "this is Lloyd," and then pointing at the woman said, "and this is Alys, my wife."

In turn Alys said, "shwmae," and when Lloyd had finished the food in his mouth he smiled and said, "shwmae."

Jac said something to Lloyd in Welsh, and he rose from the table. George noticed that he stood with some difficulty and as he went out through the door, he dragged his left leg behind him.

Jac, realising that George had noticed the boy's disability said, "typical farming accident. A horse rolled on him when he was four years old. Not been able to use the leg properly since; but he's our treasure."

Jac also noticed that George may have been aware that Alys had not spoken and pointing at her he said, "she can speak!" He laughed. "Sometimes I can't shut her up. She struggles with English and so chooses to say little." He rose and slapping George on the back, causing him to splutter his tea out, said, in a booming voice "a Godsend sometimes, eh?"

George could hear Jac chuckling to himself for a few minutes afterwards.

Alys, suddenly realising that Jac was speaking about her and understanding what he had said turned and gave a beaming smile - and then shook her finger at Jac's indiscretion.

When George had finished, he rose and said, "diolch," remembering the little bit of Welsh he had learned.

Alys turned to George and clapped her hands and said, "da iawn."

Jac who had returned to the kitchen door said, "we'll make a Welsh speaker of you yet." As the two men stepped outside, Alys gave a demure smile and Jac turned to speak to her in Welsh.

Jac followed George to the main road and said, "anytime you are passing we expect you to call in and see us mind, and I'm sure you would enjoy a break with some food and there's always a panad."

In the next few weeks, George would often break his walks with refreshments at the Jones' farm and when Jac went back to work, he would entertain Lloyd by playing at pitching horseshoes. Lloyd's

English was quite good, and he would chat away to George; who loved spending time with the boy. Lloyd liked to hear about the war and life in the trenches. George was careful to remember that the boy was only nine years old, and he ensured that he always censored his own opinions and descriptions. He became conscious that he enjoyed spending time with Lloyd perhaps as compensation for time lost with his own son.

One day, when George was about to leave the Jones' farm to complete his walk before returning to camp, Jac asked if he was able to help him repair a barn the following day. George said he would be glad to oblige. He arrived early at the farm and started the day with a cup of tea. Jac and George, with Lloyd in tow, crossed to the damaged barn. George could immediately see a layer of brickwork had collapsed, bringing down the wooden wall which stood above it. To reinstate the wooden barn wall the brick wall, which stood about four feet high would have to be replaced and then a new wooden wall would have to be laid above it, all the time taking care not to cause the collapse of the roof, which Jac had temporarily propped up.

The two men set to work to repair the brickwork, with Jac constantly talking, constantly instructing George on how to lay bricks, "now see, I always do it this way." By the end of the day, the wall was complete, and George had a feeling of satisfaction that he had not had for a long time - at a job well done.

Jac said, "on a farm you have to be able to turn your hand to anything. There's no money to employ specialists, so you have to learn."

George said, "thanks Jac, I feel I owe you more than you owe me. I feel now that I could do a half decent job of bricklaying after your instruction."

Jac turned and patted him on the back. "Works both ways, as they say. I couldn't have done the job without your help, so teamwork is the winner."

They went into the farmhouse, closely followed by Lloyd, who had continued to chat to them throughout the day, sometimes in Welsh, sometimes in English.

Even Alys spoke up as they got to the house. "Came out to see the wall a few minutes ago. Bendigedig! aye, da iawn, to you both." She followed that up with "and it kept Lloyd busy all day. Stopped him from getting under my feet."

George said in return, "and your English is bendigedig too," causing Alys to blush.

Jac said, "ready for the wood to replace the wall now."

George said, "well, I would love to help you with that, but I've got to be at the camp for the next three days. We've got a new contingent coming in, but I'm free Saturday and I would be delighted to help."

Jac said, "it's a job I can't do on my own, so Saturday it is; if you are sure?"

Early the following Saturday, they began work on the wooden walls of the barn. Jac could see that George was keen to learn. He took time and care to show George how he measured and cut the wooden planks with precision so that little of the materials were wasted. By Saturday evening, the job was complete and Jac took away the temporary buttresses. Both men and Lloyd stood back to admire their handiwork. George smiled as he noticed Lloyd copying their stance.

Jac took off his cap and scratched his head. "Duw, that's a good job if ever I saw one - you're a true apprentice, George Williams. We'll make a craftsman out of you yet."

George returned to camp that evening, proud of his efforts.

The following week, George collected a letter from the mail office at the camp. He had continued his habit of walking down to the office but for many weeks he had not received any mail. He was quite surprised to be passed a letter which he took back to his dormitory. On opening it he quickly identified Elizabeth's handwriting. It read-

George,

Hope you are well?

I'm afraid I have bad news for both of us, though it seems that this war brings only bad news.

Thomas was released from Winchester prison two weeks ago. He managed to find his way home. God knows how!

He had only been home for no more than an hour when a knock came at the door and there were two soldiers there to arrest him. He had not even had time to have a bite to eat or a cup of tea. They bundled him into the back of a truck and drove off. A few days later I received a letter which was signed by him, but he had not written it. It said that he had been sentenced once again and had been returned to Winchester Prison, this time for twelve months as it was a second offence.

The short time he was home he hardly spoke. He was a skeleton, and his hands shook the whole time he sat at the kitchen table. He had scars which had healed on his neck and face and his colour was almost yellow. I honestly cannot see how he will be able to live in the condition he is in for much longer and I have a real worry that he will do something drastic.

I don't want to burden you with concerns about Thomas when you have enough to worry about, but I really don't know who else to turn to.

Please try to find time to write.

I was wondering if it might be possible for you to accompany me to visit Thomas when you are next on leave. I know it is an imposition when your leave is short and precious, and you would want to spend as much time as possible with Maud and Joan, but I know how much it would mean to Thomas. I will await your reply and then perhaps write to Maud and O.H to explain that it is I who have asked you to accompany me.

Best wishes your loving sister-in-law

Elizabeth

George had been in a pretty good frame of mind. He was receiving letters from Maud and things were going well between them. Summer was coming and he was beginning to enjoy his time at the camp and with the friends he was making in the area. The letter darkened his mood. He threw the letter down in frustration. Dammit, why couldn't Thomas have gone to war as I did and Ben? He could have found himself a cosy little number like I have and seen the war out. Why did he have to be so principled? It'll be the death of him.

Within the next few days, George penned a letter to Elizabeth to explain that he would be only too glad to visit Thomas with her, but he wouldn't be getting leave until at least the end of August, four or five months away. George also asked Elizabeth to write to Maud to explain that she had asked him to visit Thomas and not the other way around so that Maud didn't think he was trying to spend his leave away from his home and the family.

31

Jac laughed until the tears rolled down his cheeks. Eventually he got control of himself and said, "duw, duw, that's one of the funniest things I've ever seen."

George was not so amused and tried to stand but he fell again. He tried to extricate his foot from the mud and only succeeded in pulling his foot out of his wellington boot and landing his stockinged foot in the mud.

Jac started to laugh again, "stop it, stop it, George." He held his sides as they began to hurt.

George failed to see the funny side of his predicament and while trying to control his language in front of Alys and Lloyd said, "isn't someone going to give me a hand?"

Alys said, "Jac," in a very peremptory manner, but Jac could not answer and shook his hands back and fore to show that he was not capable of helping.

Lloyd and Alys gave him a hand each and eventually George was pulled free of the mud at the edge of the stream. However, his wellington boot remained firmly in the grip of the mud about ten feet from the banking.

Jac had asked George to help Alys and Lloyd shepherd about fifteen cattle from the bottom field to one of the mountain fields. It was now early Summer and Jac was trying to move the cattle to the upper pasture. It was always a difficult task with just a few bodies to stop the cattle wandering off wherever they felt like going. George was asked to stand on a track which led down to a stream. Jac had said that the cattle would probably head for the water in the stream, and it was George's job to shoo them away from the stream and towards the gate that led to the upper fields. The larger cows had led the move up from the lower field with Jac and two dogs behind them.

At one point Jac had shouted, "they are coming your way George, make sure they don't get down to the stream."

George had been equipped with a stick and waved his arms about and shouted but the cattle had ignored him and continued on the trajectory towards the stream. He had shouted louder to no avail. The lead cow had simply brushed him aside. George had tried to pull her back, but the cow had leaned into him, causing him to slide down the banking and fall head-first into the stream. He managed to stand but lost his wellington boot in the mud at the bottom of the stream causing him to once more fall into the water. By the time Jac got to him, George was covered from head to foot in mud and was completely unrecognisable. Alys and Lloyd were more concerned with George's welfare, but Jac could only see the funny side and couldn't stop laughing.

Eventually, the cattle were retrieved and led on up to the upper pastures. By the time Lloyd and Jac got back to the farmhouse, George had stripped down to his trousers and socks. Fortunately, it was a warm day and bowls of water were brought out to the hardstand outside the farmhouse. Alys told George she was going inside the house to preserve his dignity, and he managed to strip off completely, and wash the mud off, and dry himself. He had borrowed a set of Jac's old clothes to work on the farm and these could easily be washed and so after towelling down he then proceeded to dress in his uniform once more.

George sat on the wall alongside the farmhouse smoking a cigarette. Jac had emptied the bowls of dirty water and came to sit alongside him, with Lloyd on the other side.

Lloyd cheekily said, "duw, you could come and work for Dad after the war if you wanted?"

George laughed and ruffled his hair. "I don't think so somehow."

Jac said, "well, you are obviously a good soldier, and in time you could be a good carpenter or bricklayer." He stopped for effect, shaking his head. "But a farmer?" After a moment's comedic hesitation, "I'm not so sure."

All three burst out laughing as Alys came out to call them all in for their food.

A few weeks later, George was returning to his dormitory after a P.T. session when Captain Parker came across the parade ground, waving a piece of paper. "Sergeant Williams, Sergeant Williams, a moment of your time."

George stopped and waited for the captain to catch up with him. The captain immediately caught his breath and said, "I'd like you to escort a group of men to make a delivery to Plas Penhelig, a manor house in Aberdovey, at about two o'clock this afternoon. You'll need a pass to get in and I'll get Major Fisher to sign it."

George nodded to the captain but looked puzzled. "That's fine, sir, but why will I need a pass to get in? I've gone out with the men to other establishments in the area, manor houses included, to do all sorts of things and I've never needed a pass before."

The captain shrugged his shoulders "don't know, the colonel who telephoned this morning asked for the delivery and said that all the men involved in the delivery would need a pass signed by a senior officer."

George said, "seems odd, but ok I'll get some men together, I'll give you their names and you can arrange the passes, and we'll meet near the main gate at two o'clock."

Captain Parker stood and saluted. George still looked a little puzzled but strode off to wash and dress.

On arrival at Plas Penhelig George showed his pass and those of the men to an armed guard. He counted six soldiers with rifles on their shoulders. He drove the truck up the steep drive and parked it alongside the tradesman's entrance and strode across to a water trough strategically placed alongside a tree at the top of the roadway leading to the house. He splashed water on his face to cool himself on this warm day. He walked the few yards to the house, noticing two very large guard dogs tethered alongside the entrance. George gave instructions to the three men who jumped down from the back of the truck and unloaded it.

He then went to sit on a bench overlooking the sea. The view was astonishing. You could see right across the broad estuary to Aberystwyth and beyond. The whole of the south coastline of Cardigan Bay lay before him and the sun produced a dappled effect on the gently rippling water. George thought he could stay there all day, just mesmerised by the scene in front of him and the atmosphere of peace and quiet. He thought, how strange it is that you can look for hours at a marvellous view, with nothing moving and nothing changing, yet it is magnetic, it holds your attention and is so relaxing.

George was barely aware of a figure who sat on the bench next to him until the man asked, in a strong yet cultured Welsh accent, "any chance of a cigarette, sergeant?"

Without turning to glance at the man, George took a cigarette out of his packet and passed it to the man, who then asked, "can I trouble you for a light?"

George took a box of matches out of his pocket and turned to the man. "Here you are mate, keep 'em."

The man didn't answer but pocketed the box of matches.

George, whose thoughts were elsewhere, was barely aware of the man with a mop of white hair falling to his collar. He spoke with a slightly guttural accent, as did all North Walians, but his voice had refinement. George turned for a closer look and wondered where he had seen this bloke before.

George immediately became fearful of turning to check that the man was who he thought he might be, but he looked a lot like Lloyd George.

Silence prevailed for a few minutes and for anyone observing the scene it looked like two mature men enjoying the peace and quiet while seeking to escape the worries of the world. However, it was only

215

one of them that was truly escaping the worries of the world, just for a few moments.

Lloyd George spoke first. "I see from your row of medal ribbons that you've seen service at the front. What was it like?"

George wondered what he could say, thinking I could easily be locked up for saying something out of place here. He answered "pretty bad, I was at 2nd Ypres when they used gas. A lot of men died, and I lost a lot of friends."

Lloyd George replied, "and it's the same battlefield they are fighting over again, as we speak, near to Passchendaele." After a little more thought, he continued, "we have to stop this awful war, but we can't let the Germans off the hook, otherwise that might lead to another war in the future. I'm confident that when the American troops arrive in numbers, we will be in a much stronger position."

It crossed George's mind that Lloyd George was speaking to him as if he was addressing Parliament or a political colleague. He seemed to be unaware he was speaking to a lowly sergeant who was woefully ill equipped to debate with the likes of this man. He couldn't believe that the Prime Minister seemed to be so indiscrete. Both men sat in silence for a few moments.

George asked the Prime Minister "with respect sir, are you here on a holiday? I know that you've got your work cut out in London and nobody would deny you a break."

Lloyd George looked at George with a weary smile as he said, "I'm on my way to the Birkenhead Eisteddfod. I thought I would stop off here to visit friends and have a round of golf, so yes it's a short break for me before I return to the bear pit of London politics." He then continued, "you are Welsh, but not Welsh speaking I suspect, from South Wales, judging by your accent, where are you from and why are you up here?"

George said, "I'm from Treafon. Do you know the town?"

Lloyd George nodded. "I do. I don't say I know it well, but I have

216

been there. I have been through the town many times."

After a further period of silence George returning to the topic of war said, "I was in the territorials before the war and so joined up immediately, going to Belgium in 1915," he paused for breath and continued "I was wounded twice and I was brought home to Reading Hospital and I've been assigned as a P.T. instructor at Tonfanau Camp, a few miles down the road, since last Summer."

Lloyd George puffed on his cigarette and blew out the smoke, but did not respond for a few seconds, eventually asking, "you have a family?"

George looked down at the ground beneath the bench. "Yes, a wife and a little girl. I had a son - but he died," and after a moment, "consumption."

Lloyd George gave a huge sigh and said, "I can sympathise, we have something in common, sergeant. I had a daughter, Mair, who died after an appendix operation went wrong. The loss of a young one causes you sadness that never goes away," and then "but I think it makes you appreciate your other children, in a strange sort of way." After a while he asked, "have you brothers who are still fighting?"

George answered, "I have a brother Ben who is on the Western Front somewhere, and…" He hesitated and then possibly based on the great man's seemingly genial nature he ploughed ahead. "I have a brother Thomas who is a conscientious objector." His pulse raced as he wondered what the Prime Minister might say.

Lloyd George simply shook his head slowly and pursed his lips. "Hmm"

George was confused by the reply and prepared himself to have his family denigrated by the Prime Minister when Lloyd George said, "yes, a very sorry state for those men. As you can appreciate, we have to have men to fight this war and we cannot be seen to give the conscientious objectors an easy time as then many others who have been conscripted will opt out of the fighting and we would lose the war."

He stayed silent for a time and then said, "the way I see it if we prosecute this war with vigour, it will end all the sooner and then we can release the conscientious objectors back into society. I have thought long and hard about these people and I have discussed the issue with religious men and pacificists and realise that the decisions they make to go to prison and to be vilified by the rest of society are brave choices. They are making conscious decisions and these people with their strong opinions, will be needed in the future to produce a country of people who will stand by their principles." He remained silent after these comments, but then turned to George and gave a wicked chuckle. "But don't tell anyone I said that - whatever you do."

George looked around and the Prime Minister gave him a cheeky grin and winked. A further silence followed this, and George looked back out over the estuary. When George looked around again, he noticed the figure retreating to the manor house doorway with his white hair streaming down the back of his dark cape.

George stood and taking his cap off, said to himself, "Jesus, who would have believed it?"

On his return to camp, he was approached by Captain Parker who said, "everything go alright? Did you find out why the colonel had demanded a pass to enter Plas Penhelig?"

George grinned at the captain. "Yes, Lloyd George was staying there."

The captain rose his eyebrows in surprise.

George continued, "he came out for a chat, just to make sure I agreed with his strategy for the war over the next few months. Incredible really that he bothers to travel all the way here from London just to check that I thought he was doing a good job. If he should call for me, give me a shout would you, sir." With that, George walked away.

Captain Parker was not sure whether to reprimand George for his impertinence or treat it as a joke. He walked away and laughed, deciding on the latter course as George had clearly made a joke about meeting Lloyd George and having a chat with him about the war. He watched George disappear and smiled at the conversation, saying quietly to himself, "cheeky blighter."

32

George reflected many times on his conversation with Lloyd George. He told the story of his meeting the Prime Minister many times around the camp and in the Sergeant's Mess where the telling was always met with disbelief and shakes of the head. No one had witnessed the event and its unlikelihood helped to develop George's reputation as a good storyteller. It lost its impact after a while, so George gave up telling it.

The following month, they permitted George a week's leave which would begin in early September. He immediately wrote a letter to Maud and a further letter to Elizabeth to inform them. On the second Saturday of the month, George threw his kitbag over his shoulder and headed to the small railway station, ready to begin the long journey back to Treafon.

As he came through the front door, he spotted Joan running to hide behind the fireside chair. Instead of ignoring her, he made it a game and sat at the kitchen table with two large apples in front of him. Mockingly, he spoke to Maud saying, "Joan obviously doesn't want these two lovely apples. I think I'd better eat them."

Joan stayed quiet for a while, looking longingly at the apples through the wooden slats at the back of the chair, contemplating whether to be brave and collect the apples or stay where she was. Eventually, the temptation became too great, and she sprinted across the room and reached for the apples.

George grabbed her and lifted her on to his lap saying, "you can't have the apples unless you eat them on my lap."

Joan stopped struggling and bit into one of the apples. George nuzzled her ear and she lay back on his chest. The process of getting used to him was certainly quicker than the previous time.

Maud had given George a kiss as he came through the door and seemed genuinely pleased to have him home. She said, "try to spend as much time with Joan as you can, particularly if you are going to be off visiting Thomas from Monday. She misses you when you leave to go back to camp, but she always asks about you now. She's getting older and she loves spending time with you." She continued, "I've spoken to your mother and O.H. is going to come with you."

George said, "I thought I was going with Elizabeth?"

Maud replied, "yes, there will be three of you by the looks of it. O.H. has booked rooms in a guest house and insists on paying for everybody. You'll be there for two nights."

George was a little confused at first and worried in case O.H. had heard something of the night George had spent with Elizabeth and decided to chaperone the pair of them. Then he thought, no, it can't be, it must be a coincidence.

The following day, George helped around the house and played with Joan and the three of them went for a walk to the park with Maud even missing chapel. George put Joan to bed and sat on the bed alongside her, telling her a story about princesses and giants that he had just made up. He looked across at her as she slipped into sleep with a contented grin on her face and George thought he had never seen such a peaceful human being.

He quietly went downstairs and was shocked that Maud had cooked a piece of meat with small potatoes and some vegetables from the garden. Alongside George's plate was a bottle of beer and in the centre of the table was a candle. They chatted while they ate their food and George was pleased that they could still make each other laugh. They then went to sit in the back living room where Maud had lit a fire. George could not remember that happening at any time other than Christmas. They cuddled up on the settee and began to kiss. After a while, they both made their way upstairs with each of them shushing the other in case they woke Joan. They quietly undressed and got into bed, making passionate love for the first time for perhaps three years. Maud turned to George who had pressed up against her back and said, "we are married. Why do I feel guilty when that happens?"

George said, "because it doesn't happen often enough. We become like strangers to each other when we are apart, and we have to get used to each other again."

George felt a deeper love for Maud than he could ever remember, and he turned to her to make love again. They both began kissing and George stroked her hair. She loved that and responded immediately. She sat up and George could see her body in the twilight. Hard work had given her a taut body with beautifully shaped breasts and George immediately became aroused. He stroked her skin which felt soft to the touch and then his hands crossed to her breasts, stroking her nipples. He moved his hand down her body slowly and placed his fingers between her legs. She gave a slight moan and George moved on top of her as she lay with her eyes closed. She gave in gracefully and allowed him to penetrate her and come inside her.

After a few minutes she said, "twice - that's never happened before," and after a brief silence she kissed him saying "or I would have remembered it."

She lay wondering whether she wanted to make love to George more often, as it would inevitably result in another child. She felt happy and decided not to start what might be a difficult conversation and spoil it all. A short time later she slipped off into a deep sleep. George had enjoyed making love to her, but now found himself wide awake. He looked down at Maud, who was fast asleep, and he realised he had a very contented wife, and with Joan, a daughter he loved very much; he was a luckier man than many.

By the Monday morning Maud had laid out George's uniform and she and Joan walked alongside him as he made his way to the railway station. When they got there O.H. was waiting for the train which would take them first to Caerphilly where they would meet Elizabeth and then on to Cardiff, and finally Winchester.

O.H. greeted Maud and kissed Joan but his tone changed when he spoke to George. "You didn't have to wear a uniform to visit your brother in prison, you could have worn something a little less..." he stopped and thought and then said, "provocative."

George said, "I have civilian clothes in my bag which I can put on tomorrow if you think they are not so...," he waited for dramatic effect "provocative." He followed that up with a smile, which was George's way of trying to be less antagonistic. He had made his mind up that he would use the journey to build bridges with O.H. and not argue, despite the day getting off to a poor start.

The train arrived and George and O.H. got on. George remained at the window to wave to Maud and Joan as the train pulled away.

George looked around the carriage as they slowly headed towards Caerphilly. O.H. had sat in the seat next to the window and had fallen asleep almost immediately. George was at the other end of the carriage, penned in by a very large lady with her large and boisterous boy of about five years of age. George had been tempted a few times to reprimand the youngster, as the woman seemed incapable of doing so. He had trampled all over George's feet and if he hadn't been wearing his army boots, his feet would have been black and blue.

As they pulled into Caerphilly station, George and O.H. were the only ones to leave the carriage, carrying their small bags behind them. They put the two bags together on the platform and George went off to look for Elizabeth. He spotted her as he was about to enter into the waiting room but quickly noticed that she was deep in conversation with a younger man wearing a check jacket, scarf and cap. She had picked up her valise and turned to give the man a quick kiss and a hug. George hurried back to where O.H. was waiting. As George got back to O.H. he could see him looking over his shoulder and shouting, "there she is, Elizabeth, we are over here!"

Elizabeth came up to them and quickly gave each man a peck on the cheek. George said nothing about the young man he had seen, and Elizabeth did not mention him. They chatted together for a few minutes and then the train arrived, enveloping the platform in steam, with its distinctive smell which George did not find particularly repellent.

They got onto the train for the brief journey to Cardiff and waited on the platform there for the train that would take them on the last leg of their journey to Winchester. O.H. purchased a newspaper from a vendor and the train pulled in.

The three of them got into a carriage that was empty and settled themselves down, with O.H. once again in the window seat with Elizabeth opposite him and with George sat alongside her. After a few stops, a smartly dressed elderly man got into the carriage. He politely doffed his hat to them and settled down next to O.H. The man quickly gave in to the movement of the train and fell asleep.

O.H. read the newspaper he had bought, giving a running commentary on each article he was reading. He seemed not to consider the sleeping gentleman who woke at the sound of O.H.'s booming voice. He reported, "the submarine war is continuing with enormous loss of life amongst German submariners." He turned to the gentleman next to him and nodded his head.

The gentleman looked at him with a bemused expression but remained silent and folded his arms.

He continued, "now this is interesting. Last week it was the Birkenhead Eisteddfod, and the chair was awarded to Hedd Wyn who apparently was killed at Passchendaele at the end of August. The chair has been taken to his home in procession draped in black." He stopped to turn the page, "well, well, I've not heard of that before."

George looked up. "It's probably never happened before," and after a few seconds added, "and Lloyd George was there."

O.H. put down the paper and looked across at George. "it doesn't say that - so how do you know?"

George smiled and put his finger to the side of his nose, tapping it.

O.H. folded the paper and looked intently at George, as did the gentleman sat next to him. O.H. said, "Come on, you can't leave it like that."

George, with a smug expression said, "I was talking to him about ten days ago."

O.H. disbelieving said, "Lloyd George?"

When George didn't elaborate, O.H. looked dubiously at him. As George maintained a serious face, he considered he might possibly be telling the truth.

"Yes, he was at a manor house called Plas Penhelig when I took a group of men there to deliver food."

"And you saw him?"

George folded his arms "and spoke to him."

All three in the carriage looked at George. The gentleman opposite was clearly not really sure whether to believe him or not.

O.H. said, "what did he tell you?"

George pulled a serious face and leaned forward at the same time as O.H. and the smart gentleman, who both copied his actions. "He said he'd get in touch to discuss how to win the war."

O.H. and the man opposite George both pulled back at the same time and looked at each other with almost the same expression "pfft.," and immediately lost interest.

O.H. looked out of the window and said, "you had me believing you there for a minute."

George laughed. "Well. I did see him, and I did speak to him. He wanted to know about my experiences in the war, oh and he bummed a cigarette, and a box of matches off me." George thought for a minute about repeating what Lloyd George had said about conscientious objectors but with Elizabeth and this stranger in the carriage he decided not to.

The gentleman opposite said to George, "you fought on the Western Front, young man?"

George nodded. The man continued, "I was in the South African War, fighting to keep the Empire safe, so I respect your service for your country."

O.H. muttered, "poppycock."

The man glanced across at O.H. a little confused, "and where are you going?"

George quickly said, "Winchester to visit my brother," and turning to Elizabeth he said, "and this is his wife, and my father," indicating O.H. George suddenly realised he might have given too much detail away and that the man might ask why George's brother's wife was going with his brother and father to visit him in Winchester, and so he quickly tried to change the subject. "And where are you are going, sir?"

The man said, "I have a small factory which has changed production to making gas masks. I am to visit an army camp in Salisbury where they are carrying out trials. Just trying to do our bit."

George said, "I was at Ypres when the Germans first used gas. We could have done with your gasmasks then."

O.H. muttered, "well, at least your factory is in the business of saving lives."

The gentleman, a little confused at O.H.'s comments and attitude, said, "yes, yes, quite so."

After about an hour, the stranger had nodded off to sleep and O.H. had got up to stretch his legs in the corridor. Just after O.H. left, he could feel Elizabeth's hand reaching for his. He felt acutely embarrassed and stared at the stranger opposite in case he should wake up. Elizabeth nuzzled into George's shoulder and whispered in his ear. "I've missed you. I was hoping this trip would be just me and you, but I couldn't refuse O.H.'s offer. He was most insistent. I hope

226

there will be other times?"

George was sure he saw the stranger's eye twitch and he tried to drag his hand back; but Elizabeth had it in a tight grip.

She said, "will you try to come down to see me before too long?" and after a few minutes silence "my bed is a lonely place without you."

George, very embarrassed, leaned across to her and whispered, "who was that man in the waiting room at Caerphilly station?"

Elizabeth drew back immediately and responded in a flustered tone and a raised voice "why, um, he's ... just a friend - he was carrying my bag down to the station for me."

George kept his voice low. "He looked like more than a friend, Elizabeth."

Elizabeth rose her voice and looked straight at George. "Well, he's not - there's only you George."

The man opposite had been woken by Elizabeth's raised voice and a second or two later, O.H. returned. Elizabeth and George slowly slid away from each other. George was not certain whether the man opposite had heard or understood what had been said.

The three of them alighted at Winchester station. They had said their goodbyes to their fellow passenger, and he returned their parting comment with what George thought was a knowing look. George picked up his bag and Elizabeth's valise and they left the station.

O.H. had the name of a small guest house and he asked a young lad outside the station of its whereabouts. He explained to George and Elizabeth that he had written a letter some two weeks before booking two rooms at the guest house for two nights. They found the guest house and after booking in, George carried Elizabeth's bag into her room. Before he could leave the room, she grabbed him and kissed him saying, "he is just a friend George, you don't have to be worried." She looked down and said, "he does some gardening for me and helps out around the house where jobs need doing. You don't

227

know what it is to be a woman living on her own."

George pulled away. "I'm not worried Elizabeth," and at the door "and you have a husband who we will visit tomorrow." He reached the door of the room he would share with O.H. and stopped and shook his head in frustration at the hypocritical statement he had just made.

George spent a sleepless night. Partly because of O.H. snoring loudly enough to wake the dead and partly because he was trying to work out how he could extricate himself from Elizabeth without hurting her feelings.

33

The following morning the three trudged up past the huge structure of Winchester Cathedral and onto Romsey Road. O.H. had gone out earlier for a newspaper and had asked the vendor the direction to the prison. As they came to Romsey Road, they could see the high, imposing walls of the prison. O.H. led the other two to the prison door, which was a small door incorporated into a much larger door. He tapped on the opening and eventually a small, barred recess opened at about head height. A conversation began with neither party able to see the other. A disembodied voice came out from the recess. "Yes, what do you want?"

O.H. said, "we've come to visit my son Thomas Williams," and then he added as he thought it would help, "he's a conscientious objector."

Both George and Elizabeth stood back apprehensively. George was now dressed in what he called 'his funeral suit'.

The voice could be heard to say, "a chap here with two others to visit a conchie."

A different voice said, "has he made an appointment and what's the visitor's name?"

The first voice said, "have you made an appointment and what's your name, and the names of those with you?"

O.H. stated, "Yes, I wrote a letter and received a reply. I have the reply here with me. I'm Owen Williams, and George Williams and Elizabeth Williams are here with me."

The voice asked, "relationship to the prisoner?"

O.H. said "father, brother and wife."

After a few minutes, they could hear bolts being drawn back and they were ushered in by a prison warder. They followed the warder to an area where there was a long counter and little else. Two other warders were on the other side of the counter.

One of them was writing in a ledger, and without looking up asked, "full name of the prisoner, date of application for visit and former place of residence of the prisoner?" He then looked up and held out his hand, "and the letter of acceptance."

O.H. thought for a few seconds and then placed the letter the prison had sent him on the counter. He said, "Thomas Williams. The application was made in the last week of August. I can't remember the actual date and the prisoner would usually live in Caerphilly."

The warder huffed at O.H. not being able to remember the actual date and gave the letter a cursory glance. He then took a piece of paper he had been writing on and disappeared through a door at the back.

After ten minutes he reappeared and looking very accusingly at the three of them he said, "O.K. one visitor at a time, five minutes each and in the order of wife, father, brother. Wife, please follow this gentleman." He indicated the second warder - a young lad of about twenty.

The three of them looked at each other and then Elizabeth stepped forward and followed the younger warder who had come to the front of the counter. The warder led her to a second room and closed the door behind him. He looked at Elizabeth, who was very composed. She looked back at him with her beautiful blue eyes, causing him to cast his eyes down as if overawed by her presence.

He said, "Uh, I'm supposed to search you but ..." he looked up and blushed at her expression, stopped and thought about his next words "if you tell me you have no knives or uh, files or weapons then I don't think there will be any need for a search."

Elizabeth smiled and seemed very pleased with that and nodded and then said, "I have nothing on me," and then she thought, "well, I brought a book for my husband to read, is that allowed?"

The warder said, "can I see it?"

Elizabeth produced a Charles Dickens novel she had found at home and passed it to the warder, who opened it and held it up by the binding to check that nothing was hidden in it.

The warder said, "you can give him that, but later it will have to go into the prison library."

Elizabeth replied, "that's fine."

The warder said, "I'll have to stay in the room while you speak to your husband. I have to be close enough to hear your conversation."

Elizabeth nodded.

The warder opened the door and walked perhaps thirty yards to a further locked metal door. He produced a key, unlocked the door, and the two of them went through. Another warder stepped into the corridor and locked the door behind them. They walked along a further corridor where an opening led off to the left through which Elizabeth could see a two-storey layer of grills and gates, with several warders walking as if on patrol. She assumed these were the cells. They came to another door and the warder tapped on it. It was opened by another warder who ushered them in and then left.

The room had a table in the middle with a vertical grill rising above it splitting the table in half, and another chair on the other side of the table. Elizabeth was ushered to the chair and the warder took a half step back. A door opened at the back of the room on the opposite side to Elizabeth and a warder entered with Thomas, with his hands bound. His face lit up as he shuffled to the chair and sat. The warder who had escorted him left, leaving only the one who had escorted Elizabeth.

Elizabeth leaned towards the grill and grabbed it.

The warder shouted, "don't touch!" Elizabeth's hand went back to her side.

Thomas said, "how are you? Who is here with you? Where are you staying? How are the rest of the family?"

Then he realised he was bombarding her with questions and said, "sorry, they only told me yesterday that you were visiting. I couldn't sleep last night, and these questions just piled up, forgive me."

Elizabeth, realising time was short, explained who she was with and how they had travelled and where they were staying. She told Thomas that the family were all fine and then she couldn't remember whether she had told him that Evan had been killed, but before she told him she managed to hold back the information for fear it might add to his depression. She noticed that the whole of the time she spoke to Thomas, his hands shook badly and the metal cuffs around his wrists rattled. She also noticed that he kept throwing his head back involuntarily. She noticed bruising around his face and across his neck. She said, "how did you get those bruises?"

Before Thomas could answer, the warder shouted out, "don't answer that." After what seemed a very short time, the warder called "time's up," and he stepped forward to prompt Elizabeth to rise to her feet.

Elizabeth was shocked at the very short time she was allowed to be with Thomas. She turned to leave and then when she reached the door she turned back, blowing Thomas a kiss as she reached the door. She suddenly remembered the book in her bag and handed it to the warder, who passed the volume between the grill. Thomas tried to grab it in his bound and shaking hands. He failed, and the book fell to the floor. Elizabeth became very upset, as if the falling book was synonymous with the circumstances both she and Thomas found themselves in.

The warder tapped the inside of the door, and it was opened from the corridor side. As she stepped out, O.H. stepped in, brushing past her, touching her arm with feeling when he noticed how upset she was. She was escorted back to the room they had entered originally and passed George on the way.

He stopped and said, "you ok?"

He could see she was very upset but the warder escorting him interrupted by saying "hurry along there, sir." George got annoyed with the warder and turned saying, "this lady is very upset, have you no feelings?"

The warder, a man in his early fifties with a sullen expression said, "do you want to visit your brother or not?"

George was starting to get irritated at the warder's tone and said, "we've travelled all day for a five minute visit. What's in there, cold steel?" pointing to the warder's heart. He continued, "I don't know how you can work in this shithole every day. No wonder prisoners continue committing crimes after they leave prison when they are treated like this."

The warder was starting to lose patience with George and as he opened a side door to the right of the corridor he said, "in this room, sir, we haven't searched you yet."

George huffed but followed the warder into the room. He was asked to remove his overcoat, jacket, shoes and socks and to remove his trouser belt. He did this while grumbling about what a waste of time it was.

The warder patted him down and then asked him to put his clothes back on. While Thomas did this, the warder kept saying, "hurry along sir, if you please."

George dressed and followed the warder out of the room and along the corridor. They stopped outside a door on the left and the warder stopped, waited for a minute or two and took out his fob watch. He studied it in silence and then said, "sorry sir, times up. It's the prisoners' lunchtime. You'll have to come back another day." He leaned forward in an intimidating fashion and looking George in the eye, he smirked and said, "following a formal application, that is."

George was furious and shouted out, "I hope you enjoyed that performance."

The warder said, "we can always offer you a longer stay, sir."

233

George was just about ready to reply but composed himself, realising that there was no point in losing his temper, much as he would like to give the warder a piece of his mind. He clenched his fists but held them at his side and leaning towards the warder he said quietly "I hope one day you have a relative that you love dearly in much the same situation as this and then you are refused permission to see him or her. I've been on the front line seeing my best mates die to keep you back here in safety and to create a better world for the likes of you."

The warder leaned towards George and said, "you might have better spent your time trying to persuade your cowardly shit of a brother to fight for his country."

With that, the warder who was considerably taller and broader than George rose to his full height and, throwing his arm out, indicated the way they had just come, ushering George back to the waiting room where Elizabeth and O.H. were waiting for him.

As they left the prison gate, O.H. turned to George and said, "what did you think of Thomas?"

George, through gritted teeth said, "I don't know. I never got to see him. That evil bastard stopped me," pointing his thumb back towards the prison door.

O.H. could see George was trying to control his temper and so walked on in silence.

34

That afternoon, the three of them wandered around Winchester, where the weather matched their mood. It was a grey, depressing day with light rain in the air. People were bustling around the town, shopping or, for the most part, queuing to purchase what might be available in the third year of the war. George passed two soldiers in uniform who failed to salute until he remembered that he was in civilian clothes. They eventually found a small respectable tea-room and were shown to a table. They ordered sandwiches and cups of tea and sat for a while in silence.

O.H. asked George, "what happened? Why did they not let you see Thomas?"

George looked down a little abashed. "My fault. I could see Elizabeth was upset and when I stopped to ask if she was alright, the warder started getting uppity. He then made me suffer by taking me to a room to search me and then he wasted time outside the room where I presume Thomas was, and then proceeded to tell me we had run out of time, and I would have to visit another day after making another formal application. He was just being difficult because I had questioned him - my fault completely."

O.H. thought George's answer very different from one he might have given a while ago; almost an acceptance that he was to blame.

George then turned to them both and said, "well, as I didn't get to see him, I think both of you should say what you thought and said during your visits. That way, I might think this trip was not a complete waste of time."

Elizabeth said, "well, when he got into the room, he just bombarded me with questions, one after the other. I just answered his questions about how we had travelled here and how well members of the family were. I didn't mention Evan's death, as I thought that might upset him. He must have wondered where George was after I had told him who was at the prison. I just told him things like that. I was shocked at how much weight he had lost, and his hands shook all the time and I noticed he was bruised about the face and neck."

O.H. said, "I don't think any of us should mention what he looked like in front of his mother. She would be very upset if she found out about Thomas' physical state."

Elizabeth and George both nodded in agreement.

O.H. continued, "I tried not to speak too much as I wanted to know what conditions in the prison were like, and how Thomas coped with them."

Elizabeth said, "I wish I had thought of that. That was very clever of you, O.H. I spent most of the very short time telling him about my life and what life back home was like. I learned very little of what he was experiencing."

O.H. continued, "if you told him about back home and the family and then he told me about prison life, then I think we all benefitted from the visit. I'm sure it will have helped Thomas to see us and to hear that life continues outside prison and that people are thinking of him, and that he will be cared for when he is released."

George muttered something and O.H. asked him to repeat it.

George said, "you both benefitted. I never got to see him."

O.H. replied, "that's your own fault for being difficult."

George looked up, "what do you mean by that?"

O.H. said, "I just meant that we got an indication of what Thomas is experiencing and we helped to give him a taste of what life was like back home," he hesitated and then "it's just you never got in so you couldn't tell him anything and you couldn't learn about his condition."

George started to lose his patience. "I apologised, it's me that's lost that opportunity, not you, so let's just let it lie."

There was silence for a while as George and O.H. calmed. O.H. continued, "Thomas said that there was a prison newspaper which was printed on toilet paper as prisoners were not allowed pens, pencils or paper - these had to be smuggled in. He said it was like a proper newspaper with cartoons, news and humorous stories. He said that the newspaper was very secret as the warders would carry out detailed searches if they got word of it. I thought that was very clever."

Elizabeth said, "how did he tell you that? Didn't the warder step in?"

O.H. said, "the one with me didn't seem so bothered. He left the room for a time and I'm sure he was gone for more than five minutes."

O.H. continued, "he said that the conscientious objectors were all in two of the wings of the prison and so were quite close together. However, they had little time together and were more often in solitary confinement. He said he had been in solitary confinement for the whole of the first month of his sentence. One of the prisoners had told him that he had managed to get two books from the prison library, but they had been quickly confiscated." O.H. laughed as he recalled what Thomas had told him. "He said some of the prisoners were good fishermen and when I told him I didn't understand, he said that one of the prisoners had made a fishing line and had fished for books out of the cell window from the cell below. He also said that one of the prisoners had learned morse code - you know tap tap." He tapped on the table to illustrate his point. "He had taught this to other prisoners who tapped on the water pipes to speak to each other." O.H. sat back, proud of the information he had collected. He looked at the other two. "Clever lot these objectors, to think of things like that."

Elizabeth said, "phew, that was very impressive O.H. There are obviously a lot of things going on that the authorities know nothing about."

O.H. said, "Thomas said that it was these things that kept the men's spirits up and that there was real camaraderie amongst the conchies." He stopped and looked at Elizabeth and George. "Sorry, that's what he called them." He elaborated, "that's what they call themselves."

The three sat back in silence. George broke the silence by saying, "everything depends on how long the war goes on as I can't see them letting any of them out at least until the war is over. It's vital that Thomas keeps his spirits and his strength up until then, and that he stays healthy, or as healthy as he can."

Elizabeth said, "I suspect that even when the war is over, they will keep them in prison for a while, otherwise they will be competing for jobs with those who have been in the army. They've been pretty vindictive so far; I can't see that changing."

O.H. blew out through his teeth. "What jobs will be left when they do eventually get out. Soldiers first, then perhaps the disabled and wounded and then the conscientious objectors. In a peacetime world with less employment, there won't be much left for them, and that is perhaps what the government intends." He turned to Elizabeth. "I'm sorry to paint such a depressing picture."

Elizabeth looked down. "Not much to look forward to. Perhaps I need to find work to support Thomas when they let him out."

O.H. shook his head "I know you don't agree George, but these are men who are in prison because of their beliefs and their principles. I see them as brave, and they are being made to suffer unduly because of their beliefs."

George, remembering his conversation with Lloyd George replied, "that's as may be, but it's not the way the government sees it."

Most of the remaining time they spent in the tea-room was in silence as each of them thought about Thomas and contemplated their futures and the futures of other members of the family. They left, thanking their waitress. They walked around the small centre of

Winchester, spending time in the park, feeding the ducks with bread that they had saved from the tea-room, and visiting the Cathedral; not wanting to go back to the guest house too early.

The following morning, they made their way back to the railway station and retraced their journey of two days earlier, this time not really wanting to engage in conversation with their fellow passengers. At one point, George followed Elizabeth out into the corridor of the train when O.H. had fallen asleep. He found her leaning out of an open window. She had partly loosened her hair, letting it blow with the speed of the train. They both laughed as she had to pull back quickly as the train entered a tunnel and the corridor filled with steam. George thought he had never seen her look so beautiful as she did with her hair looking untidy as it had been pulled out of a tight bun and was streaming around her face. She blew her hair out of her face and laughed.

He said, "you ok?"

She nodded with her eyes closed but a look of contentment on her face and eventually said, "I will be when things get back to normal."

She passed George, touching his arm as she went back to the carriage and for a while George stayed by the open window, wondering what she had meant. However, he was comforted by the thought that she was still hoping and waiting for Thomas to return home.

It was late when George got home carrying his bag from Treafon railway station. Maud kissed him as he came through the door and all thoughts of Elizabeth immediately left him. She realised he was very tired from his journey and so said she would ask him about the visit in the morning after he had rested. She made him a sandwich and a cup of tea, and he made his way up to bed, thinking what a different life he was now leading compared to his brother and sister-in-law.

35

George slept for much of the journey back to Tonfanau Camp. He had spent the remaining few days of his leave with Maud and Joan. They had gone up to visit his mother. George was genuinely relieved that his father was not there, as he had gone to a chapel meeting. He didn't want to rehash the same old conversations with his father, and he enjoyed chatting to his sister and mother without the conversation being overpowered and directed by his father's strong views. He had a long conversation with Esther, who was still living there, and he came away surer than ever of Esther's resilience and quiet confidence. Although devastated by Evans' death, she was determined to put on a brave face. Her attitude in the light of her immense loss had a powerful influence on George as he became more determined than ever that he would spend every minute of his leave with his family.

The weather was distinctly autumnal, with cold days but no rain, allowing the three of them to wrap up warm and to walk every day, to feed the ducks, to climb the mountains around Treafon and to visit Maud's sister, who seemed shocked at seeing George and continued throughout the visit to shake her head and say, "I can't believe it." Joan cried when George climbed onto the train to go back to camp, but he promised to write her a letter of her own which Maud would read to her and that pacified her a little. In a strange way, Joan's tears warmed his heart as he felt that she would miss him and that she was showing a genuine love for him.

A few weeks after George had returned to the camp following his leave, he found himself fully occupied picking stones from one of Jac's fields. Jac, Alys, Lloyd and George were spread across a large field picking up stones and stacking them ready to be taken to the edge of the field.

Jac stood up straight, holding onto his back. He smiled, as he could see George doing exactly the same thing. "Backbreaking, isn't it?"

George replied, "you hadn't noticed but I was standing upright for quite a while. I didn't think my back could take much more of it."

Jac said, "has to be done otherwise when we come to plough the field the stones will blunt the plough, but I have to say it's not a job I look forward to. He looked across to Alys, "panad, cariad?"

Alys squeezed past George whispering, "thought he would never ask"

George looked to Lloyd, who didn't seem to require a break at all. He said, "how does he manage it?"

Jac replied, "I think when God took the strength from his leg, he transferred it to his back. Duw, he's a good worker and strong for a youngster, tarw," he hesitated, "a bull in English."

Jac called Lloyd across and the three walked down to the farmhouse.

Jac suddenly remembered something. "I meant to ask you. Alys and I and Lloyd, of course, would love it if you could persuade Maud and Joan to come and stay for a few days, now like, before the weather gets worse."

George looked across. "You have enough to do without more mouths to feed."

Jac said with a very serious face, "George bach, we wouldn't ask if we didn't want them to stay, and the farm means we always have enough for ourselves and visitors to eat."

George didn't want to upset Jac, and he said he would ask Maud in his next letter. When he got back to camp that night, he immediately penned a letter to Maud and another one to Joan. He missed them both and it would be a way of seeing them both.

Maud replied quickly that she would love to come up to Tywyn, and Joan would really enjoy the experience of staying on the farm.

George then asked to speak to Major Fisher, explaining that his wife was going to visit the area, and would it be possible, if the other sergeants and corporals agreed, to change his work patterns and then carry out some of their activities at a later date. The major agreed and George went to the N.C.O.'s mess to put his proposal to the others. They agreed, and all was well.

Two weeks later, George and Jac met Maud and Joan on Tywyn station platform and took them by horse and cart to the farm. They stayed for four days; the weather remained mainly cold but crisp and dry and the two families walked in the surrounding hills. Lloyd loved having a companion in Joan to play with and he would begin each of the walks with the rest of them, only giving up when his leg hurt to return to the farm to await their return. George couldn't stop smiling to see Joan and Maud enjoying the walks in the fresh air. George thought how this air would benefit their health if they could live in it all the time.

A day later, Joan and Lloyd were building sandcastles on Tywyn beach and competing to see who could build the biggest and best, badgering George and Maud to give their judgement. George and Maud were reluctant to move the few yards to the sandcastles as they were cosily wrapped up in coats and blankets against the cold wind.

The one day, which turned out to be a wet day, George had to remain at camp for the bulk of the morning and early afternoon as a new contingent arrived, and were settled in. In the late afternoon, he walked to the farm where Joan very proudly offered him a cup of tea and a piece of cake. They had spent the day baking, with Alys instructing Joan in how to bake a Victoria sponge, with a few replacement ingredients to cover those no longer available due to wartime rationing. Maud was deep in conversation with Alys comparing different foods which were not available and how Maud could replace them with alternatives. Jac and George retired to the living room and the peace and quiet.

Jac looked across at George and asked, "look, I've not asked before, but I have been curious as to what it was like in France or wherever you were. That's all the local farmers talk about is the war, but none of us knows what it is really like."

George leaned forward and looked at the floor. "It was awful Jac. Try to imagine going to war with some of your best mates, some of the farmers you like and know very well, and then imagine them killed in an instant at your side. Nobody should have to experience that. That's besides the conditions, the trenches where you live, eat and sleep. The rats, water up to your knees sometimes and then the shelling, the bullets flying over you, waiting for you to make a mistake and put your head above the trench line and get it blown off. Worst of all, you stay in the same position for months on end wondering why you are there. So frustrating." He shook his head and repeated, "awful, just awful."

Jac looked across at George. "Weren't you scared?"

George sighed, "all the time, Jac. All the time."

George went quiet and then said, "and perhaps the worst of all is that you can see no end to it. The war could last a year, two years, ten years. Nobody knows, and the dying just goes on."

Jac looked abashed, "sorry George, I shouldn't have asked, but I had to know the real truth. You hear so many stories and you never know what to believe, but I trust you to tell me the truth."

On the last evening, they all went into Tywyn, to listen to a concert given by local choirs and singers. The look of contentment on Maud's face gave George a warm feeling as they walked back to the cart holding hands. It was with much sadness that he waved them off on the platform the following Saturday morning.

George went back to the farm with Jac and as they sat drinking a cup of tea. Lloyd said he was very sad as he had said goodbye to his friend.

Christmas 1917 was a subdued affair. Many of those at the camp were depressed that they were spending their fourth Christmas away from their families. The normally sociable and buoyant Captain

243

Parker seemed not to be bothered to arrange any Christmas activities and the permanent soldiers at the camp did not mention Christmas. They appeared to be happy just to be left alone with their own thoughts.

Maud's visit had provided a few days' respite from the boredom and loneliness of this fourth Christmas away from home. George continued to walk in the hills whenever he could and trudged up to the farm through deep snow at the end of January to help Jac dig out some of the sheep and cattle that had got trapped in the blizzards of the previous day.

His mood brightened in early March when Spring flowers appeared on the grass banks alongside the roadways. The weather became showery but there were enough bright spells to lighten everyone's spirits.

The war was dragging on, with little ground gained by either side.

36

The Americans had entered the war the year before but there seemed to be little evidence of their contribution up to this point. In early April, news began to arrive at the camp of a huge German offensive. The unofficial word was that they had attacked before the bulk of the American troops arrived and could provide an imbalance of troop numbers on the Western front in favour of the Allies. The offensive was proving successful and for the first time since 1914, one side looked as if it was making progress. The conversation in the N.C.O.'s Mess was one of concern. The Russian revolution and the resulting peace treaty between Russia and Germany had allowed large numbers of German troops to be transferred from the Eastern front to the Western front, allowing the offensive to take place.

George continued to take his regular strolls down to the mail office and one morning in early April, a letter was waiting for him. He immediately recognised Elizabeth's handwriting. He stopped to read the letter outside the office.

Dear George,

I hope you are keeping well?

Thomas was released from prison ten days ago and returned home. He is much the same as when we saw him. His hands still shake, and he has difficulty sleeping but in himself he is not significantly worse. He was able to remain at home for two days before the inevitable knock on the door. Two soldiers said that he had been charged with desertion and they put him in the back of a truck. Thomas did not complain, and he seemed resigned to the fact that this was inevitable. I managed to get an early train to Cardiff and waited outside the court.

Thomas appeared and was sentenced to twelve months in prison. However, after the hearing a smartly dressed captain came up to me and asked if I was Thomas' wife. I said that I was, and the captain explained that he hadn't spoken to Thomas as yet, but he was going to offer him a place on what he called 'a Home Office Scheme'. He said that it had become policy to offer conscientious objectors the possibility of working while in prison. They would have much better living conditions and he said that he didn't think that Thomas would complain as the work wouldn't contribute to the war effort.

He said that the government seemed to be concerned with the conditions conscientious objectors were kept in and this was one way in which their health might be ensured until the war came to an end. I asked if I might speak to Thomas to perhaps persuade him to take part in the scheme and the captain said he would see what he could do. To cut a long story short both the captain and I were able to speak to Thomas. We explained the scheme to him, and he thought for what seemed a very long time. He asked a few questions about the scheme and then thankfully he agreed to sign to take part in it. Consequently, he has been moved to Princetown prison on Dartmoor. I have not heard anything from him yet, but I will keep you in touch.

I sincerely hope this is for the good and may keep Thomas alive until his release at the end of the war. I thought you would like to hear of this encouraging news.

Your ever-loving sister-in-law

Elizabeth

George put the letter into his pocket and felt slightly more cheerful after reading it as the thought that Thomas might not survive the war was constantly with him. Elizabeth obviously thought that conditions might be improved for Thomas in Princetown and so George had to be hopeful.

The following week, George received a letter from Maud explaining that she had heard that John Walters had been wounded somewhere near the Somme in Northern France and he had been brought back to a hospital in Bristol to recover.

A few weeks later, a further letter appeared from Elizabeth. When George opened it, there was only a short note from Elizabeth explaining that she had received a letter from Thomas. She was clearly overjoyed, as this was such a rare event due to his poor health. She explained that she had copied out Thomas' letter as she wanted to keep the original, but she thought that he would like to read Thomas' description regarding living conditions in Princetown.

The criminal prisoners have been moved out of Princetown and the prison is now called 'Princetown Work Centre'. There are about 1,000 men here and I am a recent arrival as most have been here for many months. We are allowed to wear our own clothes and I am very glad to be rid of the scratchy prison uniform I was forced to wear in Winchester. There are no locks on the doors and the men can chat and socialise as they wish. At first this came as a shock to me, and I found it difficult to speak to other men here and to leave my cell as this was something I had not been used to.

However, it is so comforting to be in normal company, to sit and speak to men from a range of backgrounds. Some are very well educated men who take their beliefs very seriously. Many have strong religious beliefs, they are Jehovah's Witnesses, Roman Catholics and even Methodists. Some are from wealthy backgrounds while others are dockers and miners who have developed communist beliefs. They debate and sometimes try to convert others. On very rare occasions this can erupt into physical violence which amuses me as these men will fight to protect their beliefs but will not fight to protect their country, an interesting philosophical debate.

We have to work, and while some work on local farms, some break stones for roadways and some work on improving the drainage of the area around Princetown. I began to work on digging ditches but unfortunately, I collapsed from exhaustion and had to be moved to work sewing mail bags as this was less arduous. I wish I could have continued to work on the drainage ditches as it was outside work. Sewing mail bags is giving me large blisters on my fingers. I shouldn't complain as life is so much more pleasurable than in Winchester where life was very hard. I must try to keep healthy as there is little provision for any medical care and those who have health problems seem not to get any better. I will leave it at this point as I am beginning to tire but I will write and give you more of an insight in a future letter.

George noted that something had been written above the name Thomas but had been scribbled out. George sat on a wooden step leading into one of the huts in the camp. Reading the letter made him feel guilty once again. Some people were having a tough time, Thomas in Princetown, John Walters now wounded and in hospital and the women back home struggling to put food on the table, while he seemed to have such an easy life here in Tonfanau. George tried to put it out of his mind. He had been ordered here by the army and his position was not one of his own choosing.

37

As George walked through the camp on a misty morning in late May 1918, one of the corporals came running across to him. "Sarge, Major Fisher wants to see you in his office. He said if I saw you to let you know."

George thanked him and made his way to the major's office, a little disgruntled as he had been planning a walk for later in the day after the early morning mist had risen.

He tapped on the door and Major Fisher called out, "come in."

George walked in and saluted smartly.

The Major said, without looking up, "at ease, Sergeant"

For a few seconds, the Major continued to write in a large ledger and then closed it and gave George his full attention.

He continued, "I thought you ought to know that the camp is to change in the next few weeks. A camp in Pembrokeshire is going to take more of the Royal Artillery training and we are to become a German P.O.W. camp. Bigger camps in England are full and they are looking to move some German and Austrian P.O.W.s elsewhere. Over the next few weeks, we can expect perhaps fifty or sixty men. The War Department felt that we were in a perfect position to take extra men and put them to work. Many of the P.O.W.s in other camps in the country were becoming troublesome as they had little to do and the War Department thought it might be a good idea to 'farm out'.....," the major stopped and laughed heartily at the joke he had just made, albeit inadvertently.

George looked nonplussed.

After a few seconds the major continued, "anyway, these boches P.O.W.s are to be used locally. Over the next week or so, you and I will think up where they can be best put to use. I've already thought that some might be used to fill in potholes on the local roads, some can stay here to repair parts of the camp and perhaps some might be put to work on local farms. It must be remembered they are P.O.W.s and the local population might not be pleased at their presence. However, they will get used to them in time and I have been reassured that none of those coming here have been troublemakers in other camps." He looked directly at George. "Any questions Sergeant?"

George was surprised by the information and had not really had time to digest it. He replied, "uh, no sir, I don't think so."

Major Fisher said, "ok, so you and I will meet on Friday morning at nine o'clock sharp to discuss possibilities, that gives you four days to think of where we might use these people and for you to go around and canvas opinions in the local community. That'll be all Sergeant."

"Sir."

George left, scratching his head. He immediately crossed to the Sergeant's Mess. Sergeant Major Ross and Corporal Rogers were there chatting and sharing a pot of freshly brewed tea. George poured himself a cup and sat and listened. At a break in the conversation he said, "don't know if either of you can help but Major Fisher gave me a little bit of surprising information this morning. Seems we've got a few German visitors coming." George, expecting equal surprise, waited to see the two men's reactions.

Ross said, "yes, we've heard."

George was taken aback, as he had only just heard, so he couldn't understand how they knew. He decided not to pursue the point but put it down to camp gossip. He continued, "any ideas of possible things we can get them to do?" While the two appeared to think he said, "idle hands are the devil's workshop," suddenly remembering an oft used proverb of his father's which he would use when he needed to encourage George or one of his siblings to engage in some activity. O.H. deplored boredom and George remembered it was fatal to ever show any signs of it when O.H. was about.

Ross seeming to be deep in thought said, "well, there's always the local farms and the allotments outside Tywyn."

George said, "yes, I've thought of that."

Rogers said, "what about improving the beach defences on parts of the coast?"

George thought that was a good idea and said so.

Ross said, "and perhaps offering to repair people's houses."

George said, "now that is a good idea which would help the locals accept the P.O.W.s if they could see a benefit."

Ross said, "important to check with the prisoners when they arrive to see if they have any special skills, plasterers, plumbers etc."

The discussion continued and it allowed George to go to his meeting with Major Fisher with a range of ideas. George spent the week sounding out his ideas with the local community.

He realised that immediately he told people the gossip would begin. He had to admit that most people he spoke to were vehemently opposed to the idea of bringing German P.O.W.s into their community, while just a few could see how they might benefit. Most hated the thought that the enemy would possibly be free to wander and might even violate their womenfolk. Some even talked of locking up their daughters and not letting them out until the end of the war. Fisher accepted most of George's ideas but suggested that they hold back on the repairs to the camp until they could be assured that the P.O.W.s would not sabotage any remaining artillery training activities.

Two weeks later, five trucks pulled into the parade ground in the centre of the camp and the P.O.W.s piled out of the backs of the trucks and formed up in two rows. They had been escorted by a small detachment of armed troops who would remain at the camp to help guard the prisoners. A corporal in charge of the detachment shouted at them to come to attention but George had to smile at the response of the group who slowly formed up but continued to slouch in front of a welcoming party, many ignoring the guards and continuing to carry on conversations with each other. George considered their dissension understandable under the circumstances. They seemed to be wearing a wide array of clothing of both German and British origin.

Major Fisher took up his position in front of the P.O.W.s and George noticed that one of the German sergeants stood alongside Major Fisher and was ready to act as interpreter for those who spoke no English. He wondered if the major would try to force them into a more military bearing.

He wisely didn't, and shouted out, "welcome. We hope your stay with us will be short and when the present war ends, you will be returned to your families."

One or two of the P.O.W.s laughed out loud, and one said something in German which caused the rest of the group to laugh. Every statement of the major's was followed by a pause allowing the German sergeant time to repeat the statement in German. Fisher continued, "we have tried to make your sleeping arrangements as comfortable as possible, and we have designated one of the huts as an area where you can collect and eat your food. We will put up a list of mealtimes on the notice board over here, and we will use the noticeboard to convey any other important information," as Fisher pointed to his left at a board that had been put up in front of one of the huts. "You will have a bathhouse where you may wash in the mornings and evenings, which also has a latrine. While you are here, you will be expected to work." This statement was met with silence until one of the men at the front relayed the information in German. His translation was met with a degree of derision and a few shouts and wolf whistles.

As Fisher was speaking, George cast his eyes across the P.O.W.s but his eye kept returning to one man in the second row. He pondered on why this particular chap was drawing his attention and then he thought he must look like somebody he knew, but he couldn't place who that was. The first row of P.O.W.s were led off to their dormitory by a group of the armed detachment. Major Fisher and Captain Parker moved off to the main office and George crossed to have a closer look at the man, who looked familiar. As he got nearer, the man looked up.

Before George could speak, the man stared and said, "mein gott! It is you George," with a look of total surprise.

George stopped. "Bloody hell, Isaac, I can't believe it. What are you doing here?"

Isaac Gaba stayed where he was as George came nearer. The rest of the line of men moved off but George indicated to the armed guard that he was perfectly safe with this man.

Isaac smiled, "well George, I am shocked." He hesitated and shook his head and then continued by explaining what had happened to him during the last few years. "I found selling was more difficult around Treafon. Being a packman was never easy. People were more reluctant to buy from me because I was German. A German and a Jew!" He shook his head and laughed. He continued, "and so in 1913 Rachel and I and the two children left to go back to Germany. We lived in Hamburg. I worked in the dockyard until I joined the army in 1914. I was captured in France in 1916 and I have been in a camp south of Birmingham until now. How are you and Maud and the children?"

George related what had happened to him and Maud in the last few years and the sad story of what had happened to Willie.

Isaac said, "oh George, I am so sorry to hear about Willie. He was such a lovely little boy; you must be so sad?"

A few yards away, an armed sergeant shouted a command and Isaac smiled. "I think that was for my benefit. See you George," he turned, and as he walked away and with ironic humour said, "perhaps we could have a beer sometime."

George grinned at the statement and walked away.

A few days later, a second letter came from Elizabeth. Once again, it contained only a short note from Elizabeth but a longer letter which she had copied out, which had come from Thomas.

I have tried to continue in my worship, but this has proved difficult. You know how important Christianity is to me, well, apparently the Bishop of Exeter, whose diocese covers Princetown has refused to allow 'prisoners' the use of the chapel at the prison. Many of us here are devout Christians and this has upset the men here more than anything, I think. We got together and decided to hold a service in the assembly hall in the centre of the cells. We constructed posters and explained that the service was open to everyone. We thought this would help many cope with the privations of their stay at Princetown. However, when we started to sing the first hymn and later when we decided to sing the National Anthem to show we were patriots we were drowned out by the communists singing 'The Red Flag'. This caused much anger amongst the men.

A few months ago, one of the inmates became very ill with pneumonia after being out on the moors working on drainage ditches. Medical care is (the next few words were crossed out) and he failed to improve and eventually died. The whole contingent, some thousand men tried to give him as respectful a send-off as possible by escorting the coffin to the railway station while singing 'Abide with Me'. It was very moving.

We have our own gymnasium, games room and library and we provide our own entertainment, from poetry readings to debates, though some of the debates can get a little heated. Our food is (the next part was crossed out in Thomas' letter).

We suffer from boils and rashes because (the next part was also crossed out).

We go out to work and at present I am working on improving the road which goes down to the river. We have started calling it 'Conchies Road'. During bad weather we get very wet and there are no facilities to dry clothes. Some men get very bad colds and cough all the time. We work long hours, ten hours each day and six and a half hours on Saturdays. Fortunately, we are not expected to work on Sundays allowing us time to have church services, however difficult that may prove.

As you can see the conditions are better than in Winchester but not quite like home. We all pray for a speedy end to the war and the hope that we will be allowed to come home to see families again.

All my love

Thomas

George was left with the same feeling that he had after reading the first letter; relief that conditions were better in Princetown and that Thomas seemed in better spirits but with little chance of him being allowed home yet.

He said out loud to no one in particular, "this damned war puts a hold on people's lives and continues to bring death and misery to the families of people throughout the world. I pray that it ends soon."

38

George was allowed a week's leave in June. He was excited to be going home, if only for a short time. However, he found the journey to Treafon slow and mind numbing. Two days of his leave were wasted in traveling. He rushed from the railway station to the front gate of his house, keen to be home with his family. It was quite late but still light in the bright summer's evening. This further lightened his mood as he thought it would lengthen the time he might spend with Maud and Joan walking outside in the warm evenings or playing in the garden. He had informed Maud by letter that he was coming home, and he hoped that she and Joan would be as excited as he was.

He couldn't be bothered to look through his kit bag for his key, so he knocked on the door. It was opened immediately by Maud, who kissed him with no little affection. His smile broadened as Joan came hurtling from the next room to throw her arms around her father. "Daddy, I've been waiting for you."

George was speechless at the welcome given by his little family, and he felt a tear come into the corner of his eye. He said, "and I've missed you both." After taking off his heavy boots, he asked, "so what's been happening?"

Maud left him to bring a plate of sandwiches and to put the kettle on the stove for a cup of tea. She said, "let me get you a cup of tea and I'll tell you, though I'm afraid it's not good news." She came back into the room and quietly said to Joan, "why don't you go and play with your dollies in the front room while daddy and I have a chat, and he will give you a cwtch after."

Joan toddled off, pulling a face, and Maud brought George a cup of tea. George was ravenous as he had not eaten all day and he began to eat the sandwiches and sup his tea. Maud sat opposite him and began her tale, with her sad face preparing George for bad news. There had been so many times during this war when he had received bad news, he was becoming used to it.

She said, "O.H. came down yesterday. He said that the day before they had received a letter from the War Office telling them that Ben was missing in action. The letter had a note in it from Ben's commanding officer. Apparently, Ben's company had been involved in an attack on German positions. The attack had only been moderately successful, and the company was forced back to their own trench. When they got back, Ben was nowhere to be seen. One of his friends had seen him falling after being shot but they couldn't find his body. O.H. was in a bit of a state and he didn't stay long. This morning, I left Joan with Annie and I went up to see them. As you can imagine, your mother and father fear the worst. All O.H. would say is that he would pray for Ben's safe return and that he hoped that he might have been captured. Then he went into the other room. I spoke to your mother in a quiet moment, and she told me she was sure Ben was dead."

George could not trust himself to speak without breaking down. He stood up and walked out to the back garden. It was just getting dark, and he sat on the low stone wall between them and next door. Maud did not follow him out, as she could see that he needed to be on his own.

George's mood changed from pleasure at seeing Maud and Joan to deep despair at the news of his brother. Ben was probably closer to him than any of his siblings and the information about his possible death dug deep into his soul. He sat and thought of the times he had played with Ben as a youngster, the times he had stood up to older boys in defending his younger brother. How would the other members of his family be able to cope with this loss? He always felt Ben was his mother's favourite. He had a wicked sense of humour, and he could make his mother laugh. He would charm her, and she would push him away saying, 'get on with you, leave me in peace'.

Would they never hear his voice or see him again?

The following day, George, Maud and Joan walked up to the park

257

and George sat on the grass in the sun watching Joan play. Maud tried to encourage George to play with Joan, but he showed no enthusiasm and no energy. He felt miserable and just wanted to be left to his own thoughts.

Maud suggested, "why don't you go on up to your parents. You are going to have to see them before you go back, so you might as well get it over with. I'll take Joan home and you come home when you are ready."

George agreed eventually. He wasn't looking forward to going to his parent's house, but he knew he had to do it. At first, he suggested that they all go there, but Maud thought that wasn't such a good idea under the circumstances.

George walked to their house at the other end of town and was greeted by his mother with more affection than usual. She kissed him on the cheek and ushered him into the kitchen where his father sat, seemingly in a daze. George thought his father had visibly aged since he had seen him last, only a few months before. He seemed to be preoccupied and looked unkempt. His hair had not been brushed and his braces were loose around his waist.

George sat opposite him, "afternoon sir."

O.H. mumbled something in reply.

George said, "you ok? No more news of Ben?" really just for something to say.

O.H. shook his head, "ah, no, nothing."

George prepared himself for a difficult few hours, as neither parent seemed keen to talk. He continued, as his mother joined them, "he's missing - it doesn't mean he's dead. When I was on the front line, this would happen loads of times. In the chaos of battle, men would go missing. They would turn up hours or even days later. It's madness out there. Groups get separated and have to find their way back. Ben might even have been captured. I know that's not good news but after this is all over, he'll come home."

George's mother said, "yes I've heard that, but I've also heard of men getting blown up and their bodies blown into a million pieces, so there's no evidence of them anymore. We've heard that Ben was wounded. Imagine if Ben...," she dropped her head and gave a deep sigh before breaking down completely and leaving the room.

O.H. looked up. "Probably best not to talk about it in front of your mother. It's taken me a long time to calm her down and every time she thinks about Ben, she breaks down again."

George asked, "do you want a cup of tea?"

O.H. said, "answer to every problem," but then realising that he was only trying to help he looked down at his hands drawn together on the table-top, "sorry son, I've been drowning in tea. Seems to be the only thing you can do which takes your mind off Ben for just a minute."

George was content that he had shown his face and now it was best if he left. As George moved towards the front door, he shouted "bye," up to his mother upstairs. There was no reply. He asked O.H. if he could do anything for them and then he was completely taken aback when, before he walked out through the door, his father grabbed him in a huge hug, then pushed him away as if he suddenly realised what he was doing in such an unusual show of affection.

George walked back through the town in deep despair. As he passed the Castle Vaults, he walked in through the door as if he was some sort of mechanical toy, completely without a conscious thought. He looked around and not recognising anyone, he went to the bar. "Afternoon Maldwyn, I'll have a pint of ale," and as an afterthought "and a glass of whisky."

It was as if Maldwyn could sense his mood. He nodded and left George to his thoughts.

George sat, quietly sipping his beer and taking an occasional sip of his glass of whisky. The afternoon and then the evening slipped by. George would go to the bar and Maldwyn would pour the same combination, without any conversation between them. George spoke to no one until late in the evening, he slurred his order to Maldwyn and then realised his pockets were empty. Maldwyn said, "you can have this one on the house, George - then you go home," and then he added "with no fuss."

George nodded and after being refused his next order, left the pub swearing under his breath. He later had no recollection of his walk home, but could remember Maud quietly saying, "come on, let's get you up to bed." Maud placed a bowl alongside George's bed and left the room. It was well past midday when George surfaced the following day. He quickly apologised to Maud and sat with his head in his hands. Maud brought him a cup of tea, but he was surprised that there was no admonishment as there had been in the past.

Later in the afternoon Maud suggested "how about if we go for a walk, the fresh air will do you good." George was not convinced, but he later admitted that the walk had made him feel better. He thought that Maud had realised that the afternoon's drinking had probably been what he needed to get the sadness and despair out of his system.

The following day, he took Joan up to town to give Maud a little respite from her daily chores. Joan was delighted when George bought her some pieces of ribbon for her hair, and he bought a bunch of flowers for Maud from the florists.

That evening, Maud cooked George a piece of meat with some peas from the garden and a few small potatoes. She placed a candle on the table, and they chatted quietly. George apologised for his behaviour on the previous day and Maud brushed it away as if it was of no importance. After the meal, they sat either side of the fireplace and talked about what they would do after the war. As it got late, they went up to bed, George getting into bed without his usual night shirt on. Maud glanced around and after giving George a knowing smile, she copied him. They fell into each other's arms. George kissing his wife and then stroking her skin lovingly. Maud responded by giving a slight moan and gently throwing her head back. George moved down to kiss her breasts, nuzzling her nipples. After such a long period without making love to his wife, George quickly became aroused and moved across on top of her, gently penetrating her. She gasped and gave in to his movements. He could not hold back and quickly came inside her. Rolling back onto his side of the bed, he felt a deep sense of satisfaction in realising how much he loved his wife. He cuddled up to her and she fell asleep in his embrace, both of them content that they seemed to have once again-found the love they seemed to have lost.

She was everything to him. She was kind, gentle, thoughtful and he realised that he was still excited by her body and that he would never want any other woman and no one else could love him and know him as she did. They looked at each other and George stroked her cheek. He said, "how can you love me like you do when I've done so many stupid things?"

Maud smiled and said, "yes, you have, but I felt that I just had to be patient for you to appreciate how much I loved you. Remember when we married the minister said, 'for better or worse'? Well, we've had the worse now we'll have the better."

George lay on his back with Maud looking across at him, stroking his chest and smiling.

George spent the rest of his leave with Maud and Joan, walking most days when the weather would allow and playing with Joan inside when the weather was wet. George became adept at making up stories for his daughter, who was now very interested in farms after her stay on Jac and Alys' farm.

Maud and Joan came to the station to see George onto the early morning train back to Tonfanau, and George felt a deep sadness that he had not felt before to be leaving them.

39

George had already checked out the places where the P.O.W.s would work before his leave started. He had reassured the people they would be working with that they would be supported and protected and that these men posed no threat. They had got used to moving the P.O.W.s around in the trucks provided and they got used to the abuse from some of the local population. Just the appearance of the men in grey would be enough for some of the locals, both young and old, to direct a torrent of abuse. The P.O.W.'s had got used to it and generally ignored it.

Once however, when George had taken a truckload down to Tywyn beach just for a change of scenery, a shower of pebbles came out of the sky. These were probably hurled by a gang of youths hiding behind the rocks at the head of the beach. George could not leave the prisoners to investigate, so they were quickly herded back onto the truck with a great deal of muttering and complaining. Corporal Rogers had also been involved in a stand-off with a group of older men who were army veterans. When George discussed the incident with Jac, he laughed and said, "that'll be Ieuan Withers, spent the whole of his war service in a canteen in Norwich, never saw a bullet fired in anger. He's got a mouth as big as Cardigan Bay."

With the P.O.W.s ignoring the abuse, the local boys soon lost interest and eventually it stopped. George had heard that a local man who had been a boxing champion had had a word with the youths as the P.O.W.s had been repairing his roof. The irony amused George.

Four trucks were used to take the P.O.W.s out onto their first day's work. George and one of the privates from the camp had eleven men in the back of their truck, and they dropped them off at a range of farms in the area. George was extremely apprehensive as he pulled away from the first farm. He desperately wanted this scheme to succeed, and he would spend each day and all day driving around the farms to check that all was well. That way, he could easily respond to any problems. He drove up the lane to Jac's farm with Isaac and Karl. He felt he owed Jac a favour and he made sure that Isaac was working on Jac's farm, because he trusted him. Karl, he was less sure of; he said little and was surly when he did speak. Isaac said he could speak little English, and that he became frustrated when he could not find the words he needed to express himself.

George put Isaac and Karl together because Isaac had befriended him and acted as his translator. In a conversation a few days before, Isaac had told him that Karl was from a town in Westfalia. He talked all the time about Helga, his wife back home. He carried her photo with him and showed it to all those he met. George had seen the photo. Heini, one of the other P.O.W.s, who came from the same town, had told him that Helga had gone off with another man two years before. It seemed that Karl just could not accept it, and it had made him bitter. George had told Isaac to keep an eye on him.

At the end of the week, all had gone well. George could hear the Germans talking with some exuberance in the back of the truck, and though he couldn't understand what they were talking about, their manner seemed happy and contented. He could even hear Karl's deep voice. George was satisfied with the work arrangements and hoped the P.O.W.s would be just as happy working outside when the winter came, as it was one thing working outside in the Welsh mountains in August and something quite different in December and January.

During their second week of working, George called in on Alys and Jac at lunchtime. Isaac and Karl sat outside eating their packed lunch and drinking from their water bottles and Jac and George sat at the table chatting. Lloyd was sat at the end of the table listening to their conversation, copying their mannerisms.

This made George smile. He said, "how are you getting on with the two German workers?"

Lloyd said, in a strong Welsh accent, "the one Isaac is very nice. He asks me what I want to do when I grow up, but the other one

263

doesn't say much. I asked him if he wanted me to teach him some English or Welsh even, but he just grunted. Isaac's English is very good, so it is easier to speak to him." Lloyd stopped and gave a chuckle and with a wicked grin he said, "I didn't like the other one, so I told him when we win the war, he will have to speak English. I think he was angry, and he just spat on the floor while Isaac laughed. I think he knew I was making a joke."

Jac and George laughed at Lloyd's cheek and George noticed Alys taking a piece of cake and a cup of tea outside to Isaac and Karl.

After a while Karl brought the plates and cups back in and in a very slow speech said, "tha…nk. yoo veery much," with a very respectful bow.

Jac and George applauded and for the first time George saw the hint of a smile cross Karl's face.

After Karl had gone back outside, George turned to Jac and said, 'do you think we might be winning?"

Jac shrugged, but there was no reply.

George was sat on a wall at the back of the P.O.W.s dormitory chatting to Isaac, but away from the sight of the other P.O.W.s. Isaac said he felt more comfortable away from their sight as otherwise his conversations with George might be viewed as spying. He said, "the men generally seem very happy with their situation. You always have a few sullen ones who won't be happy until they go back to Germany and those on the road gang complain that their foreman tries to belittle them all the time, even telling them they must have been cowards to have been captured. These men resent him, and I think he will have to be careful that the men don't turn on him."

George said, "I will have a quiet word with him and hope that things improve." After a short silence he continued, "I don't want you to think of yourself as betraying your comrades. If we chat like this, then we can give all of you a more comfortable time while you are here. I appreciate how difficult it is for you. You don't want to be here. I have a brother-in-law who is a P.O.W. in Germany and all I hope is that he is treated as well as we think we treat you. We just want the war to finish so that we can get on with our lives. However, if you think it causes problems, we can stop seeing each other."

Isaac said, "no it is all for the good. Now you are able to speak to people who cause us difficulties and I can do the same with the other German soldiers."

George looked at Isaac. "P.O.W.s"

Isaac nodded and smiled.

40

As Summer moved into Autumn, the sea became greyer and the sky less blue with thicker and denser cloud. September became October and the news from France became more encouraging. George was buoyed by the thought that perhaps things might be coming to some sort of final stage. The German attacks of the Spring and early Summer had petered out and the ground lost by the Allies was quickly regained.

George had spent two weeks relieved of his supervisory duties with the P.O.W.s to chaperone an American captain, Roy Kowalski, who had been directed to Tonfanau to learn about artillery training. Clearly, the Americans had not heard about the changes that had taken place in the camp's duties and that most of the artillery training had been moved to other camps.

George sat down with Captain Kowalski in Captain Parker's office. Parker had been given instructions that he was to be transferred to France in December and was packing up. He passed Kowalski on to George on the basis that George was a trusted individual with years of experience at the camp and he would be remaining at the camp whereas the captain would not be. Kowalski, in his relaxed American way told George to call him Roy, something that would never happen in the British army. Kowalski said, 'suppose you'd better call me captain or sir when we are outside - just in case anyone is listening."

George was amused by the fact that the American army was equally out of touch with reality in sending one of their captains to look at artillery training in what in effect was a P.O.W camp. He said, "don't worry, the British army sent me here as a P.T. instructor after I had been wounded and was using a stick to help me walk."

Kowalski laughed at the madness of the instruction. He said that he was a professional soldier who had joined up in 1912 and that he was from Montana in the Mid-West of the U.S.A. He had been shipped out in 1917 and spent six months on the front line after a period of training in France. Whereas when he arrived he thought the German army unstoppable, now he said, "you can see that they have overrun their supply lines. Troops have ended up miles in front of their supplies and have had to surrender because they don't have food or ammunition." He went quiet for a second and then said, "of course, now we are here to help you lot out there's no chance the Germans can win."

George looked to see if there was a hint of a smile to suggest that Kowalski was joking but his face was deadly serious. George said, "you do know that we have been fighting this war for over four years?"

Kowalski looked up and said, "yeah, but in my opinion making a hash of it. Look, you've been in the same trenches in the same positions for all that time. Surely, if your commanders had been any good, they could have found a way to get around the German front line." George was flabbergasted at what he believed to be ignorance on the American's part, and he became frustrated and angry with the American's attitude.

George was keen to change the subject and stood up and said, "do you want to have a look around?"

He didn't give the American much of an option as he started to make his way out. Kowalski stood and followed George out of the door. They passed the solitary armed guard, who had taken up a relaxed position slouched against the wall just in front of the German quarters. George pointed out the mailroom, the N.C.O.s Mess, Admin offices and Major Fisher's office, the area where the guards ate and the area where the P.O.W.s ate and where their latrines were. Finally, he said, "and they are in here," pointing to a row of huts on his right, "its Saturday today so we give them a day off from their work details." George thought Kowalski might not be interested in the P.O.W.s and he was surprised when he walked towards their quarters.

Several of the P.O.W.s were slouched near the door, some sat on the step at the entrance and some inside playing chess or reading newspapers. Kowalski walked in and immediately greeted them in fluent German. The P.O.W.s were as shocked as George. Kowalski sat and chatted to several of them and after thirty or forty minutes, walked back out with George. Kowalski turned to George and said, "they are very keen to hear about what is happening on the Western front. One of them is from the same town in Eastern Prussia my grandfather was from. When they moved to America, oh.." he thought for a second, "fifty years ago, they moved into a German community in Montana. They could barely speak any English and so my dad was brought up speaking both German and English," he hesitated, "and so was I."

George stopped. "Well bugger me, you are a turn up for the books and no mistake."

Kowalski said, "I don't know why you are so surprised. There's probably as many Germans in the U.S.A. as there are in Germany. The Germans have a lot of support in the U.S.A." He stopped and the two carried on walking. After a while he said, "they think you are ok, 'a fair person' one of them said." Kowalski carried on, "but I would watch out for a few of them. There were a group in the corner who were very sullen, they still seemed very bitter and said they would like to have the opportunity to go to war again. They would not make the same mistakes and would no longer be led by old, stupid generals."

George remembered to bear Kowalski's advice in mind. The American might have a big mouth but he could learn more about the P.O.Ws and their views because he could speak and listen to them in their own language.

George was a little disappointed when Captain Kowalski left after only a few days, citing his own army's error in sending him in the first place. Though the captain got on George's nerves with his brash comments, he had been really helpful in giving him an insight into the personalities of the P.O.W.s. It certainly helped in knowing how to deal with them.

At the end of October, George picked up a letter in the mail room, which, from the handwriting on the front of the envelope he realised, was from his mother. It contained more very bad news.

Dear George,

I hope you are well? We have still not heard any more news of Ben.

The family have received more bad news I'm afraid. Your father received a letter last week from a neighbour of Elizabeth's who had found our address. It seems during September Elizabeth contracted Spanish flu. She became so ill that she had to retire to her bed. This neighbour came in to help her several times a day, to feed her and to change her bedclothes. She also picked up her medication regularly. After two or three days, Elizabeth worsened and became delirious, the doctor came but said that she could not be moved to hospital as the wards there were already full of flu victims. In the meantime, the neighbour came down with the flu as well and the doctor said that he would send a nurse to help both patients. Sadly, when the nurse called the following day Elizabeth had died in the night. It seems the neighbour has recovered. There was a quick funeral as at that time no family could be found to be contacted.

So, I'm afraid there is one more piece to be placed in this jigsaw of despair that the family has faced in the last few years. Your father has said prayers for her in the chapel and has written to Esther and Thomas to let them know. How much worse can it get?

Your father and I have discussed the circumstances and as it appeared that Thomas and Elizabeth were renting their house in Caerphilly it is only right that Thomas will come here to live when he is eventually released. I'm afraid that Thomas will take this news very badly.

Your ever-loving mother

Ann

George found himself once again in a very depressed state. He wondered whether the war was to blame for all this tragedy. It was not the war that took Willie and seemingly it was not the war that took Elizabeth. However, if there had been no war, Thomas would have been at home to look after Elizabeth and he would have been at home to look after Willie. Would that have made any difference?

George felt guilty but with Elizabeth's death, no one could inform Maud about his indiscretion with her. Not that Elizabeth would ever have said anything, but in a rash moment, people were capable of anything. It played on his mind that he had thought that Elizabeth's death had salved his conscience at the terrible deed he had done to bring disgrace on himself and that now he would never be found out.

He considered telling Maud, but then realised that the upset that would cause her would do nobody any good. He felt selfish and self-centred, but it helped him commit to Maud wholeheartedly and to do his very best for his family. George felt guilty that he even thought about what he had done with Elizabeth, and he felt sad that she had died in loneliness. He should be more concerned about Elizabeth's sad passing and how Thomas would cope in his state with the passing of his wife, not that he had now been 'let off the hook'.

The following week, George received another letter and found himself almost afraid to open it in case it brought news of yet more sad tidings. He took a deep breath and looked carefully at the front of the envelope. He recognised the handwriting as Maud's and thought perhaps it was a letter which says the same as his mother's, as Maud might not have realised that she had already written. He opened the letter and began to read.

George,

You have no doubt already heard the sad news of Elizabeth's passing. We are all stricken with more grief.

However, for the first time in many months I have some good news to pass on to you. Ben is alive and in Queen Mary's Hospital in London. It seems that stretcher bearers had picked up someone wounded in no-man's land. He had been struck by a bullet in the shoulder and more seriously several in the legs, one had also struck a glancing blow to his head. He was left unconscious on the battlefield. When he was found he was taken immediately to a casualty station. It was several days before he came round and was able to tell them who he was. He had lost a lot of blood and the wounds had become infected. The lower half of his body was in a bad way, and they had to amputate both legs while he was still in France. Later he was moved back to London for rehabilitation – I hope I've spelled that right. Your father tried to contact the hospital and he was told that Ben was as well as could be expected under the circumstances. O.H. said he is going to try to go up to London to see Ben in the next few weeks.

I hope you are pleased as Ben might be badly wounded, but he is alive and hopefully he will not have to endure any more suffering as his war is over.

Hope you are well and that this war ends soon?

Love Maud

George was cheered by the news of Ben's survival but constantly thought about how Ben would cope without his legs. He had always been so active and lived life to the full. Would he become miserable and depressed? George then wondered about all the men who would be permanently disabled - how would they work? How would they live? Oh God, please let this war be over soon so that there is no further suffering.

41

George put his greatcoat back on to ward off the cold wind. He had taken it off to help Jac, Lloyd and the two German P.O.W.s herd the sheep into a field nearer to the farm.

Jac said, "by doing this it will be easier to keep an eye on them and to get feed to them should the weather turn bad over the next few weeks."

George was sweating a bit after the activity and after putting his coat back on, he made his way back to the truck, cold and shivering. He stopped and turned at the same time as Jac, as he could hear one of the dogs growl at Karl. In response, Karl swung his coat at the dog. The two Germans climbed into the back of the truck.

Jac turned to George, "really unusual. I've not heard Griff growl before except when a tramp took a swipe at him with his boot. He obviously doesn't like Karl."

George shrugged and started to walk away.

Jac shouted to him, "very perceptive dogs are - mind you."

George rose his hand in farewell.

As the two P.O.W.s got out of the truck back at the camp, George beckoned to Isaac, "what happened with the dog back there. Jac was very surprised, he's never heard him growl before. Well, almost never."

Isaac looked up. "Karl tried to kick him as Griff ran in front of him. He just caught him a glancing blow, but the dog understandably didn't like it. Griff doesn't like Karl, anyway. He's mistreated him before."

George returned to the dormitory and lay down on his bed, ready to read the letter which had arrived from Maud. He prized open the envelope apprehensively as so many letters he had received in Tonfanau had brought bad news. He read-

Dear George,

Hope you are well? We are all fine. We get news and gossip about the war while shopping in town and some of the women have said that the letters they have been getting from their relatives who are fighting at the front are very encouraging. One woman in chapel said that her husband told her in one letter that they were having difficulties containing all the German prisoners that were surrendering. I so hope all these encouraging signs prove to be true, so that we can begin to get back to a normal life. It would be good to have you back here all the time.

I spoke to your mother last week and she said she had received a letter from Ben and confirmation from the War Office. She said her prayers had been answered, he seemed in good spirits and said that he had lots of good mates on the ward he was on, and that all of the men on his ward had lost one limb, and some like him more than one.

He said they played cards a lot of the time and the nurses were all good looking. He had already asked five of them to marry him. He also said that the weather was good, and the nurses would take them out in their wheelchairs. They were even having wheelchair races. However, I have to say that your mother thought that Ben was being over-encouraging and that she would not really know what Ben was feeling like until she had seen him in the flesh. O.H. is planning to go up to see him this weekend.

Your mother also said that there had been a bit of a fuss with Esther and that she had moved back to Rhymney, though not to the house she was renting with Evan but to Evan's mother's house. In a conversation Esther had with your mother she let slip that she had been seen walking out with Gwynfor, Evans' brother.

Apparently, Richard Elias had come to see O.H. and told him that people in Salem chapel were talking. There was a row as O.H. said that she should not be seeing other men so soon after Evans' death. Your mother said that she defended Esther to your father, but she thought it was also a little early. I don't think they liked it when I said that Evan had died in December 1916, nearly two years ago and that perhaps Esther should

273

think about moving on with her life and that she could not grieve forever.

When O.H. started to argue that it was unseemly I pointed out that after so many men had died in the war there would be very few men for the many women left, and that if Esther was happy that was all that mattered and that she should not deny herself a future. O.H. got a little hot under the collar and said marriage was not a numbers game and Esther should not be running after the first man she found after her husband's death. He went quiet for a while and then suddenly said, 'and she will be living under the same roof as him'.

I wonder if after this war people will have a different view of life and be more willing to accept things at face value and not as a result of convention.

I wanted to calm the situation down and so I told them my news, that I was expecting. That seemed to shut them up and cheer them up at the same time.

All my love

Maud

George stopped, and then quickly read the end of the letter again. Maud said she was 'expecting'. George pondered on the word, almost afraid to believe that she meant 'expecting a baby', but what else could she mean. George firmly decided that she could only mean one thing. All other alternatives were pushed out of his mind. He stood up and walked around the room, not knowing what to do.

He suddenly went out of the dormitory and seeing Captain Parker talking to Corporal Rogers a few hundred yards away, he sprinted over to them. As he arrived in their presence, the two stopped their conversation and looked at George, still holding the letter in front of him, "I'm going to be a father," and then after a few seconds "again, ah sir."

Captain Parker, a little bemused by George's interruption, looked quizzically at him. "Congratulations, I suppose," and then before

George could respond, "I've got three, expensive little blighters."

Corporal Rogers, a little more expansively, with a broad smile said, "well done George," and then "when?"

George, still looking at the letter said, "no idea."

George went back to his dormitory to write home to Maud to tell her how wonderful she was. He planned to write to his mother and father to express his views on Esther's relationship with Gwynfor. He thought for a second and suddenly said out loud, "bloody Richard Elias, what has Esther's relationship got to do with him, or any of the chapel goers from Salem?" His letter to his father and mother would have to wait, he was in too good a mood.

George spent the next few weeks telling everybody he met of his marvellous news. Some like Jac, Alys and Lloyd were genuinely 'over the moon,' and asked George to pass on their congratulations to Maud and to tell her not to work too hard, while some others said, "we know George, you've already told us."

They received news at the camp regularly regarding the progress of the war, but when the news came in early November that the war was over, it still came as a complete surprise. George had often thought about what the end of the war would bring, the celebrations and the elation everyone would feel but when the news eventually did come it was met with relief and was celebrated in a very muted way, as if everyone was exhausted by it and just wanted it gone from their lives. George celebrated in the N.C.O.s Mess but by ten o'clock most had gone off to bed and the following morning, the first morning after the armistice, the day started in exactly the same way many other days had started. George, at one point, sat on the wall which ran alongside the road that ran through the camp. He was soon joined by Sergeant Major Ross who sat on the wall next to him.

Ross said, "so a new day begins."

George looked at Ross and said, "do you feel any different?"

Ross said, "it's strange isn't it. I thought I would feel ecstatic after all this time, but I realise I just felt fed up with the whole thing. I just want to be able to go home. I signed up before the war and I should have finished in 1916, so the last two years were extra time for me, but I'll just be damned glad to be going home." He stopped to look across at a group of P.O.W.s making their way across to the latrines. "They look just as fed up as they did yesterday."

George looked across at them. "Yes, you'd think they'd be really pleased at now being able to think about going home." They both sat in silence until George said, "feels a bit flat really, but you know what, I don't care."

Ross said, "perhaps the boys at the front feel differently. They now know they are not going to be killed in France or Belgium or wherever they are. They know they will be going home."

George stood up, and as he crossed the roadway, he noticed Isaac coming back from the latrines. He stopped and looked at him, saying, "good news, eh Isaac?"

Isaac gave a broad smile, "yes, we all want to see our families again."

George said, "everybody happy with the news?"

Isaac pursed his lips. "Well, most. Karl and a few others were shooting their mouths off that the German army is still the best in the world and that just because some cowards wanted to give in …" he hesitated "but then Karl knows he has nothing to go back to, even though he persuades himself his wife is waiting. One of the others said that in time the Allies would suffer for this and that we should have carried on fighting." He waited a second and added, "some of the younger men agreed with him but almost all of us are glad it is over." He rose his hand and walked away.

42

Throughout late November, the conversation amongst the men, both German and British, at Tonfanau camp was usually a version of the same thing, and often ended with the same question, 'when do you think we will be going home'?

Isaac told him that the conversation amongst the German P.O.W.s was exactly the same. George tried to put thoughts of going home out of his mind, as it just brought frustration. He found it difficult as his mind often turned to Maud's plight and his concern that she would try to do too much housework and place the unborn child in jeopardy. He tried to remember that life goes on, and the P.O.W.s still had to be taken and collected from their work places.

George parked the truck alongside Jac's barn and walked around to the front of the farmhouse. He spotted Karl sat on the wall with Alys alongside him. Karl had not seen or heard him, and Alys was trying to teach him Welsh and English. George could hear her saying, "cwpan" and then "cup," pointing to the cup of tea she had just brought out to him. When he repeated the words she said, "da iawn, Karl." and gave him a broad smile.

As Alys turned away to draw her shawl around herself, Karl could just be seen putting his arm around her, seemingly to help, but he kept his arm around her just that second or two too long which heightened George's concern. He quickly withdrew it as he saw George coming nearer. Alys had not seen George and very quickly but innocently shrugged away Karl's arm with a discontented scowl.

George wondered if he should be concerned, but he chose to say nothing. However, he thought he would log it away for the future. He had coughed so that Karl could see him coming. Karl frowned and looked down, pretending to re-tie his boots.

George walked into the kitchen and came up behind Alys saying, "you ok?"

Alys replied, "of course."

George said, "I noticed Karl becoming a little too friendly. Has he ever tried to do that before?"

Alys became embarrassed. "He was just helping me with my shawl," she looked away and then continued "if he did anything I'd hit him with my saucepan." She immediately shuffled into the next room and George did not pursue the issue as it would cause her further embarrassment.

George wondered whether Karl had understood the consequences of his action and thought it was a good job it was him that had seen what had happened and not Jac.

Alys came back into the room but quickly changed the subject. She said, "have you heard any more from Maud?"

George replied, "no, nothing after that first letter giving me the good news."

Alys said, "I almost forgot, it's Lloyd's birthday next week, hard to believe he's un ar ddeg, eleven. I'm going to bake a cake for him and on Wednesday we are going to have a few friends around for him. Will you be able to come?"

George said, "yes, I'd love to. What time?"

Alys said, "the friends have been told to come about two o'clock in the afternoon. It gets so dark early on in December that you can't have it any later. They have time to get their children home then before it gets dark."

George thought and then said, "is it ok if I come when I have to pick up Isaac and Karl? What I mean is, is it ok for them to wait here while the party is on before I take them back to camp?"

Alys said, "of course. Lloyd likes Isaac and he would want him here and Karl......well, it'll be fine."

George said' "that's great, thank you for asking me."

Two days later Major Fisher approached George as he made his way to the canteen. "Sergeant Williams, I was wondering if we could have a quick word?"

"Certainly sir," replied George, giving a smart salute.

"Well, you've heard that Captain Parker is to be transferred to France or possibly Germany, he doesn't know which yet. He's to help to try to sort out the mess that's out there.

Well, I thought we might give him a bit of a send-off, just a few drinks and some speeches. I will say a few words and I was rather hoping that you might also say a few words. I think that would go down well with the captain, seeing as how you have been here for so long."

George reluctantly replied, "of course sir, no problem," thinking that Captain Parker had wanted little to do with him while he was at the camp, but there we are, he is a decent sort.

"I thought next Wednesday afternoon about one thirty in the canteen, thank you Sergeant Williams," and with that the major walked off.

George didn't have time to think, and it was only a few minutes later he remembered that he had agreed to go to Lloyd's birthday party that afternoon. He said under his breath, "Bugger it, nothing to do for much of the time and now two things at the same time."

George couldn't make his mind up whether to approach the major to ask whether he might miss the 'do' for Captain Parker, but then he thought that wouldn't go down well. Fisher would look at George astounded at his request to go to a child's birthday party rather than making a speech for a colleague who was leaving. The speeches would be at one thirty and Lloyd's party at two. Well, I'll just have to arrive at the party a little late.

The following day, George explained the circumstances to Jac and Alys, and they said they understood.

279

George spent the Saturday afternoon looking around the shops in Tywyn to try to find something that Lloyd would like for his birthday. He settled on a pen knife, and then he went to buy some sweets which the shopkeeper put into a decorative box as it was a present.

George attended Captain Parker's party at one thirty on the Wednesday afternoon and got a little frustrated when it didn't start on time. It was well attended, and George made a short speech praising the captain for his help and support and wishing him all the best for the future. George approached the captain and shook his hand instead of the usual salute. He then deliberately moved to the back of the group at the canteen door and eventually quietly slipped away, hoping to get out unnoticed. He made his way to the back of the latrines where he had parked the truck.

George arrived at the farmhouse just before two thirty, and even outside in the farmyard he could hear laughing and shouting, and as he knocked at the door Alys came and ushered him inside saying, "you will need ear plugs I think."

George could see Lloyd and four friends, three boys and a girl, playing 'blind man's buff', shouting at each other in Welsh. At the end of the game, George gave Lloyd his present. Lloyd's eyes lit up when he unwrapped the present and he thanked George profusely and gave him a very formal handshake. Lloyd then showed George the present Isaac had given him. It was a small cigarette box with German writing on it and inside Isaac had laid out in order the buttons of his greatcoat which had his regimental insignia on them. Lloyd said that Isaac had told him they may be worth something in the future. George considered how thoughtful Isaac had been.

George said, "mind you take care with the pen knife otherwise you could cut yourself." After a while, he looked around and noticed Alys, her friend Mair, whose young boy was one of the guests. Stood in the corner alongside the dresser, were Isaac and Karl. George rose his hand to them, and Isaac acknowledged him, but Karl didn't. Karl stood with his arms folded and a permanent scowl on his face. George thought - nothing strange there.

George asked Alys, "where is Jac?"

Alys replied, "he should be back soon. He had a call from a local farmer to say that a fox had been seen and a few of the local farmers had gone off to see if they could catch it before it did any damage."

Twenty minutes later, Alys got them all around the kitchen table to sing "Penblwydd Hapus" to Lloyd before he cut his cake. The cake looked amazing, bearing in mind that Alys had few ingredients to bake it. Lloyd blew out the three small candles and they all clapped. Nobody had noticed Jac coming in through the back door, placing his shotgun alongside the doorpost, and emptying his pockets onto the dresser. Everyone was aware of his return when he joined in the singing with his booming tenor voice. George sat eating his piece of cake, drinking his cup of tea, and chatting with Jac.

Their conversation abruptly ended when they could both hear a scuffle near to the door and raised voices. Jac got up to see what it was. George stood up just behind Jac, but before they could move towards the door, there was a piercing scream. Jac rushed towards the door only to see Karl with his one arm tightly around Alys' neck, with Alys looking very frightened. Karl was moving backwards with Alys in front of him, looking up at Jac. Karl's other arm held Jac's shotgun with his finger on the trigger and the barrel pointed towards Alys' head.

The small porch area between the kitchen and the door to the farmyard was quite cramped with Karl and Alys with their back to the door and the bulk of Jac, Lloyd and George in the doorway between the porch and the kitchen. Jac quickly looked across at the dresser where he had lain down the two cartridges for the gun, which were no longer there. He realised that Karl had probably loaded the gun unnoticed by anyone.

Lloyd had shouted in fright and frustration as Jac pushed him backwards into the kitchen. He said in his booming voice, "I think you had better let her go."

Karl in his halting English said, "I don't want to hurt her, but I want to go home," and after a few seconds "to my wife."

George said, "you are making a big mistake Karl, if you harm her you will end up in prison when the others go home."

Karl had a determined look on his face as he said, "I have waited many months to go home to her. Now I have run out of patience. There is no more war, so we should go home."

George replied, "Karl, we all want to go home to our families, but believe me, this is not the way."

George was aware of Isaac standing just behind him, and saying something in German to try and defuse the situation.

Jac was becoming more concerned for Alys as Karl tightened his grip and she began to struggle for breath. He said in a menacing way, "let her go now, or..." He never completed the sentence as he lurched forwards to grab Alys from Karl's clutches. Karl pushed Alys away from his body as Jac came forwards. As they collided, Alys fell in front of him causing him to stumble over her. Karl took advantage of the chaos to hit Jac firmly across the forehead with the butt of the shotgun and Jac fell to the floor unconscious, with a streak of blood running down his forehead. As Jac fell, Karl reached and grabbed Lloyd's sweater, pulling the boy into the porch and grabbing him around the neck as he had done with Alys.

He spoke quietly to Lloyd, telling him to grab his coat off the rail as he walked backwards to the outside door. Karl reached behind himself and unlatched the door, walking backwards through it with Lloyd stumbling in front of him. After Karl had passed through the door to the outside, he slammed the door shut and while still holding Lloyd; he put the gun down for a second to grab a wooden post to jam the door.

George left Alys to tend to her unconscious husband, after checking that his injuries seemed not to be life threatening. He rushed to the outer door, but it stuck as he tried to push it, with the post

282

further embedding itself into the ground as he pushed on it. Both Isaac and George quickly put on their boots, which they had left in the porch and then put their weight behind the obstructed door. The door wouldn't budge. They both ran through the house, unlocking and leaving through the front door. When they got around to the farmyard, they could see the dim figures of Karl and Lloyd in outline in the distance. They were at the end of the first field and Karl seemed to push Lloyd through the gate. Karl had about a five minutes start on them, but he was being held up by dragging Lloyd with him. However, it was now getting darker, and George realised it would soon be very dark as he moved away from the light given off by the farmhouse.

43

George realised he was perhaps only a few minutes behind Karl and Lloyd, but as darkness fell, that would become irrelevant. He strained his eyes as he tried to follow the movement of the two figures. Isaac was just behind him, but he hadn't had the walking and mountain climbing experience George had over the last year or two. George's leg still ached from time to time but he had built up his stamina and a climb like this did not concern him.

George looked up at the half moon in a cloudless sky, which helped them stay on the worn path. It was a frosty evening but luckily there was little wind. The fields of grass led onto the rocky lower slopes of Cader Idris which George had climbed many times, but not in darkness. George kept in contact with Isaac but after an hour there was no sign of Karl or Lloyd.

The wind increased slightly as they climbed and the surface became rockier and more uneven, George and Isaac tried desperately to stay on the path, but Isaac was struggling and felt he might have to give up when George realised that there was no point in trying to pursue Karl and Lloyd in the dark, as clambering over the rock was dangerous in the black of the night. They tried to huddle together in a cleft in the rock where they were protected a little from the wind. They would then try to pursue them in the early light of the following morning. It got colder throughout the night and both men had to stand, stamping their feet every so often to increase their circulation.

They both expressed their concern about how Lloyd might fare in these conditions, and this almost persuaded them to continue their pursuit in the dark, but George could see that pursuit was impossible until the light of the morning.

Isaac turned to George and said, "perhaps it was a silly thing to rip the buttons off my coat to give to Lloyd as a present. I could do with those buttons now," as he drew the coat around himself.

They spent a miserable night on this unforgiving mountain. They both had coats but were worried that despite Karl and Lloyd having coats, it would not provide enough protection against a December wind. They both shivered uncontrollably and slept fitfully, and the night dragged slowly. At about seven o'clock, they tried to move up the mountain despite it still being quite dark. As morning light came, they could see no evidence of Karl or Lloyd, but they kept climbing. Their bodies warmed with the exertion of climbing, and both George and Isaac felt better as they moved up the mountainside.

All at once, George noticed a movement across a small dip in the rocky surface, perhaps three or four hundred yards ahead of them. Not a great distance, but not easy to cover climbing the steep rocky surface. He said nothing as any noise would carry but he tapped on Isaac's shoulder and pointed towards the movement. Isaac nodded and George whispered that he thought they should split up and try to get around the dip from different directions.

After a few minutes, George had nearly caught up with Karl and Lloyd and he slipped down behind a rock to observe. He could see that Karl still held the shotgun in one hand and was pushing Lloyd with the other. He could hear Karl shouting at Lloyd in what seemed to be German, but he could see that Lloyd was having real difficulty in moving with his damaged leg, and he looked as if he was shivering with the cold.

After a few minutes, George noticed Karl resting on one of the rocks with Lloyd a short distance away. Karl was still pointing the shotgun at Lloyd, and he seemed to be agitated, continually drawing his hand across his brow. George hid behind a rock and watched the two of them for a while, trying to think how he could separate Lloyd from Karl. He thought that he would have to do something quickly, as Lloyd seemed to be suffering from the cold, which George thought was hardly surprising.

George was startled when suddenly Lloyd lurched towards Karl. He noticed that Lloyd had the small penknife in his hand which he had managed to keep hidden. Karl was taken aback momentarily, but then regained his composure and made a grab for the knife. Lloyd went to swing the penknife around in an arc towards Karl. Karl pulled back to avoid the penknife but at that moment lost his balance as he tried to grip with his foot. George could see Karl slip backwards towards the edge of the rock but he couldn't understand why he was having so much difficulty in standing until he noticed Isaac's hand coming up from below Karl to make a grab for his leg. Karl swung the shotgun at Isaac's hand, catching him on the wrist but Isaac managed to maintain his grip.

Lloyd took advantage of the attack from Isaac to put space between himself and Karl, and he hid behind a rock. The thought flashed through George's mind that it was a good job Lloyd didn't attack Karl because with his disability, he might well have lost his balance and toppled over the ledge. Karl took another swing at Isaac's hand, but Isaac brought his other arm up and knock the shotgun from Karl's hands. George could see it fall from the ledge of the rock onto other rocks some distance below.

Karl reached Lloyd's penknife and used it to stab at Isaac's hand, catching him painfully and causing a line of blood to run down from his hand. George quickly climbed up from his hiding place, dislodging some stones and this distracted Karl, allowing Isaac to climb up onto the flattened area of ground using only his undamaged hand.

Karl attacked Isaac first and he swung the penknife towards him. Isaac moved his body back from the swing but lost his balance and slipped back over the edge of the rock, just managing to grab hold of the jagged edge of the rocky ledge, leaving him suspended in mid-air. George heard a cry of pain from Isaac as he tried to hold on with one hand. George could see blood dripping from the other hand, and he realised that if Isaac took his hand away from the ledge, he would slip several hundred feet onto the jagged rocks below. He was struggling as he seemed to be unable to use his damaged hand.

George had little or no time to think. He launched himself at Karl, bundling into him. In turning to defend himself against George, Karl swung around but lost his footing and fell backwards over the ledge. George made a dive to grab his hand but just as Karl's fingers touched George's sleeve, gravity took him away from his grasp and with an ever-diminishing scream, he fell onto the rocks below with a sickening thud.

George shut his eyes as Karl fell, as he knew he would see that vision for the rest of his life, and he felt angry with frustration that he could not save him. He dropped his head onto his outstretched arm as he remained in a crouching position, turning to Lloyd and then momentarily remembering that Isaac was only holding onto the ledge by the fingertips of one hand. He pulled Isaac back up and the three of them stood in silence.

A short while later, they sat in a small circle trying to regain their breath, too shocked to speak. Lloyd seemed to have stopped shivering and George asked him if he was alright. Lloyd nodded. George took off his coat and put it around him but then had to sit down again.

Isaac looked up after a few seconds and was about to speak when Lloyd said, in his strong North Walian accent, "bloody hell, what a day," and then quickly added "and a night. I won't be forgetting this birthday."

George and Isaac both laughed and then Isaac turned to George and said, "you saved my life." George ignored the comment as he tried to rip off a section of his shirt to bind Isaac's hand.

Isaac repeated the statement and George shook his head and looked back at Isaac. "Call it quits for a broken window."

Isaac looked confused and thought for a few minutes, and then looked at George curiously as it seemed to register. "Were you one of them, back then?"

George looked back. "Shamefully yes, I needed something to atone, to tell him when I got to the pearly gates. Now I have it."

Isaac gave a wry smile. "This is perhaps the first British German cooperation after the armistice."

George said, "I'm sure it won't be the last."

Lloyd stood up and with a broad grin said, "look what I found," holding up the pen knife.

George smiled back. "Didn't think it would come in handy quite so quickly mind you. Come on, let's go down before we freeze to death."

Isaac smiled ruefully, looking down at the damage the penknife had done.

Isaac and Lloyd moved off and George took a brief moment to look out onto the beautiful but unforgiving terrain in front of him. This mountain he would never forget.

They began to trudge back down the side of the steep surface of the mountain and as they got nearer to the farm, they could see that the police and the camp had been alerted. The farmyard had several policemen and several armed soldiers, looking as if they were ready to go up into the mountains to search, and looking relieved that with the arrival of the three, they would probably no longer have to go.

Jac was sat on the farmhouse wall looking like a deranged pirate with a large bandage over one side of his forehead and one eye, but with his cap on top. He shouted across to George, "where is the bastard then?"

George looked back at Jac and drew his fingers across his throat.

Alys rushed out with a blanket to drape over Lloyd and take him inside, with Lloyd protesting "not in front of everybody, mam."

Two policemen went to take Isaac into custody, and one held out a pair of handcuffs. George intervened. "There'll be no need for those. He's a hero and he's coming back to the camp with me in the truck." The two policemen withdrew and the one put the handcuffs back in his pocket. George went up to the police sergeant in charge of the detachment to explain what had happened and where they could find the body of the dead German. He looked across at Jac and said, "any chance of breakfast?"

Jac got up from the wall and grabbed George with one arm and Isaac with the other, "come on you two, I bet you are both starving," and a second later his voice boomed out, "Alys, a bacon sandwich please."

After an hour or two, the truck trundled into camp and Isaac turned to shake hands with George.

George said, "get that hand seen to before it falls off."

Isaac smiled and turned to go, and George went in to report to Major Fisher.

He tapped at the door and on the command to enter, he stepped inside. George saluted smartly and the major said, "at ease. When you and the two P.O.W.s didn't come back to camp yesterday, we sent out an armed detachment. We guessed something was wrong." He sat back in his chair and asked George to explain exactly what had happened.

George explained and at the end, Major Fisher looked up and said, "quite an ordeal. I would normally recommend you for a bravery medal," he hesitated, "for tackling an enemy," he smiled "but he wasn't technically an enemy anymore," he turned his pencil over in his fingers and then said, "and I would have difficulty in explaining clearly how you were at the farm when I had expressly asked you to be at Captain Parker's farewell. You were disobeying an explicit order. Perhaps this is one we will just have to let go as perhaps a quid pro quo."

George didn't have a clue what he meant by that, so he simply smiled. However, he understood the circumstances and to be honest, he didn't care. Lloyd was safe. Karl probably got what he deserved. Captivity had done him no good - he had just become more bitter. All George really wanted was to go home. He was buoyed by thinking

289

that Isaac was a good bloke in whichever army he had been fighting, and a man's attitude to life was more important than whether he was British, German or any other nationality. George took his leave, thanking the major and went straight back to his dormitory to sleep.

The following week, George went out to the farm to take Isaac to work. He stayed for a cup of tea and then Jac took Isaac to show him his work for the day. George could see that Lloyd seemed unaffected by his ordeal, but asked Alys if she thought he had recovered.

Alys said, "to be honest, he seems fine. A few of his friends have called with their parents to check he is alright, and he seems to quite like telling them about what happened. He skips over quite quickly the part where Karl fell."

George said, "fortunately Lloyd had drawn himself away from the ledge when Karl fell and so he was not near." He was silent for a few seconds and then he said, "mind you, it was a harrowing experience for any young boy, so keep an eye on him for a while."

Jac came into the kitchen at that moment slapping George on the back and almost knocking him off the chair, "shwmae, how is the hero?"

George said, "a hero in no one's books, I was lucky to get away without a reprimand as I wasn't supposed to be at Lloyd's party in the first place."

Jac looked shocked. "I'll go down to that camp and tell them what for, saving my boy and all that, a row of medals is what you should be getting." He repeated, "yes, I'll go down to the camp and tell them."

Alys immediately stepped in, "you'll do as you are told Jac Jones. If George says it is as it is, that's the way it will stay and there'll be no interfering from you."

George had never heard Alys speak so forcefully or for so long in English. He laughed. "That's telling you Jac, best you listen."

HOME

44

The family shuffled along the pew in Salem Chapel. Thomas on the inside followed by George, Maud with baby Wesley, who was now eight months old and fast asleep, Joan, Ann and then Ben, who required help to sit alongside his mother and to ensure there was room for his crutches. After the family were all settled, George looked across to the end of the pew. Esther had just arrived and had come down the aisle to speak to her mother. Ann moved along the pew to make room for her, but she made it clear she was not going to sit in the pew and George, even though he couldn't hear what was being said, could see her point towards the back of the chapel. Ann glanced back as Esther chatted to Ben.

Immediately Ann squeezed past Ben, not a difficult manoeuvre as Ben had no legs to obstruct her leaving the pew. Esther continued to chat to Ben as Ann strode to the back of the chapel. George could see her engaging in conversation with Gwynfor, Evan's brother, in the aisle at the back of the chapel and then grabbing his arm and almost frog-marching him to the front and their pew. She beckoned to Esther to move in alongside Ben and pushed Gwynfor to sit alongside Esther. Ann sat in the only remaining seat in the pew. It was a bit of a squash, but Ann leaned forward and looked across the row. She smiled and said, "there we are, a proper family!"

George looked at Esther and both smiled. He then looked across at Gwynfor and reached across to shake his hand. Ben did the same as George then turned to Ann and said, "well done Mam."

It was Sunday 16th November 1919 and the service was to remember those lost in the war which had ended just over one year before. The chapel went quiet as O.H. rose to the pulpit. He gave a very short prayer as the congregation bowed their heads. He then quickly introduced the eighty-five year old previous minister of the chapel, Ifor Roberts, who gave a short sermon on 'Forgiveness', using several texts from the Bible which he could recite from memory. The congregation then rose and sang 'Calon Lan'.

The chapel then went silent once more as O.H. rose to the pulpit. George watched carefully as O.H. looked around the congregation and nodded, at first saying nothing. The chapel was full and there were many stood at the back.

He began, "after the turmoil of the last five years, it does my heart good to see those who have returned." He hesitated and glanced at his family on the pew below, and George wondered if it was for effect. Then O.H. took out his handkerchief and brushed away a tear at the corner of his eye. He gave a little cough and then continued, "now is a time to mend the hurt of the past. After all that we have been through, there should be no need for hatred as we can all see what hatred brings us." He stopped and looked around once more. "Loss and misery." He shook his head in sorrow.

O.H. then asked the congregation to stand in silence and remember those who had been lost. He added, "I'm sure God understands that those who have given so much of themselves can continue to give from a seated position." This brought a smile of understanding to a few faces. George looked around and noticed a few who could no longer stand, such as Ben. He also noticed Alfred, his brother-in-law, returned from a P.O.W. camp in Germany, looking thinner but otherwise seeming to be fine, and further back on the other side Rhys Jones' wife and children.

George thought of Elizabeth, who was indirectly a casualty of the war, he thought of Brinley, Rhys and Captain Gattick, casualties of the war. Ben, whose life would never be the same and he thought of Karl who although an enemy for a time, was also a casualty of the war. George then thought of Willie, who, while he was not a casualty of war, deserved to have his father at home to look after him in his hour of need, instead of being away fighting. George wondered whether he would have died if there had been no war - possibly not. He wondered whether politicians thought of these sorts of casualties when they made speeches sabre rattling about the need for conflict.

After the two minutes of silence, the congregation sat once more. George expected a religious sermon from O.H. who in the past was adept at dealing out 'fire and brimstone' from the pulpit with a good deal of warning about retribution and constant reference to the Bible. This sermon was different. George assumed he would nod off during the sermon or at the very least let his mind wander, but O.H.'s speech from the pulpit grabbed his attention.

He talked of 'rebuilding', he talked of people enjoying their lives more than they had ever done, enjoying more of their free time with their families, of neighbours looking after those in need, of people using their energy for a greater good, to take the country forward, and he talked of ensuring that people remembered the sacrifice of those who had been lost. George almost wanted to applaud at the end of O.H.'s speech as he wondered whether it could really be described as a sermon with not one mention of the Bible. It was more of a social plan that paved the way for people to live their lives in the future.

As they sang their last hymn, 'Abide with Me', O.H. left the pulpit and walked slowly to the door at the back of the chapel. He made a point of greeting everyone who left the chapel and wishing them well. Many stopped to tell him how much they had enjoyed the service and when it came to his own family, who were almost the last to leave, he had a special word for each of them. George was particularly pleased that he stopped to speak to Gwynfor, holding a tight handshake for some time, but then only had a very short chat with Ben, who he could see was clearly struggling to stay upright on his crutches.

George, holding Joan's hand and Maud carrying baby Wesley, went back to his parent's house. The whole family squeezed into the small house, and it became so much of a squeeze that George and Maud went into the front room.

As George entered the room, he noticed Esther's wedding picture of the whole family on the windowsill. He took the photograph and sat with it. He looked carefully at the photograph. No Willie, no Evan, no Elizabeth and Thomas, now a different man, and likewise with Ben. He stared at the photograph, not noticing Esther and Gwynfor coming into the room. Maud nudged George and he quickly went to put the photograph back. Maud tried to ease the photograph past the curtain so it could not be seen. Gwynfor, noticing what Maud was trying to do, stepped past her and pulled the photograph back into the centre of the windowsill where it could be clearly seen. He said, in a quiet voice, "that photograph is a part of this family's history and should always be seen. Remember, it is also my brother we are remembering." George stood and shook Gwynfor's hand. He laughed. "Welcome to this mad, wonderful family."

On leaving his parent's house, George walked alongside Maud as they returned to their house. Maud carried baby Wesley and nine-year-old Joan skipped in front of them, Thomas shuffled along behind them, now completely white-haired, and with his unusual stooping gait, carrying his hands in front of himself.

Thomas now lived with George and Maud so that George could help him try to make his life as pleasurable as possible. He felt he owed him that. Though Thomas had aged considerably, and despite being only forty-one, he looked seventy. He rarely spoke and George noted he had not spoken all that day, despite friends of the family coming up to him and asking how he felt. He would merely smile in response and look down at his feet.

The following morning, George sat at the kitchen table finishing his cup of tea. It was early and still dark. Maud had gone into Thomas' bedroom and woken him. George could hear him getting dressed. His cup of tea and a piece of toast waited for him on the table.

After breakfast, George shepherded Thomas out through the door and turned to give Maud a kiss. "See you this evening, cariad."

George had been given a key to the Drill Hall, which was at the end of the street. The Drill Hall was no longer used to drill soldiers but was now being used as a centre to develop skills in many of the men who had come back from the war with horrific disabilities. The men were taught simple carpentry, basketry and sewing, hoping they could contribute to society and perhaps be able to hold down a job in the future. He unlocked the door and took Thomas in and sat him down on a seat at a large table in the centre. "I'll be about an hour. You ok to carry on with the sewing work you started yesterday?"

Thomas nodded, and George quickly left. It took him about thirty minutes to walk up to his parent's house where Ben was living. O.H. had got Ben up early and sat at the table waiting for George. Immediately upon George's arrival, Ben got up with the aid of his crutches so as not to keep him waiting. He said his goodbyes to his parents and George helped him out through the gate.

With a few stops, it took George and Ben a little over forty minutes to walk back down to the Drill Hall. Ben felt the times spent at the Drill Hall were invaluable for learning new skills and to socialise with men of their own age. He lived at home with his mother and father, who could help him get about, though he was severely disabled. He had been promised prosthetic legs and had been given a date for his first fitting. George would never cease to be amazed at Ben's ability to be sociable and to make people laugh. It pleased him particularly when he saw Thomas give a little smile at some of Ben's jokes.

After safely delivering Ben and checking that Thomas was fine to be left, he would return to the back of his own house where he had built a small shed. There he would collect his tools in a small canvas bag, and he would go off to do his work, which might be brick laying, carpentry or plumbing, referring to himself as 'a George of all trades'. George would also help with work at the Drill Hall when he had any spare time between jobs.

Esther still lived in Rhymney and planned to marry Gwynfor the following Summer.

George had returned from Tonfanau in May of that year. The P.O.W.s had been moved to camps in England before returning to Germany. He had said his goodbyes to Isaac and wished him the best for the future, telling him that if he wished to return to Treafon, he would always have a friend there. He spent time with Jac, Alys and Lloyd, saying goodbye and promising to write, telling them there would always be a welcome at his home for them. He promised to try to bring Maud, Joan and Wesley up to visit them.

He was desperately excited to see Wesley, who had been born in March and was two months old when George first saw him. George was formally demobbed from the army and for two weeks, he spent some time with the family. The weather was pleasant. He walked with Maud and played with Joan and Wesley. He spent time with Joan in the back garden and took her out to the park and bought her ice creams to give Maud a much-needed break.

After two weeks he went to the colliery to see if he could get his job back but those in charge made it quite clear the need for coal had declined after the war was over and there would be no work for many returning soldiers in the foreseeable future. George was secretly glad that he would not have to go back into the depths of the earth once more but would now do work he really enjoyed. He had given up smoking and he felt healthier for it. He found his skills were much in demand after the neglect of the previous years. He got more work as his name became known as a reliable, skilled and not too expensive craftsman. He realised that if his success continued, he would have to think about taking on an apprentice to help him as the offers of work poured in.

Despite the difficulties, the family was closer than ever.

It's a strange thing that it often takes terrible events and all the misery and loss associated with them to bring people together with perhaps more love, care and happiness. Perhaps it's not surprising that we often need something devastating to make us appreciate the value of what we have.

You might also like…

If you enjoyed this story, you might like a previous book by Phil Morgans. Available from all book shops, Amazon and direct from Cambria Books.